Also by Tobly McSmith
Stay Gold

ACT COOL

TOBLY McSMITH

Quill Tree Books
An Imprint of HarperCollinsPublishers

Content Warning: This novel depicts transphobia, homophobia, misgendering, deadnaming, and suicidal ideation. If you feel that any of these subjects may trigger an adverse reaction, we advise that you consider not reading this book. If you do read the book and some part of it is beginning to distress you, please stop reading immediately. If you are experiencing suicidal thoughts, feeling hopeless, and need a safe place to talk, many resources are available to you, including the trained counselors at the TrevorLifeline at 866-488-7386 or www.thetrevorproject.org. If you are in immediate crisis, dial 911. As someone who has been there, I want you to know you're not alone, you're important, and the world needs you in it. Never ever give up.

Quill Tree Books is an imprint of HarperCollins Publishers.

Act Cool
Copyright © 2021 by Tobly McSmith
All rights reserved. Printed in the United States of America.
No part of this book may be used or reproduced in any manner whatsoever without written
permission except in the case of brief quotations embodied in critical articles and reviews. For
information address HarperCollins Children's Books, a division of HarperCollins Publishers,
195 Broadway, New York, NY 10007.
www.epicreads.com

ISBN 978-0-06-303856-1

Typography by David DeWitt
21 22 23 24 25 PC/LSCH 10 9 8 7 6 5 4 3 2 1

First Edition

To my best friend, Bob McSmith.

ACT ONE: NEW YORK

ONE

Sunday, September 8, 2019

12:00 P.M.

If you saw me now, you'd say my dreams are coming true. I'm about to audition for a spot at the most prestigious art high school in the country. That'd be any actor's dream. But last night, I dreamed I was naked in a classroom full of people. Will that be coming true? What about the one where I'm onstage and can't remember my lines? I'll pass on both. But this dream, I wouldn't mind if it came true.

I smooth out my shirt, run my hand through my hair, and walk into the classroom. Unlike in my dream, I'm wearing clothes. It's a regular classroom except for the fact that there's a stage and a Steinway piano. Back home, we'd push desks out of the way and roll in the slightly out-of-tune piano from the band room. Other than that, it's a normal classroom that could possibly change my life forever. No big deal.

The man I assume is Mr. Daniels looks up from his tattered paperback. He's got messy gray hair and a slightly less messy gray beard. Glasses sitting low on his nose—all smart people wear glasses—and slumped posture. Beside him sits a girl—a cute girl—possibly the same age as me. I notice her eyes first, big and brown. She has black hair and high cheekbones, reminding me of a young Idina Menzel. She smiles at me. They both make me nervous for different reasons.

"I'm here for the audition," I announce in the deepest voice possible.

"Ah, you must be the infamous August Greene."

"Yes, sir," I say, wondering what's so infamous about me.

"I'm Mr. Daniels and this is Anna, my assistant."

"Very nice to meet you. Thank you for taking the time—"

"Let's get started, shall we?" he asks, cutting off my hashtag-blessed speech. I drop my backpack on a desk and find center stage. "Did you bring us a headshot and résumé?"

"No, sir," I admit. "But I have played the lead in every musical at my school."

"How charming. Did you at least prepare two monologues?"

"I did," I nearly yell, relieved to have something. "First one is from *Cat on a Hot Tin Roof.* But—could I have a moment?" I ask. I need to ground myself.

"Whenever you're ready, Mr. Greene. We will wait."

"Thanks," I say, ignoring his sharp tone. His words have bite, but his eyes are kind. I turn my back on my audience of two. A rush of nerves hits hard, causing my muscles to clench. I shut my eyes and take a deep breath. Right now, I'm not the "infamous" August Greene auditioning at the School of Performing Arts. Right now, I am Brick. It's summertime in Mississippi. I'm sweaty, angry, and tired. Also, drunk—very drunk—and secretly gay. I direct my anger and confusion toward my wife, Maggie.

I face my audience. Mr. Daniels flips a page in his book, almost challenging me to keep his attention. His assistant gives me a big smile, making me feel things. Holding myself up with a stool—Brick has a broken leg—I step into character. "All right. You're asking for it . . ."

I put everything into the next two minutes, ending the monologue feeling spent. Last night, I read audition tips online—one suggested watching the "signs" from the people across the table. Anna snaps to show her support. Good sign. And from what I could tell, Mr. Daniels kept his eyes on me and not the book. Another good sign.

"August, nicely done. I see why your aunt speaks so highly of you."

He's not a fan of nepotism. Bad sign.

He continues, "Do you know how often a spot opens up in the drama department at SPA?"

"Not often?" I guess.

"Never," he says, then pulls an orange out of his desk drawer and starts peeling. "A student relocated to London last minute to join the cast of *Pippin* in the West End. This has only happened a handful of times in my tenure here. . . ." He stops himself. "So please know how rare an opportunity like this really is, son."

I stand up straight to show my readiness to accept the great weight of this opportunity. "Thank you," I say, having no idea how to respond.

He eats an orange slice. "Not saying it's your spot. I'm merely confirming the existence of a spot."

That's a bad sign. I shift my weight from one foot to the other, uncomfortable in this moment. This audition means everything to me. Based on this man's decision, my life could completely change for the better, or get much worse. I'm freaking out and he's having a snack. I need to connect with him. "I love oranges," I offer.

"This is a tangerine," he says, then Anna laughs. "Now that I think about it, August, I wonder if your aunt sent the student to London herself."

He appears to be half-kidding, half-serious. "Honestly, I wouldn't put it past her," I joke, earning a smile from Mr. Daniels. That's a good sign—one small step closer to becoming a student here.

"I'm late for a chess game in Central Park. What's your next monologue?"

I unzip my backpack and dig around. "Another one from *Cat on a Hot Tin Roof*."

He shakes his head, disappointed. "Brick again?"

"No," I say. That would be a mistake. I did some research about the audition process at SPA after my aunt called two days ago. Everything I could find online said two diverse monologues that show range. I've got the range but had no time to prepare, so I went with two monologues from the play we did for sophomore showcase at West Grove High.

"Big Daddy?" Anna guesses.

I pull out a blonde wig from my backpack and put it on my head. "Maggie."

They laugh—not at me, at the surprise. (I hope.) For the second time, I turn my back to my adoring audience. I am Maggie. Born poor, married rich. A fighter. I love my husband, but he's not interested. I loosen up my body and slowly turn back around. Here goes nothing. "Oh, Brick. I get so lonely. . . ."

After the final words leave my mouth, I crumple to the ground and hold there, the blonde hairs falling over my face. Maggie leaves me feeling frustrated. I stand up, remove the wig, and dust my shirt off.

Mr. Daniels takes his glasses off and rubs his eyes. "Tell me, why did you leave Pennsylvania?"

"I had to," I say without hesitation.

He nods, hopefully understanding everything I don't say. "One more question. Why do you deserve this spot at SPA?"

"I don't," I say, pausing to watch his expression—he cracks a little. I guess this is my third monologue. I am August, desperate to go to this school. "Like you, Mr. Daniels, I'm not a fan of getting something because I know somebody. But my situation back home isn't great. And there's no way to study at this level in West Grove, Pennsylvania. Just give me a chance, sir."

He smiles. "August, you'll hear from someone soon. If accepted, you will be starting classes on Tuesday. Will that work for you?"

I'll take that as a good sign. "Absolutely," I say.

"But if you're not accepted, I wish you the very best of luck."

Dammit. Bad sign.

"Oh," he continues, "please say hello to your aunt for me?"

"Will do," I say, while stuffing the wig into my backpack. I say my thank-yous and goodbyes and walk out with no clear sign on how that went.

12:25 P.M.

Having nowhere to go, I sit on the cement benches in front of the school and process how I did. Before today, I've only auditioned in front of my teachers for school shows. Not really high-pressure situations. Also, I didn't sleep much last night, my mind running lines from the monologues over and over to avoid thinking about other things.

I untangle my phone from the Maggie wig, ignore the five voicemails on it, and dial my aunt. I promised I'd call after the audition. She dropped me off on her way upstate to sell art. No clue what "upstate" is exactly, but it sounds fancy, bucolic, rich. Nothing like downstate. I picture Aunt Lillian driving her bright yellow vintage truck. After two rings she picks up. "Tell your favorite aunt some good news."

I wish I had good news to deliver to my only aunt. "I'm still alive," I announce.

"Hallelujah," she sings. "And how was the audition, my love?"

"I truly don't know, but I did my best."

"Good," she says. "That's all we can do in life."

"I don't think Mr. Daniels warmed to me," I admit.

She laughs. "Yeah, he can be a real sonofabitch, but there's a heart somewhere in that chest of his." The way she says "chest of his" makes me wonder if they once dated. I don't know much about my aunt's love life. "Now, how will you spend your first day in the city?"

I look around at the concrete buildings stacked up over me. "I'll wander around. And try not to get kidnapped."

"Wonderful. I'll be home for dinner. Call if you need me. Bye, love."

When I end the call, there's another voicemail waiting for me. And twenty-one unread texts. All from Mom. Each one more urgent and angrier. The most recent text mentions the cops. I should call her before I end up on a missing-child commercial, but Aunt Lil and I made a plan to call her after we find out if I get into SPA.

This is my first attempt at running away from home. It's too early to write my official review—I'm only twenty-four hours in—but so far, it's been a roller coaster. For the most part, it's one long adrenaline rush—*I'm free! I can do anything!*—and panic attack—*I'm going to jail! Or worse!*

When I look up from my phone, there's a new friend at the end of the bench. "Hello, pigeon," I say to the bird. He stares at me intensely with one eye while the other wanders. His feathers look like they were glued on by a child. The bird hops closer to me. Is this how I die?

"What are you doing?"

I look up, thrown by the interruption. Mr. Daniels's assistant is standing over me, blocking the sun. "Just making new friends," I say, nodding to the pigeon. She laughs, then claps twice—effectively frightening the dirty bird to the ground—and sits down beside me.

"I feel like we haven't had a proper introduction. I'm Anna."

"And I'm the *infamous* August Greene."

"What was that about?" she asks.

"No clue."

"August, your audition was something else. You killed it."

"Did I?" I ask, unsure.

"Um, yes. I think you have a real shot."

"I don't think Mr. Daniels was impressed."

She waves off my comment. "Oh, that's just him. But he knows talent when he sees it."

"Thanks," I say, then take my first deep breath of the day.

Anna squints. Sizing me up. "Can I ask a personal question?"

"Yes," I say hesitantly.

"You nailed both Brick and Maggie. I haven't seen that before. Does being transgender make playing both boy and girl parts easier?"

How did she know I'm trans? Maybe my aunt told Mr. Daniels and he told her. Or could she tell by looking at me? I wonder if it's obvious. "As an actor, I can step into both genders, if that makes sense. I can play any character on earth."

"Bold statement, sir," she says with a sweet smile.

I first heard the word *transgender* in my eighth-grade history class. I'd heard the word before (I don't live under a rock), but never really *heard* it. It was end of the year—my last days in middle school. The teacher was giving a lesson on LGBTQ history for pride month. The teacher was talking about the L, and G, and B, and I was Z(oning) out as usual. But then he got to the T, talking about how transgender people feel uncomfortable in their assigned gender, and everything he said fit me to a T.

I went home after school—locked my door—and looked online. I took a quiz called "Are You Transgender?" and it said I was, in fact, transgender. I took three more, just to make sure, all with the same result.

Those "Are You Transgender?" quizzes suggested that I talk to someone. But in a conservative town like West Grove, who was I supposed to talk to? I didn't know any transgender people. I couldn't tell my folks. I knew what they would say. I decided not to tell anyone else—not even Hugo, and he's my best friend. It was just this big secret that I carried while wearing Mom-mandated dresses.

Anna taps on my shoulder, bringing me back to earth. "So, August, you've got me curious. What's your deal?"

Good question. My deal is complicated, and I don't know how much I should tell the assistant of the man who has my future in his hands. I need to play this cool. For Anna, I'll be the Chill Guy. Unfazed, unworried, aloof. I sit back, spread my legs. "My deal is that I moved here. Living with my aunt."

She tilts her head. "You just moved?"

"Yeah," I say, so very chill-like. "But I've been here tons. Most weekends," I lie.

She gives me a look of major doubt. "How many Broadway shows have you seen?" she asks.

"Lost count," I answer. Translation: I lost count of the bootleg recordings I've watched on my old scratched-up laptop.

"Vague," she announces. "I've seen twelve. Where do you live?"

My aunt told me the neighborhood last night, but I can't remember. "Somewhere in Brooklyn off the orange subway line," I say.

"Orange subway line?" she repeats.

One thing is clear: Chill Guy isn't working. I don't know enough to act like I don't care. Time to flip the script. For Anna, I'm Bright-Eyed New Guy. Naive to my new world and easy to excite.

"Actually," I admit, "it's my first day in New York."

"I knew it." Anna throws her hands up. "A real-life New York virgin!"

My face reddens up. "Go easy on me."

"No promises," she says, then pulls out sunglasses from her purse. The glasses are oversized—cartoonishly big—but stylish. I see my reflection in the lenses, almost unrecognizable from two days ago. Goodbye, flowery shirt and long skirt; hello, white tee and jeans. I run my hand through my short hair, still not used to it. Aunt Lil gave me a haircut last night. We printed out a picture of Shawn Mendes for inspiration and she did her best. The sides of my head are super short with a nice patch of curly hair on the top. Nothing like Shawn, but a lot more like me.

My phone starts vibrating in my lap. Anna peeks at the screen. "Answer it," she says.

"It's probably a robocall."

"Dude, I can see it's your mom. Maybe she wants to, *I don't know*, hear how your audition went?"

Or maybe she wants to know where the hell I am. She's worried, and she loves me, but she doesn't approve of me being transgender. I send the call to voicemail. "I'll tell her about it later," I say, losing my cool a little.

"Someone's hangry," Anna says, then pulls a tinfoil ball from her purse. "Do you know what a bagel is, newbie?"

"Of course I know what a bagel is," I say, but lean into my newbie status: "And of course I've never had one."

She laughs and unwraps the bagel. "That's cream cheese."

"Wow," I say, pretending like I've never seen cream cheese before. Anna hands me half and I take a big bite—too big a bite—letting the carbs and cream cheese wash over me.

She takes a picture of me. "Baby's first bagel."

After a few seconds on her phone, she looks up. "What's your Insta? I'm trying to tag you in my Story."

"Oh," I say, swallowing. I haven't had time to create a profile for August yet. "I'm not online."

"What planet are you from?" she asks.

"Pennsylvania," I joke, leaning into New Guy. "Do you think I should?"

She rolls her eyes. "Yes. Obviously. That's how people get noticed. And every casting director and producer checks that stuff. They want to know you have built a following that will follow you to the theater and buy a ticket."

"How do you know that?" I ask.

She waves off my question and continues, "At SPA, your social media is everything. It's how you tell your story and control your narrative."

I laugh a little. I don't mean to—it just slips out.

"Laugh all you want, buster, but look at mine," she says, and shows me her phone. There's over three thousand people following her. Who are all those people? She scrolls through her page, stopping to show me photos and announcing how many likes or views they got.

My old profile had fifty-three followers, mostly people in Theater Club. I don't know anything about brands or narratives. I nod and pretend to understand as she explains the algorithm.

"So, new friend," Anna says. "I'm guessing you haven't actually been to countless Broadway shows?"

"No," I admit. "I've only watched them on my laptop and phone."

Anna covers her mouth. "That's so sad."

"Tragic, really," I confirm.

"Well, would you be interested in attending the matinee of the newest show in town?"

My heart jumps. I could be going to my first Broadway show. I know there's some rule about stranger danger, but Anna doesn't fit the profile of a serial killer. And to see a Broadway show, it's worth the risk. "I'm interested," I say.

"Would you still be interested if the musical probably sucks? And will most likely close before opening night?"

The worst Broadway show in person is better than watching the best one on my laptop. My phone vibrates in my pocket. And I could use a distraction. "I would say I'm still interested."

She claps, excited. "The show is called *Last Tango in Paris.* My friend last-minute canceled on me. She probably looked up the reviews. Anyways, would you like to join me?"

"YES," I nearly scream, then hug Anna, celebrating as only the Wide-Eyed New Kid could.

"Okay, wow," she says, surprised by my excitement. "Be cool."

1:40 P.M.

The taxi to the theater was disappointing. I wanted my first cab ride in New York to play out like in the movies, with the driver speeding recklessly, yelling out the window, and constantly honking. None of that happened. The ride was slow and hot, but the destination—Times Square—is heaven. We passed electronic billboards stacked on top of each other like apartments. Anna played tour guide, and I acted blown away by her knowledge of the city.

While she pays the guy, I step out of the taxi and take in the theater. I can't believe this is happening. Flashing lightbulbs line the marquee, bright enough to compete with the sun. Posters of actors dancing in front of the Eiffel Tower are plastered to the walls of the theater. Maybe one day, my photo will be up there.

We walk to the end of the will-call line—almost a block away—and wait. "Okay, August, let's play a game called quick fire. I ask you questions, you answer quick—without thinking. Ready?"

"Sure," Wide-Eyed Guy says.

"Favorite musical?"

Without hesitation I say, *"Rent."*

She looks at me like she doesn't believe me. "Why?"

I shrug. "'La Vie Bohème'!"

"Favorite musical movie?"

"Don't laugh," I say. *"Hairspray."*

She laughs anyway. "Sorry, it's good, I guess. But I don't love John Travolta as Edna Turnblad."

"'Cause of his acting?" I joke.

"Well, yes," she jokes back. "Why couldn't they cast a woman to play the mother? There's plenty of hilarious women."

I've read a couple of articles about the decisions to cast Harvey Fierstein in the Broadway run and then John Travolta in the movie. "I think it's tradition," I offer.

"Tradition?" she repeats with disgust. "What does that even mean? It's the mom, it should be played by a woman." Anna shakes her head. "Let's not get into this. It's a hot topic at school now."

"John Travolta?" I kid.

"Representation."

"I don't follow," I say.

"I'm talking proper representation in theater. The stage needs more women, people of color, people with disabilities, transgender and nonbinary people," she says, and gives me a knowing look. "If a role is meant for a marginalized character, they better not cast some white dude who then gets awards and praise for his quote-unquote bravery."

"Like how Harvey Fierstein won the Tony for Edna?" I ask.

"Exactly."

"But acting is about being someone else?"

"When it comes to acting now, August, it's about staying in your lane."

But I'm transgender. Is that my lane? I'm good at playing girls and boys. Can't I play both? There are very few trans characters in theater. I want to ask her but don't want my fear confirmed.

After ten minutes of slowly inching ahead in line, we're close enough to the doors to feel the air conditioners. My pocket vibrates again. I pull my phone out and send Mom's call to voicemail, hoping Anna didn't see.

"Out with it, August: Why won't you pick up your mom's calls?"

"I'll talk to her later," I say.

"Don't be mad, but Mr. Daniels said they aren't cool with you being transgender."

My face burns hot. I didn't think Aunt Lil would tell him. "Yeah," I say, deciding how much to disclose. I need to keep the Wide-Eyed New Guy thing going and not veer into Trans Teen Runaway. "They are religious," I offer.

"Oh," she says.

"The evangelical kind."

"Got it."

My plan was to never tell my parents that I'm transgender. Maybe I'd send a letter when I was eighteen and out of their house, but not before. The problem with that plan was, once I knew I was trans, the urge to transition got louder every day. I couldn't wait years. I needed to tell my parents. I needed them to know. And I needed to say it out loud.

It was a week before my fourteenth birthday. Dinner table. My mom asked what I wanted for my birthday and I said, "Actually . . . I want to transition. I was born in the wrong body. I'm a boy. God made a mistake." My mom said, "God never makes mistakes." My stepdad stayed quiet. For my birthday, I got a new dress—and was told not to talk about that boy stuff again. God made me a girl for a reason. End of conversation.

"You ready?" Anna asks, handing me my first Broadway ticket. We pass through the metal detectors into the lobby. The air conditioner is on high, chilling the sweat on the back of my shirt and sending a shiver up my spine. An usher scans my ticket. Someone puts a Playbill program in my hand as Anna holds the other, leading the way.

I can feel her watching my face. She wants to see my reaction to walking into my first Broadway theater. I need to overact, but that's easy—this place is magical. I look around, mouth open. Endless rows of red seats. Red curtain three stories tall. Balcony with more red seats. The ceiling, far away, with swirls of fancy blue-and-white etchings mimicking clouds. Two of the biggest chandeliers I've ever seen. When I look at Anna, she snaps another picture. "Baby's first Broadway," she says.

Another usher (in a beret) leads us to our seats. The theater feels old and unchanged, and there's a musty smell of moldy carpet and popcorn. We find our seats, and Anna calls aisle. The seat beside me is empty, and I hope it stays that way. The well-worn chairs are too close together and too small. There's an outline of Paris projected on the curtain. "I'm suddenly in the mood for French fries," I joke.

"*Oui oui*," Anna says, then checks her phone. "Five minutes until curtain. Back to the quick-fire questions?"

"Bring it on," I say.

"Why acting?"

I shake my head. "You want a short answer for *why acting?*"

"Just try," she suggests, flipping a page of her Playbill.

Things got dark after coming out to my parents. I was lost. And uncomfortable in a body that continued to defy me with the beginning of boobs and hips. My freshman year started, and I walked around in a thick cloud of blah.

My friend Hugo knew something was up—we've been friends

since fourth grade—but I couldn't tell him. Too scared he'd push me away. Being the best best friend, he came to me with the solution to my sads (that's what he called it: "my sads"). Hugo's big idea was to sign up for Theater Club. Cassie was joining, and he was looking to land the role of her boyfriend. He said it would be fun to act like somebody else, and that didn't sound bad. That's all I wanted—to be someone else.

We showed up to the first meeting, and I tried to remain invisible (my typical MO at West Grove High). The teacher asked us to break into small groups and perform for the club. I don't remember much of the performance, but it felt good. It felt right. When it was done, Hugo ran over and said, "Wow, you can really act." I didn't believe him. What did he know? But then the teacher came up and said the same thing.

After I joined Theater Club, things got better at home. Turns out, I was an actor all my life—playing the role of a girl. My anxiety calmed down when I figured out that I didn't need to *be* a girl; I only needed to *act* like one. For my parents, I played the part of their daughter. The world, I heard, is a stage. And it was working.

"August?" Anna asks. "Why acting?"

I find her eyes and smile. "It saved my life," I say simply.

The lights lower and the crowd goes quiet. My heart speeds up. I can't believe I'm here. When I go to turn off my phone, I notice there are no new calls. That's weird. Did my parents give up?

Music fills the house—heavy on the accordion—as the ensemble enters from the wings for a high-energy high-kick group number with fake cigarettes hanging from their mouths. The lights are bright, the dancing is tight and fun, and the singing is perfectly harmonized. We're close enough to see the facial expressions on the actors. Without warning, my eyes fill with tears. I'm overcome with what my life is right now. Yesterday I was on a bus heading to New York, and today, I'm sitting inside a Broadway theater after auditioning at SPA. I'm exhausted, scared, and completely inspired. I wipe the tears away, and Anna sees. She leans over and whispers, "Come on, the show isn't that bad."

When the lights come up for intermission, Anna is on her feet and says, "Follow me." I trail behind her as she heads up the aisle, speed-walking past everyone. We make it to the restrooms before anyone else. "I don't do bathroom lines," she says.

I head into the men's and lock myself in the teeny tiny stall. Barely enough room to turn around. I pull my binder up, allowing air to hit my stomach and back. I'm wearing a chest compression binder under my shirt to flatten my chest. It looks like a tight undershirt and feels three sizes too small. It's wet with sweat, and the fabric is beyond scratchy—but necessary. Lucky for me, I don't have tons of chest to compress, but the binder gives me confidence.

I ordered the binder online and had it shipped to Hugo's house. I wouldn't tell him what the box was, and he didn't seem to care. If the package had arrived at my house, Mom would have intercepted and inspected for sure. Late at night, when my parents slept, I'd wear the binder around the house, imagining how it would feel to live as a guy. Or at least dress like one.

"August," Anna yells when I exit the bathroom. I'm glad we hustled—the restroom line now snakes down the stairs into the lobby. Most of the audience is standing, stretching their legs, chatting in small groups. We head back down to our seats. "I didn't think there was a show more miserable than *Les Misérables*," she says. "But here we are."

I nod in agreement. "I'm not convinced the leads are in love," I say.

"I'm not convinced the leads remember their lines."

I laugh hard. She continues, "Did you see the juggler drop his balls? You had one job, buddy."

"It's not the worst show," I say.

"Stop," she says. "This is terrible."

"It's not great," I admit, "but think of the people who worked hard to make this happen. How many hours the set designer worked to build that Eiffel Tower. How many rehearsals the choreographer spent getting the tango right. The poor accordion player was playing so hard, I'm sure his fingers are bleeding. Even a bad show takes a lot of work and heart."

"Ugh," she says. "Please don't make me feel guilty about my shade."

We both laugh. A little too loud. The man beside me looks up from his phone. "You girls enjoying the show?" he asks with a friendly grin.

Why does he think I'm a girl? Maybe it's my voice—I haven't focused on keeping it low. My posture? My clothes? I feel caught.

Exposed. An impostor. And embarrassed to get misgendered in front of a cute girl.

Anna leans over me. "Excuse me, please don't assume our genders."

"It's all right," I whisper to Anna. "I don't mind."

She gives me a *Really, August?* look, and I nod. This is my first day presenting male—I'm bound to get misgendered. The man apologizes and goes back to his phone.

"Anna, let me ask you," I say, changing the subject. "Why acting?"

She looks up and shrugs. "It's all I know. I love being onstage. It's addicting, like a high. And I keep chasing it."

"Best drug ever," I say. The nervous energy before, the endorphins during, the applause after. Once you get a hit, you want more. Bigger stages, bigger roles, bigger audiences.

"Should we start Acting Anonymous?" I kid.

She flashes side-eye. "There's nothing anonymous about acting."

About an hour later, the last tango is tangoed and the musical ends. The applause wakes up the man beside me. The actors take their bows during curtain call as the audience claps politely. I feel bad for them. They didn't choose to do the dance with cardboard Ferris wheels, but they did a great job despite the cardboard Ferris wheels. I stand up and clap loudly. Anna gets up—after rolling her eyes so hard I swear I hear it—and does the same. Other audience members get on their feet. By the last bow, the entire crowd is up and cheering. The cast smiles bigger than before.

We walk slowly with the herd of people to the exit and play the quick-fire game.

"Favorite musical song?" Anna asks.

I think through a catalog of my favorite songs. "'You Will Be Found' from—"

"*Dear Evan Hansen*, I know," she says. "*The Wild Party* by Lippa or LaChiusa?"

"No clue?"

"Are you a virgin virgin?"

My face reddens up. This game has certainly taken a turn. "Can I go back to the *Wild Party* question?"

"No."

"Are you?" I ask back.

She half smiles. "For the most part."

"I am," I say. My only kisses have been onstage.

We exit the theater and walk away from Times Square. The sun sets, turning the sky pink. "Are you with someone?" she asks.

"No," I say with a laugh. "How about you?" I ask.

"Not really. I haven't met anyone interesting enough to be my person."

"Person?" I ask.

"Yeah, I don't care about the gender."

"Cool," I say. "I'm into girls, but they aren't into me."

She gives me a little push. "Don't worry, you'll do fine at SPA."

We stop at the corner of Forty-Sixth Street and Eighth Avenue and face each other. If this were a scene in a play, we'd kiss right now. She smiles at me and I look away, nervous. Instead of leaning in for a kiss, I ask for help calling my Lyft. When the car is one minute away, I start my goodbye. The big ending on the role of Wide-Eyed New Guy.

"Anna, this day was perfect. Thank you for being an exceptional tour guide."

"Say it," she demands.

"Thank you for taking my New York virginity."

"You are so welcome, Augustus," she says, grabbing my hand.

"Augustus?" I repeat.

"Mighty Augustus, that's what you are to me. Breaking free from Whatever Grove Pennsylvania and moving to New York. You're literally following your dreams."

"I still have to get accepted," I say, not wanting to jinx it.

"You will," she says.

My car pulls up. Anna hugs me tight—her face close to my neck. The driver honks, scaring us into letting go. I'm about to get in the front seat when Anna directs me to the back. (Lyft virgin as well.)

After we get out of the Times Square traffic, the driver passes the aux cord back. "Want to listen to music?" Big mistake, buddy. I grab the cord and plug in my phone. This guy is too trusting with his ears. I find the *Hamilton* soundtrack and "My Shot" fills the car. I look out the window and try to process the day. After the song ends, I hit the back button, starting a new round of *Not throwing away my shot*. The driver sighs loudly, but I don't care.

Three months ago, I tried to come out to my parents again. The first time I asked my parents to let me transition, I bombed. A true no-star performance. But after two years in Theater Club, I knew how to put on a show. I gave an impassioned plea to start my transition. They sat there quietly, listening. Then said no on the spot. The first time I asked, my parents could ignore it. The second time, they had to do something about it.

After that, they couldn't even look at me. Their pride for me disappeared. They made me go to church more often. I had a weekly session with Pastor Tim, who thought there was a painful event in my past that made me confused about my gender. He asked me awful questions. I felt so alone. And ashamed.

My head went to bad places. I couldn't get out of my house, couldn't get out of my body, and couldn't escape my family's disgust for me. I don't know what came over me, but I wrote to Aunt Lil and told her everything. I asked if I could come live with her. It felt like a big ask, but I was desperate. She called me and said she would start looking for a school. That was the light I needed to keep going.

While waiting at a red light on Thirty-Fourth Street, I watch the city move—people walking, biking, laughing; a dog poops while the owner scrolls through his phone. I love this city. I never want to leave. The ending *not throwing away my shot* rings out. I see the driver's eyes in the rearview mirror, daring me to play it again.

So—I do.

He looks back at me. "What's your deal with this song, man?"

"I'm having a moment," I say to him.

One of the first songs in most musicals is the "I Want" number. This is the moment when the main character sings about their dreams and sets the entire plot in motion. I want to be August. I want to be on a Broadway stage. I want it more than anything in the world. This is my chance at living my dream. I'm not throwing away my shot.

6:35 P.M.

The car pulls up to my aunt's block. Her town house is hard to miss—bright yellow, green shutters, with golden pineapple statues littering the staircase. Aunt Lil is obsessed with pineapples. Seriously, her place is pineapple everything. Pineapple cookie jars, coasters, paintings, pineapple-shaped foods.

I head up the walkway and see lights on inside. That means she's home. I can't wait to tell her about my day. I unlock the entryway and front doors. Take off my shoes. I'm doing my best to follow the few rules she laid out when I arrived from the bus yesterday. Music fills the house. Well, music is a strong word for what's happening. It's more of an aggressive bongo with a woman making noises.

I start talking before I get to the kitchen. "Auntie, you will never guess—" I stop because someone is here.

"Don't just stand there with your mouth open," Aunt Lil says. "Say hello to our guest, Davina."

"Hello," I say to the African American woman wearing glasses (smart) with her hair in a large bun on the top of her head. Aunt Lil is sitting beside her, smiling. There are plates of green things, red things, and my sworn enemy: tofu. "Pleasure to meet you," I say to the lady, not the tofu.

"Likewise, August. I've heard so much about you," Davina says with a kind smile.

"I'm apparently infamous," I say, looking at my aunt.

"Me too," Aunt Lil says, "in certain circles." She is a big fan of vintage clothes and designer glasses. Right now, she's wearing a flowy purple dress and bright blue eyeglasses. Aunt Lil gets up and turns down the "music" so we can talk.

"I came home to seventeen messages from you-know-who," she says with a frown.

My heart drops. It's not a surprise that Mom would find me here. I didn't have that many options. "Only seventeen?" I ask, trying to lighten the mood.

She shakes her head. "I haven't checked my email yet."

I sit down at the table. "You okay, Auntie?"

"Of course, sweetheart. I know in my heart this is the best thing for you, but I feel awfully guilty about stealing my sister's child," she says with a wink.

Aunt Lillian is risking so much for me to have this chance. Basically, her entire relationship with her sister. When it comes to my aunt and my mom, being sisters is the only thing they have in common. They disagree on politics, religion, ice cream flavors, whatever. Aunt Lil would drive through West Grove—maybe once a year—on her way somewhere better. We never once visited her in New York—Mom was too afraid.

Aunt Lil puts an empty plate in front of me. "August, tofu and vegetables? Maybe some brown rice?"

My stomach nearly screams. "No thanks," I say. "I need real food."

She heads to the kitchen. "I thought that might be the case." Like a magician pulling a rabbit from a hat, Aunt Lil reveals a pizza box from the oven and plates two big slices. My stomach rejoices at the smell of actual cheese and grease.

"How do you two know each other?" I ask between cheesy bites.

Aunt Lil gives her a look. "Davina is my partner."

"Oh, like art partner," I suggest. They share a smile.

"Not quite." Aunt Lil holds Davina's hand. "She's my girlfriend, although we're too old to use that term."

I stop chewing and let the information sink in. My aunt has a girlfriend. She likes women. I nod repeatedly, looking like a bob-blehead. Aunt Lil lets out a playful laugh. "You're not the only one who can keep secrets, August," she jokes. "My parents—your grandparents—were not accepting of anything outside of one man and one woman. Just like your mom. Some apples don't fall far from the tree."

"And some fall very far," I say. I don't remember much about my grandparents—they passed when I was in elementary school—but keeping a secret like this all your life must be tough. "I feel sad for you, Auntie. To keep this part of your life from our family."

She laughs again. I'm cracking her up tonight. "Honey, I may be related to them, but they aren't my family."

Davina laughs softly as she heads to the kitchen and puts her plate in the sink. She moves around the house like she knows the place well. Like she would know where every pineapple-shaped object is stored.

"Do you live here?" I ask Davina. I've only been here one night—maybe she was hiding.

"No," Aunt Lil cuts in.

"I'm allergic to pineapple," Davina says with a wink.

"And you're never too old to do the walk of shame," Aunt Lil adds.

"August," Davina says, putting her hand on my shoulder, "I'm going to head upstairs and give you and your aunt time to talk. You're a brave boy, and I look forward to getting to know you better." The way she smiles makes me think everything will be all right.

"I'll be up in a few," Aunt Lil says to her. Once Davina has cleared the room, Aunt Lil turns to me and says, "I'm sorry for keeping this part of my life from you. I had a feeling you would understand, but your mom was always around. I could tell there was something going on with you when I'd come for a visit, but I couldn't put my finger on what. I just hoped you would reach out if you needed me."

"Thanks," I say. "For being there when I needed you."

"August," she says, looking me right in the eyes. "It was your talk about ending your life that alarmed me most."

A few days ago, an envelope changed my life. Mail doesn't usually get my attention, but the address on this envelope, hand-written in tight cursive, was from Brand New Day Therapy. The name sounded familiar, but I couldn't remember from where. First result on Google was a web page promising a conversion therapy program for gender confusion. Then I remembered where I'd heard of it—the pastor had their brochures on his desk.

I didn't know much about conversion therapy. But I knew it wasn't good. I couldn't believe my parents were considering sending me. They would take me out of school and out of theater. It would probably destroy me. It felt like there was only one option left—to end this life and hope I came back in the right body next time.

In desperation, I called Aunt Lil. I told her about Brand New Day and my dark thoughts. I could hear the concern in her voice. She had made a few calls and gotten me wait-listed for a dozen high schools, but no luck. I told her I couldn't wait much longer.

She called me back the next day with the last-minute audition for the School of Performing Arts. We planned my escape and here I am.

"Thank you," I say now, "for saving my life."

"You saved your own life, August." She slides her phone in front of me. "But I decided you need to call your mom."

I slide it away. "Maybe tomorrow?"

"You need to call your mom," she repeats, sliding her phone in front of me.

I push it back. "How about you call her?"

"I already did."

"You did?" I ask, surprised. That wasn't part of the plan. She went off book.

Aunt Lil removes her glasses and cleans them with a napkin. "I'm a lot of things, my dear nephew, but I'm not a child thief. I hated the thought of your mother not knowing where you were. She needed to know you were safe." That explains why my phone stopped buzzing around Times Square. Guess that's when they talked. She continues, "And I had some news to share."

"News?" I ask.

"August, Mr. Daniels called. You're accepted into SPA."

Everything in the room slows down. My head starts spinning. "I got in?"

"Yes," she says, then kisses my forehead. I let the news sink in. I was accepted. I'm going to one of the top high schools for performing arts in the country. I want to remember this moment forever.

"I can't believe it," I finally manage to say.

"Believe it, buddy. I knew you would. You must have really impressed Mr. Daniels. You can start classes on Tuesday if . . ."

"If?" I ask.

"If your mom signs the transfer forms. So, we need her on the team."

"Did you tell her I'm August now?" I ask, worried.

"No," she says in a soft voice. I feel instantly relieved. "Call her, please."

I pull my phone out—just as it starts ringing. It's my mom. Is that a good sign or bad sign? "What do I say?" I ask Aunt Lil, freaked out.

She runs her hand through my hair. "You know what to say. You can do it, brave boy."

I wish I could believe her. I put the phone to my ear. "Hi, Mom."

"Hello, sweet daughter." She sounds relieved. That's not like her. Good sign? Maybe the stress of a runaway child has changed her forever. "Do you have any idea how worried we've been about you? I have the entire church praying for your safety."

And there's my mom in all her religious glory. "I'm sorry, Mom, I really am."

I hear her exhale. She's probably standing in the kitchen, leaning on the counter. Or organizing something—that's what she does when she's nervous. "Randy is going to drive up there tomorrow morning and get you. We need to have a long talk."

Bad sign. Very bad sign.

"Wait. Mom, please, just hear me out," I say.

"I'm listening," Mom says, waiting for me to speak.

I clear my throat, raise my voice to the girl level. For my mom, I will play the part of her daughter. "If I go to the School of Performing Arts, I'll have a real shot at being a successful actress. This is everything you want for me. I'm sorry I ran away, but my audition was today, and I knew if I told you—"

"I wouldn't have let you go. You're correct about that."

"And I need this, Mom."

She's quiet. Thinking? Talking to my stepdad?

"All your talk about changing to a boy. I need to know that's not going to happen there. You're a girl. I know how liberal that city is. Randy isn't happy."

Oh, Randy. Stepdad of the year. He barely talks to me. Barely even looks at me. I want to scream, but I'm not throwing away my shot.

"If I let you stay, I need you to promise me one thing."

"Anything, Mom."

"Promise that you won't change into a boy. Can you do that?"

My big dream won't be stopped by this little problem. I will do anything for my dream.

"I promise, Mom."

TWO

Tuesday, September 10

11:17 A.M.

As of this morning, I'm officially a student at the School of Performing Arts. Hard to believe that I was in Pennsylvania three days ago. Harder to believe I'm here now. If getting on that bus to New York was the scariest thing I've ever done, walking into SPA on my first day of school was a close second.

My locker opens after two attempts at the combination. I survived my morning classes. Assuming I survive lunch, my acting classes are in the afternoon. My day started extra early in the office of the guidance counselor—and his glorious sideburns—sorting out my schedule. Mr. Esteban rolled up his sleeves and made me a schedule for my junior year at SPA. It wasn't easy for him—lots of squeezing me into full classes, overriding systems, and playing a mean game of "Schedule Tetris," as he called it. Mr. Esteban took extra care to make sure my deadname—my legal name—wasn't listed on any attendance sheets or forms. He smiled like he was proud of me. What world have I stepped into?

Mom signed the transfer papers yesterday. I hate lying to my parents—it's not what I want to do. I missed Mom this morning. She has a cute first-day-of-school tradition of pancakes and packed lunches. A handwritten note in my sandwich bag. But Aunt Lil made a tofu scramble and ordered a Lyft so I didn't have to deal with the subway on my first day. That's a good tradition, too.

Before closing my locker door, I catch my reflection in the mirror glued inside. Talk about a fresh start. New hair, new clothes, new name, new school, new everything. And now I'm a student at that school. I can't believe I'm here. It's all happening so fast, but it helps to pretend I'm a character in a play—this play just happens to be my life.

The final bell rings as I head toward the stairs—the cafeteria is on the seventh floor. This school is big. All-caps BIG. Mr. Esteban said there are nearly a thousand students—triple the size of my old school and ten times louder. This school is loud. All-caps LOUD. In between classes, the hallways are filled with people talking, singing, dancing, making videos, and an occasional instrument will play out. The first-day excitement is palpable.

From the outside, SPA looks more like a business than a school—it's a cement building with windows lining the seven stories. The inside feels a regular high school—with white-brick walls and faded yellow lockers—but also a museum with glass cases displaying art projects, sculptures at nearly every corner, and paintings on the walls. The school feels both historic and in need of a remodel.

My calves are burning when I get to the seventh floor. This school has only two elevators—everyone takes the stairs. My legs are going to be jacked by the end of this year. Every ounce of me wants to go hide in an empty classroom instead of facing the lunchroom—but Anna texted and asked to have lunch together.

A poster over a water fountain catches my eye. It reads: "Join the LGBTQIA+ Club! Everyone welcome!" This school is so open and accepting. You can be yourself. No need to hide who you are here. This poster would not fly at West Grove. There's no LGBTQIA+ Club there, but even if there were, they wouldn't advertise. West Grove is the opposite of out.

"Augustus!" Anna yells from down the hall. I smile and wave—relieved that I don't have to look for her in the cafeteria. "My god, you exist!"

"I do exist," I confirm, happy to finally be seen. Anna's first-day outfit is well planned—black skirt, Ramones shirt, black Converse. I'm wearing jeans and a black shirt, both purchased at thrift stores near Aunt Lil's apartment.

"Welcome to SPA, August," she says, then hugs me. "Or should I say the infamous August Greene?"

She's referring to the Insta handle I created yesterday. "I go by both," I brag.

"Am I still your only follower?"

"You are," I brag again.

"We're about to change all of that." She laces her arm through mine. "Are you ready to enter the lunchroom Thunderdome?"

I can tell our friendship is exciting to her. I'm something different, and she likes something different. "I'm ready," I say, actually not ready at all.

"Walk cool," she says, then pushes the double doors open, revealing a big room with high ceilings and circular tables. Posters on the walls promote arts events, not the next sports game like my old school. Everyone at the tables looks cool. Already famous. Heads turn and watch us walk by. I straighten my posture and push my shoulders back—playing confident—and try not to look at anyone. Anna tells me things about the people we pass. "That kid was on an episode of *Law and Order*" and "That girl's sister was last season's *Bachelorette*."

I can feel eyes on me. They must wonder who I am—and to be honest, I don't really know who I am either. August has no history, only future. He's an underdeveloped character. I don't want to be the New Guy—that character isn't cool. I want to be like everyone in this cafeteria. This is the role I need to learn, and any good character development starts with research. So that's what I'm doing—researching my role as a student at SPA.

We arrive at a table with four people in the middle of the lunchroom, near the trash cans. Anna puts her arm around my shoulder—I'm more of a prop than a person. "Everyone, this is August Greene from Pennsylvania. He's here to conquer the world. I told you about his audition in the group chat—he's genius level." She sits down, and I take the seat next to her—happy to be her prop if she keeps calling me genius. "Don't be shy; introduce yourselves to August."

The girl across from me smiles warmly. She's wearing bright clothing, and her hair is in pigtails. "I'm Meena. Pronouns are she and her. Tech theater major."

"You stage manage?" I ask.

Her face lights up. "I'm lead SM for the fall musical this year."

"That's the most important job of the show," I say. "Without the crew, the actors would never make it to the stage, have lights shining on our faces, sound, or a set. We'd pretty much be help-less."

"I like him," Meena says to Anna. "He can stay."

"Jack," the person beside Anna announces, then strikes a pose. "They, them pronouns. Dance major. Tell me I'm important, too," Jack jokes.

"You're so important," I confirm. Jack looks like Alvin Ailey and carries themself like a dancer with excellent posture.

"And I'm Juliet. She and her, and art. I'm also trans," she says with a smile. Her look is striking. She's got sea-blue eyes and blonde hair with hints of pink and red making a rose-gold effect. Her nose is pierced.

They look at me, silent. My turn. "I'm August. My pronouns are he, him, his. Drama major. But I think Anna has already filled you in on my biography."

"Only up to your early childhood," Jack says. They are quick with the humor.

"Let's give August a tour of the lunchroom," Anna says, looking around the cafeteria. "See that girl three tables away? Black hair, brown shirt, looks like she's already had plastic surgery?"

"Yes," I say, not really knowing who she's talking about.

"That's Mindy Walters. She's been in three Disney TV shows."

"All walk-on parts," Jack adds.

Anna points to another table. "That handsome Asian guy in the green tank top spent the summer doing *Come from Away* on a cruise ship. Oh, and that redheaded guy models for Gap, and not Gap Kids, *Gap* Gap."

Meena points to a girl. "Bailey Jones landed one of those prescription pill commercials where the family plays catch while the voiceover lists the bad side effects like dry mouth and diarrhea."

"We have the same agent," Anna brags.

I nod. I'm definitely in over my head in this school.

"So, August," Juliet jumps in, "what do you think of SPA?"

"Still a blur," I admit. "Very different from my old school."

Jack gives a high-pitched laugh and claps. "Can't imagine there's a theater scene in Podunk, Pennsylvania. Tell me, were the chickens and goats onstage with you? Or are they the audience?"

"I bet the goats have a union," Anna jokes.

"How'd you guys meet?" I ask, wanting to shift the attention away from me.

"We grew up together," Anna answers. "Well, same neighborhood, same schools."

"Same Long Lake Theater Camp every summer," Meena says.

Anna snaps. "Where I lost my stage fright."

"And I lost my virginity," Jack adds.

"Anna took my virginity yesterday," I brag, silencing the table with shock.

"Not as juicy as it sounds," Anna adds. "I took him to his first Broadway show. Too bad it was *Last Tango in Paris*. . . ."

While Anna gives a scene-by-scene takedown of the musical, I study Juliet. I'll never tell her, or anyone, but this is my first time meeting another trans person. She looks nothing like me, acts nothing like me, but we are the same. It's comforting to be in the company of someone like me, but I'm scared of saying something incorrect, or not acting trans enough. I bet she can tell that this is all new to me. It must be so obvious.

Juliet interrupts my thoughts. "So, August, you live with your aunt?"

"In Park Slope," I announce with confidence.

"Right off the orange subway," Anna teases.

Jack shakes their head. "My parents would not let me move without them."

I'm relieved they understand. Maybe I'm not the only one with controlling parents. "'Cause they wouldn't be able to watch over you?"

"Oh, no," Jack says, then cackles. "My mom wouldn't miss out on being an active participant in my life."

"Your dance things?"

"My dance, my school, my love life. I'm sure she's tracking my bowel movements."

Meena jumps in. "When I came out to my parents as a lesbian, they were so mad at me."

"I'm sorry," I say, knowing exactly what it's like.

Meena laughs. "Oh, no, they were mad because I waited so long to tell them."

"Sounds nice," I say.

"Sounds nice until your mom throws you a coming-out party. It's so embarrassing." Meena hides her face.

Juliet jumps into the conversation. "When I came out to my mom, around ten, she wanted to throw a party for me."

"Not a bad idea," I offer. "Have the gender reveal party in middle school!"

She laughs, then continues, "I was lucky; my parents have been supportive from day one. They got me a therapist. A doctor. Books. And we go to the Philadelphia Trans Wellness Conference every year."

I shouldn't be surprised to hear stories of such accepting families—this is New York City, after all—but it's almost shocking. Our lives are so different. They are practically competing for most supportive family.

"August," Jack sings. "What's the deal with your parents?"

I wish I had a family like theirs. But I don't. If I told them the truth, they would feel sorry for me, and I'm not playing that part. I sit with four potential friends. I don't want to jeopardize that by being different.

"They weren't baking rainbow cakes for me, but they let me be me. They're cool," I say, making Anna's head tilt. "And they knew I should be here and not Podunk, Pennsylvania." I lie, lie, lie. Or better: act. Anna looks confused. I give her an *I'll explain this later* look, but I don't think she gets the message.

The energy in the cafeteria shifts—people on their feet, packing up their stuff. The bell must be about to ring. "We need to get to class, Augustus," Anna announces.

Nerves kick in. My morning is academic classes, very standard issue: teacher, textbook, assignments, and test schedules. No one noticed me this morning—there was no reason to notice me—but that won't be the same for my drama classes. I have Acting 3, Improv, Musical Theater, and Audition Technique. A schedule of my dreams—if I could shake these first-day jitters.

"Picture time," Anna says, holding her phone up and finding the angle to fit everyone into the shot. "Smile," she says, and takes the photo. I watch as she adds the text **Introducing the new star of SPA @infamousAugustGreene** and posts to her Stories. "That should get some new fans. Everyone better follow the infamous August Greene," she playfully demands.

"Done and done," Jack says, head down in their phone.

"Jack has, how many, ten thousand followers?" Anna asks.

"Ten thousand nine hundred twenty, but who's counting," they say with a smile.

"How?" I ask, stunned at the number.

"By being me," they sing, kicking their foot in the air. "Well, the online version of me."

"And that's different?" I ask.

"Social media is performative," they say. "You create a persona, make content, try to trigger people's emotions—good or bad—and build an audience."

"Persona is dramatic," Anna decides.

"It's me," Jack says with an eye roll. "Just a bigger, brighter, more beautiful version. I'm going to be an international pop star *someday*, so why not act like one now?"

"Or you could be yourself," Meena says.

"And that's why you have two hundred followers," Jack jokes, but it stings.

"I call them my friends," Meena corrects them.

"Don't worry about it, Meena," Anna says, coming to the rescue. "Stage managers don't need that kind of thing."

Meena shrugs off both comments and turns to me. "I post pictures of celebrities made from food," Meena says proudly.

"My favorite was Pasta Malone," Juliet says, having otherwise kept quiet through this conversation.

The first bell rings, ending the conversation like a bell concluding a round of boxing. Anna and I say goodbye to my new friends and take the stairs down to the bottom of the school. "All drama classes are in the basement," Anna explains. "Like we are little underground theater trolls."

The basement doors swing open to reveal a mob of people filling the basement from wall to wall. Everything is overwhelming—the loud voices, the people making videos, the guys running around, the hugging and laughing, singing and dancing. Unsurprisingly, Anna says hello to almost everyone we pass.

Anna stops to talk to identical twins with blonde hair and matching outfits. One of them says, "Loving that first-day look."

"Likewise," Anna sings. "That skirt is everything!"

"Thanks, girl," they say in unison.

"August, this is Brooke and Tiffany. Twin triple threats!"

Triple threats are people who can act, sing, and dance. "Twiples," one of them jokes.

"And ladies, this is August, here to conquer the world."

"You're in the right place," the other one says. They both smile at me.

"The twiples had a video go viral this summer," Anna brags to me.

"Over five million views and counting," Tiffany adds.

"We got a call from *America's Got Talent*, but we passed."

My body tightens up. There's something exciting about their fame. They are doing it, they are on their way, and maybe they can help me get there. Anna starts to say something, but it's quickly drowned out by a sudden burst of singing. Several girls near us start belting loudly. More voices join as the words grow louder, echoing around us, gaining speed, and by the time the chorus hits, the entire basement is singing. Everyone has their phone out, recording.

When the song ends, people clap and laugh. Brooke and Tiffany head to their dance class, and I follow Anna to our class. She turns to me. "Hey, Augustus, what was the deal with lying about your parents at lunch?"

I knew this would come up. "My family is different." I look away, ashamed. "I didn't want your friends to feel sorry for me."

Anna puts a hand on my shoulder. "No one is going to pity you. And if they did, who cares?"

I shrug. "They would think I'm weird. I want to be just another student at SPA."

"There's not enough time to unpack all of that," she says as we arrive at the door. "You ready for this class? It's the big one."

"I was born ready," I say, hiding my panic.

We pause at the door before heading into the classroom. I recognize the room—it's where I auditioned. This is Mr. Daniels's room. Go figure his class is "the big one."

"What?" Anna asks, noticing my hesitation.

"This is *his* class?"

"Yes. Don't put your hand in the cage and he won't bite."

We enter the room and the air feels different. The students are muted, calm even, leaving the manic energy and wild screams in the hallways. Anna and I grab desks in the back. The bell rings and the strangest thing happens: the class does nothing. At West Grove, a teacher-less room would turn chaotic within thirty seconds. Desks would be destroyed after two minutes.

Mr. Daniels enters the room with his head down, reading a paper. He's wearing a brown corduroy blazer with brown elbow patches. Whenever there's a teacher onstage, they always have those patches. Mr. Daniels's messy hair and wire-rim glasses finish the professor look nicely. "Hello, students," he says, finally looking up.

"Hello, Mr. Daniels," everyone chirps in chorus. There's clearly a high level of respect for him, and he holds himself with confidence—a slightly slouched confidence, like Bernie Sanders.

"Welcome to Acting, level three—in my humble opinion, the most important class in your time at SPA." He grabs a stack of papers off his desk and begins walking between the rows of students. "Shall we begin the first lesson?"

Notebooks open and pens wait at the ready. "This is a script," Mr. Daniels announces while holding the papers over his head. "You hopefully learned that in your first two years at this school."

Everyone laughs. He continues, "In this script, like all scripts, there's friendship, conflict, love, possibly death, betrayal, or injustice, and maybe even a lion king. But what's missing from the script?" he asks, looking around the room for the answer. A few hands sheepishly go up.

"Daunte, what's missing from this script?"

I duck down in my seat. Daunte answers, "The director?"

Mr. Daniels throws the script on his desk. It's more poetic than aggressive. He's the star of this show and I'm here for it. And relieved I wasn't called on. "The actor is missing from the script. These are just pages, scenes, character descriptions, but it's up to you to bring the words to life. To give them depth and meaning. The words on these pages are not your character. Neither are the scenes. Not even the character descriptions are your character. Daunte, who decides your character?"

"The director shapes the character," Daunte says.

"What's your deal with directors, son?" Mr. Daniels asks. "You create the character, Sasha. You embody the character, Daunte." Mr. Daniels pauses and scans the class. "You're the character, August."

My cheeks go hot. Would it be obvious if I hide under my desk? Mr. Daniels continues, "And to be that character, you must find yourself in each role. Your fear, your love, your jealousy, your truth. The great Laurence Olivier once said, 'Acting is an everlasting search for truth.' I'm here to help you on that journey."

The class is motionless. Full attention on Mr. Daniels. He continues, "This year we will develop your ability to deepen your characters and make them feel real. We will learn from the masters, taking our notes from Lee Strasberg, and we'll study the Meisner technique, we'll study the Meisner technique, we'll study the Meisner technique," he repeats, making a joke of the repetitive exercises that Meisner teaches. The class laughs.

"And we will start with my favorite, the Stanislavski method, in which you learn to use your own experiences and truth to develop the character," he says, then makes his way to the whiteboard. He opens a marker, smells it for some reason, then scribbles: OBJECTIVE / SUPER-OBJECTIVE.

"Justin," he says, spinning on his heels with a mischievous grin. "What's the difference between the objective and the super-objective?"

The guy I suspect is Justin sits up and clears his throat. Anna turns around and whispers, "His dad is Robert Sudds."

"No way," I say, trying to get a better look. Anna smiles with the satisfaction of delivering juicy gossip. Robert Sudds was recently cast as the new James Bond. Justin's just as good-looking as his dad. He runs his hand though his hair and begins, "Objective is the motivation for the scene, and super-objective is the play's overall motivation."

"Close," Mr. Daniels says. "But let's think about it in terms of your character. The character's objective is something they want in the scene, and the character's super-objective is the character's overall goal, the thing that drives their every movement, decision, and interaction with other characters. You want to find love. You want revenge. You want to be in the room where it happens. You just can't wait to be king."

A redhead raises her hand. "What's your super-objective, Mr. Daniels?"

"To retire and play chess in the park. And help you become good actors. Sometimes characters have two super-objectives."

"How about three?" a kid asks.

"Don't get greedy, Mr. Griffith. I'll be proud if you can conquer one," Mr. Daniels says with a wink. It's clearly in good fun, but Mr. Daniels is in control and won't be shaken by hecklers.

"August Greene?"

I reluctantly raise my hand—like I'm volunteering for the firing squad. This is not how I want the class to meet me. Mr. Daniels stands at the lip of the stage with his hands behind his back. He looks pleased. He likes this kind of thing. "There you are. August?"

"Yes, sir," I say, my voice cracking. The class turns around, every single eye on me.

"Class, this is August. A new student from New Jersey."

"Pennsylvania," I correct him. The class giggles softly.

"Same difference," he says. The class laughs louder. He continues, "August, what's your objective for the school year?"

"To make it to Broadway," I joke, and the class laughs. I can be the Funny Guy, too.

"So soon?" Mr. Daniels questions.

"I'm ready," I say, getting another laugh.

Mr. Daniels gets frustrated. "What's your super-objective?"

I copy the son of James Bond and run my hand through my hair. "I want to be a working actor."

"Try to dig deeper, August," Mr. Daniels says, walking toward me.

Does he want me to tell everyone I'm transgender? I'm not ready for that. What does he want? As much as I want to please my new teacher, I'm not going to spill my life story. "I want to be a busy working actor?"

Mr. Daniels turns back to the class. "Here's my first exercise for you, due Monday: a one-page paper on what your super-objective is for your acting career. I know this is personal stuff. I promise not to share with the class. Unless you say something ridiculous." He smiles. "Then you're forcing me to share it."

The rest of the class is calmer. While Mr. Daniels lectures about the life of Stanislavski, I think about my super-objective. What's my endgame with acting? Do I want to be so famous I can't even walk down the street? Or at least be a respected Broadway actor with tons of fans waiting at the side door after performances? If all my motivation comes from my super-objective, I need to figure it out. When the bell rings, Mr. Daniels waves his arms in the air to keep our attention. "Don't forget, one page on your super-objective due Monday." He lowers his arms, officially releasing us from the class.

We head into the basement hallway and the energy resumes—all the way back to one hundred.

Anna comes up behind me. "Well, you barely survived that one. But it's downhill from here. I need a costume change before improv." She points in the direction of the girls' dressing room. "This skirt isn't giving me 'yes, and' vibes," she says, disappearing into the crowd. I look in the direction of the boys' dressing room. Going in there feels overwhelming. The men's bathroom is different—there's privacy in the stalls. I don't know if I can change clothes in front of guys. Luckily, I wore improv-friendly jeans and a black shirt.

"Is that Mr. Super-Objective?" I hear from behind me. I turn around to find a girl with wavy brown hair, perfect eyebrows, and brown eyes. She's wearing a pink baggy shirt and camouflage pants. A thin gold chain around her neck. "Hello, I'm talking to you."

I puff out my chest and straighten up my shoulders. "That's me."

She laughs. "What were you thinking?"

"I wasn't." I smile and look away. "I'm August. I'm new here."

"I'm aware," she says. "I'm Yazmin. You can call me Yaz."

"Hello, Yaz," I say.

"Can I give some totally unrequested advice? You have to say yes."

"Yes," I say, having no other option.

"This school," she says, stepping closer to me. "There's a bunch of fake people here. Be careful who you trust."

"I'll keep that in mind."

Yaz picks something off my sleeve. "You'll find out soon enough," she says, then gets lost in the crowd.

THREE

11:45 A.M.

Lunch is quieter on day three. Jack left us mid-lunch to sit with their dance friends, and Meena is working on some last-minute essay for history. I'm growing concerned at the amount of homework. Last night, after hours of chemistry work, I passed out with both my jeans and the lights on. I'm looking forward to the weekend—to catch up on homework.

"August, has anyone shown you Theater One?" Juliet asks as I take the final bite of my almond butter and grape jelly sandwich.

"I don't think so," I say, covering my mouth as I chew.

"It's incredible," Meena says. "But the real view is from the sound box."

"Can I give you the tour?" Juliet asks, smiling.

I look at Anna, unsure if I should take the invitation. "Go—I need to go change anyways. This dress doesn't allow for movement."

I smile at Juliet. "I'd like that," I say, feeling a little panicked. This sounds silly, but I'm nervous to be around another trans person. I'm too new. Too inexperienced. I don't know the script between two trans people. I don't know the language. What if there's a secret handshake?

We say goodbyes and exit the lunchroom into a quieter hallway. Juliet walks slowly, with purpose, and pulls her roller backpack behind her. I haven't seen her standing—she's taller than I am, with her rose-gold hair in a half bun. "What do you think of SPA so far?"

"It's a lot," I admit. This school makes me feel behind. Behind on academics—classes move faster here. Behind on acting—everyone already has an IMDb page. And behind on being transgender—new to my new identity and new to even being around other trans people. I don't know how obvious it is, but to me it's so clear.

Trying to be a gentleman, I carry Juliet's oversized backpack down the stairs.

"Anna seems to really like you."

My cheeks get hot. I can feel her looking at me for a reaction—wanting to know if I feel the same. Instead of responding, I ask, "How does Anna know everyone? Is she the theater mob boss of this school?"

"You don't know?"

"Know what?" I ask.

She shrugs. "I think you should ask her."

We make it to the ground floor. I set down her backpack and wipe the sweat off my forehead. "What's in here? Every single book you own? A dead body?"

"Some art supplies, and maybe body parts," she kids.

We pass my new favorite place—the gender-neutral bathrooms. I nod toward them. "They didn't have those at my old school."

"So progressive, right? I don't get the big deal with bathroom politics. All the fear and the laws. It's just a place to do your business and makeup."

"And vape and text," I add.

"Exactly."

As we walk down the hallway, I ask, "How many trans people go here?"

"It's a big school, hard to know. At least two," she says, then nudges me. "I think maybe ten? There's a good number of nonbinary people."

"Like Jack?"

"Like Jack," she confirms. "I do love the singular they—not just a rebellion against gender, but also language."

Juliet stops in front of blue double doors. "Here we are," she says, "Theater One." I push the doors open and audibly gasp.

"Holy shit," I say, making Juliet laugh. I was expecting big, but not Broadway big. There must be a thousand seats. This place is the opposite of that old Broadway theater I was in last weekend—the seats are new, the carpet is fresh, and the stage is the size of a football field. To think that I might be on that stage someday with an audience full of people.

"This is incredible," I say, my voice echoing.

Juliet leans against a guardrail and watches me. "I was on that stage once."

"You did art on that stage?" I ask, confused.

"No," she says with a laugh. "I started in drama but changed to art at the end of my freshman year."

"Why?" I ask, hoping it's not too personal.

Juliet sighs. "I got shy. After my transition, I didn't want people staring at me, and that's kind of the whole point of standing onstage. So, I transferred to painting and sculpture. I like making art, not being the art. And the odds depressed me. How many transgender actors have been on Broadway?"

"Only a handful," I say.

"Only a handful," she repeats. "In the history of Broadway."

"But things are getting better," I say—to convince her, and also myself.

"Sorry, August, I imagine you have big dreams, and I don't want to rain on them, but I couldn't compete with those odds. I wasn't that good at acting."

"I get it," I say, looking at the empty stage. "I'm going to be up there. And on bigger stages. In front of sold-out audiences. I know it."

"I believe it," Juliet says.

"You're the first trans person I've met," I blurt out.

Juliet puts her hands on her mouth. Her eyes soften. "Oh, August, that's adorable."

"I feel so behind. I'm new to everything," I admit.

She puts her hands on my shoulders. "You've been transgender all your life. Just like me. Transition is a transformation, and those take patience and time. And every gender journey is different. Don't measure your transition against anyone else's."

There's something I want to ask but don't know how to. "I have this friend with a problem," I start.

Juliet crosses her arms, amused. "Ah yes, a friend."

I continue my obvious ruse. "My friend thinks that everyone knows he's trans when he walks into a room. It makes him self-conscious. He doesn't know what people think about it."

Juliet contemplates what to tell me. I'm sure she doesn't want to give "my friend" the wrong advice. "Well, August, tell your friend that they can't control what's happening in other people's heads. They don't have access to other people's thoughts, and so they will never know for sure. Unless your friend has magical powers?"

"They don't."

"Too bad," she says. "But you can tell your friend that I'm here for them."

"Thanks," I say.

"You ready?" she asks, just as the bell rings. I could stay here all day, but I don't want the wrath of Mr. Daniels if I'm late to class.

Before we get to the main corridor, Juliet points at a display box full of clay faces. "Check those out," she says proudly. "Every sophomore sculpture class does a self-portrait. The best ones live forever in this box."

"I'll guess which one's yours," I say, then study the faces, eventually pointing to the one with happy eyes and a smile. "There you are," I say confidently.

"August, no," she says, almost offended. "It's that one." She points to the face that's screaming, with eyes filled with terror. "That's me."

I look at Juliet. "That's how you feel, really?"

She shrugs. "Sometimes."

Maybe Juliet isn't as comfortable as I thought. I take a closer look at the sculpture. "It's dark and sad, but beautiful."

"Like me," she says.

I make it to class right at the bell. The only empty desks are in the back row. I'll take it—as far away as possible from the eyeline of Mr. Daniels, who is at his desk flipping through a notebook. The room gets quiet, waiting for him to begin. He stands up, his white button-up shirt puffy under his scholarly vest. "Everyone up. Let's get warmed up. Up, up, up you go."

We stand by our desks and do stretches, movement exercises, humming, lip bubbles, and tongue twisters. It's nice to get the body moving, but this means we will be performing for the class. "Now sit," he directs. "Let's continue discussing the Stanislavski method. Today we will focus on identifying your character's objective in scenes. Don't get too comfortable in that chair—we will be working on a scene in a few."

My heart jumps into my throat. This will be my first time acting in front of the class. I'm equally nervous and excited. First impressions are important. Everyone will remember this performance. I need to prove myself to this school, and to Mr. Daniels.

He continues, "The objective is your character's motive in the scene. What they want, what they need. Your actions all work toward that objective. Make sense?"

A couple of hands go up, but Mr. Daniels ignores them. "Now, let's get some stage time in, shall we? You and your partner will perform a scene. As you prepare, identify your character's objective. I want to see that in your performance. You'll have ten minutes before we begin. Your scene partner's name is at the top of the script," he says, then hands the stack of papers to Anna. She hops up and walks the aisles, passing out papers and saying hellos.

When Anna gets to me, she drops my script down. "Sorry about your scene partner," she whispers.

"What?" I ask, scanning the top of my page for a name. TESS MONTAGUE. "Who is this?"

Anna smiles and points to the girl a few rows over. She would make a great Regina George. "Is she a mean girl?" I ask.

"The meanest," Anna confirms, then continues handing out scripts. Everyone pairs off and spreads out around the room. Tess remains at her desk, reading her script. I walk over and say, "Hi, I'm August Greene."

"I know who you are," she says, not even looking up.

"We are scene partners," I offer.

"I'm aware." She puts her highlighter down and fake smiles.

She knows so much about me. "So, want to run the scene?" I ask.

"I'd rather work with my script. It's best for me."

"Okay," I say, frustrated. We should be figuring out blocking and running lines, but instead we work separately as the room explodes around us with laughter, talking, and overly dramatic readings. This is not going well. I skim the scene, but I'm too annoyed to concentrate. It's a two-page fight between a husband and wife. Full of clichés. Boring.

"Hey," I say, earning me an eye roll from Tess. "How about we switch parts? I play the wife and you play the husband. That would be memorable."

She looks disgusted. "Why would we do that? Why would I play the husband?"

"It's just an idea." I get bold and say, "I can play both genders."

Another scoff. "You can? Who says you can?"

I feel the need to defend myself. "I'm transgender," I say, hoping that explains it.

"So you can play both roles?"

"And how are we doing?" Mr. Daniels asks, standing over me and Tess.

"Hello, Mr. Daniels," Tess practically chirps. "We're doing great."

"Good, good," Mr. Daniels says. "Maybe it would help to run

the actual lines from the scene, too? You have about four minutes left." He walks on to the next group.

Tess looks at me. "Why can't I find anything about you online?"

"Excuse me?"

"Who are your parents?" she asks.

"Why does it matter?"

Tess tilts her head. "Someone in your family has to be famous. Or rich. Last I checked, they don't let some nobody from Pennsylvania show up at the last second and attend the most prestigious arts high school in the country."

I shake my head in disbelief. I don't even know what to say. I look down at my script. I need to concentrate. I'm playing Donnie. The whole scene is Donnie begging his wife to stay. She doesn't love him. My mind is racing.

"All right, thespians, time to show us what you got," Mr. Daniels yells. I'm screwed. So much for first impressions. At least I'll have time to prepare during other people's performances. "Tess and August. How about you get us started?"

Craaaaaap.

It's official—I'm finished. Tess nearly skips to the stage, her blonde ponytail almost taunting me as I follow behind. We take the stage and I'm gripping my script tight to not reveal that my hands are shaking. This isn't going to go well. Will they laugh at me? Anna will tell my new lunch friends that I bombed. And that cute girl named Yazmin is in the front row.

"Ready when you are," Mr. Daniels sings from behind his desk.

Tess and I turn toward each other. I take one last deep breath and get into the scene. I am Donnie and I love my wife (ugh, Tess), who is leaving me for a rich man (great, bye!), but I am desperate for her to stay. I start the scene, but we don't connect. Our energies don't match. Tess is too standoffish, and I'm too desperate. It's like she's not in the same scene as me. She's giving me nothing. And when we get to the end, a moment between Donnie and Jackie that's supposed to be sweet and hopeful, it comes off like we hate each other, because maybe we do?

After we finish, there's a small round of applause—more polite than real. I look at the class, who are visibly unmoved by our performance. I kind of want to throw up. Mr. Daniels removes his glasses. "Tess, what was your objective?"

"Passiveness," she says passively.

"That's an emotion. What was your goal?"

"Oh, to be passive. I hate him and I wanted it to be over."

I can't tell if she's talking about Donnie and the marriage, or me and the scene.

"And August?"

"My character's objective was to stay with my wife." I turn on the Funny Guy and give Tess a look. "I'm not sure why."

The class laughs, and that feels like fuel. Mr. Daniels shakes his head. "You can take your seats. William and Kerry, won't you be next?"

I return to the back row, defeated. I'm embarrassed and avoid making eye contact with anyone. The next scenes are great—some funny, some serious. I'm drowning in other people's talents. I spend the rest of class seething about Tess. This is all her fault. She really messed it up for me. That was my chance to show everyone why I'm here, and Tess Montague ruined that.

After the last scene, Mr. Daniels takes center stage. "Great work today, gang. Don't forget your super-objective paper on Monday. I would also like you to prepare a monologue for the end of next week. Anything you want," he says; then, like a cue from the sound board, the bell rings.

I wait until Tess walks by and follow her out. Once we're in the hallway, I tap on her shoulder and say, "Good job ruining that for me."

"You did that yourself," she says.

I puff up my chest. For Tess, I'm the Tough Guy. "What's your deal?"

She rolls her eyes. "I started acting classes when I was five. Dance, ballet, and singing classes in middle school. I had a tutor just for the audition to SPA. *Just for the audition.* We prepared, we stressed, and we even prayed for a spot at this school. I waited outside for five hours, and earned my spot here. And some of my best friends, they didn't get in. So, you walking into SPA like nothing really annoys me."

"Sorry to annoy you," I say, not backing down. "But I auditioned for my spot."

"With Mr. Daniels? I'm sure your girlfriend helped sweet-talk her dad."

"Girlfriend?" I ask.

"Anna."

"Dad?"

"Mr. Daniels," Tess says, watching my reaction. "Oh, you didn't know that?"

"Sure I did," I say, lying.

"Look, no offense, but I don't think you deserve to be here."

Before I can continue my Tough Guy act, Anna appears by my side.

Tess smiles big and fake. "You're such a cute couple," she says, then walks off.

"What was that?" Anna asks.

"Nothing," I lie. I can't even look at Anna right now. Her dad is Mr. Daniels? Why wouldn't she tell me? Did she influence Mr. Daniels's decision on letting me into the school? And worse, does everyone at SPA think that?

Anna smiles. "Want to walk to the subway after school?"

I need some time to think. "I'm good today."

"Fine," she says. "Talk later?"

"Sure," I say, actually not sure at all.

FOUR

Sunday, September 15

12:47 P.M.

"Rise and shine! This is a homework intervention," Aunt Lil sings
while opening the shades to let in the sun. I spent Saturday doing
homework. And Friday night. I was planning on doing the same
today, but I guess Aunt Lil has different ideas. "You do know you
live in the coolest city in the world, right?"

"I can see it from my window," I say, stretching my arms. I've
been enjoying a lazy morning looking at my phone before getting
back to my desk. I've never had homework to do on the weekends.
Also, I've never had this much. I'm getting concerned about the
next two years.

"It's the weekend; you should be out vaping or eating Tide
Pods," she jokes.

"I don't want to get behind."

"Maybe this will get you out?" She hands me a printout of a

ticket to an Off-Broadway show. "I became a member of the Atlantic Theater Company years ago to impress a girl. The things we do for love, August, I swear."

"Was she impressed?" I ask.

"Yes. For about a year, then she got impressed by someone else. I never went to a show, but I kept paying the dues. You should go forth, young man, and get my money's worth."

The ticket is for an up-and-coming play called *Happiness Is for Other People*. I've read reviews online, mostly positive, and it's a Critic's Pick by the *New York Times*. Maybe it will inspire me to write my super-objective paper for Mr. Daniels. The play starts at three—I need to get moving. "Thank you, Auntie," I say, excited.

"Don't come home until you have something pierced," Aunt Lil demands with a wink.

After one subway transfer, one delay due to a sick passenger, and a ten-minute walk, I'm standing in front of a church. I'm usually at a church on Sunday (not by choice), but this church is a theater (more holy, in my opinion), and I'm not sitting through a sermon, I'm attending a matinee (hallelujah!).

The place is packed, with people standing outside the theater, crowding the lobby, and waiting for the bathroom. It's unsettling to see people standing in a church holding sippy cups of wine. But I can adjust quick. I walk with confidence, pretending to be an important person. People must think I'm a celebrity, or the son of a celebrity. Or maybe they will think I've lost my mom.

I hit the concession stand. It's thrilling to be here alone. I'm good on my own. In West Grove, I'd go for bike rides by myself and go to see movies alone. I can get lost in my thoughts and not have to put on a show for somebody else.

The usher hands me a Playbill and points at my seat—back row and middle. Ten people stand up to let me by, though a couple of them move slow and act like I ruined their day. I'm deep in the middle of this row. Let's hope I don't have a bathroom emergency. This theater must have two hundred seats, all filled. It feels more like a theater than a church, but there are stained-glass windows and religious etchings on the ceiling. The stage is not impressive—about as big as the one at my old school.

The man next to me flips through his Playbill. His cologne smells expensive. He has a salt-and-pepper beard, slicked-back hair, and thick-rimmed glasses. He looks at me and smiles. "Best seat in the house," he says.

"I have to disagree," I say, not happy to be so far back.

He shakes his head. "What do you mean? We have the best view of the set, the actors, and the audience. The audience is very telling. And look," he says, directing my attention to the armrest. "We each have our own. Every other row has to share."

I guess the back row has its perks. Armrests. Full views. Talkative strangers. "It's not so bad," I confirm.

My seat neighbor smiles. "That's the attitude!" He's got a cool-dad vibe. "Mind if I get nosy?" he asks.

"Sure," I say, hoping this doesn't get weird.

"I'm curious why a young guy like yourself would be here on a Sunday afternoon?"

That confirms it; he's one hundred percent going to kidnap me.

My palms start to sweat. "Um," I finally say, wondering if I can change my seat.

"Sorry, sorry," he says, holding up his hands. "I'll explain myself. I'm a producer, and if you can keep a secret, I'm thinking about investing in this show. Maybe taking it to Broadway." He shrugs like it's no big deal. "I'm always curious about the audience. How did you hear about this show?"

I'm sitting by a producer who can nonchalantly take things to Broadway. I've watched *The Producers* and know that producers are the ones with the money and the power, but I've never met one. And now I'm sitting by one. "My aunt gave me the ticket. And I'm studying acting," I say, hoping he will cast me immediately.

His eyebrows rise. "Where?"

"School of Performing Arts," I answer with pride. This gets another eyebrow raise. "I'm a junior at SPA," I repeat, mostly because I want to say it again.

"Good for you," he says. "Lot of talented actors came from that school."

"It can be intimidating," I admit.

He smiles. "It should be inspiring."

The lights go down, and the audience quiets. As the actors take their places, I replay our conversation in my head, wondering if I could've been more charming or funny, and if he'll give me a job someday.

The lights go up, and we're in a women's shelter in New York. The characters have rough lives and dirty mouths. The group is planning a talent show, which leads to several fights, mostly with the main character, Fresco—a retired army vet suffering from PTSD. Fresco is fiery and quick to take someone down verbally. And maybe physically. I think about how I would play that part. I don't think I could scream that much.

As the scene plays out, my eyes wander to the woman in the corner of the stage. She sits with her head down like she's in pain. Fresco goes on a tear and heads over to her, pointing her finger, yelling, "Why would they let transgender people in our women's shelter? This is a women's shelter, and this isn't a woman."

I grip the armrest like I'm on a roller coaster that's plunging to the ground. My body is hot and tight, and my brain has tons of thoughts at once. Fresco continues yelling slurs and hate speech that are not only offensive—they feel like a hate crime. She continues belittling the trans woman, named Wanda, and I want to cover my ears and look away. Every mean thing feels like it's being said to me. I feel as hurt as Wanda. And I know it's not real, but it feels real, and I want to get off this roller coaster.

Fresco pulls back to slap her, but Wanda grabs her hand. "You should die," Fresco screams, then spits in Wanda's face. "You don't belong in this world."

I've heard the word *triggered*, but I've never felt it before. I'm triggered, and there's nothing I can do but sit here, hearing and feeling every word. My body is on fire. There's sweat on my forehead. I want to get the hell out of here, but I'm trapped in the middle seat.

When Wanda walks off the stage, my muscles relax. My fingers unclench on the armrest (I'm now very thankful to have my own). I scan the audience and see no one alarmed or upset. The producer looks unbothered. Why are they so calm? How could that be okay? I'm already worried about the next time Wanda enters the stage.

I have trouble concentrating on the show. I'm thinking about why the playwright used all those terrible words. What was the point? The play takes place a while ago, maybe in the 90s, when talking like that about transgender people was tolerated. But it's not anymore. There was no reason for what happened onstage. Wanda gets a few more scenes, and I swear I grip the armrest so tight I'm leaving dents.

When the lights come up for intermission, I step over my seat and get to the lobby first. My shirt is wet from sweat, and my binder feels soaked. I step outside to get some air. I should leave, but I would feel bad for the actors. When I'm onstage, empty seats after intermission make me feel awful. And the play is pretty good minus the Wanda verbal torture scenes.

Once outside, I google the playwright. He's an older man with a gray beard and thinning hair. *Happiness Is for Other People* is his sixth play, and most of them debuted at this theater. Several websites say he's gay. I think about why he chose to write Wanda this way and what he wanted to accomplish. He probably wanted to feature a trans character, and show how difficult life was in shelters, and call out the injustice. Or maybe he didn't think about it all.

I head back inside and hop over my seat from behind—successfully avoiding having to ask the entire row of people to stand up again. The producer is drinking wine from his sippy cup. "What do you think?" I ask, curious about his take.

"I'm intrigued. But I would cut thirty minutes out of that act."

I can't help but be in awe of this man. "You have the best job in theater," I say.

He laughs so loud the two ladies in front of us turn around and give a look. "What makes you think that?"

I wave my hand over the sea of people here on a Sunday afternoon. "All these people paid to be here. That's a lot of money."

This gets another loud laugh from the producer. "Let's do some math."

"Fun," I say.

"Stick with me. Assume each ticket costs a hundred dollars. And each row has about twenty seats. The first row would pay the actors, the next row the crew, the next four-ish rows would go to theater rent, two rows for the upfront money to get the show on its feet, one more row for equity dues, taxes, fees, and that leaves us"—he counts the rows with his fingers—"with two rows for producers."

"I hadn't thought of it like that," I admit.

"Shoot, sorry, one row for marketing and management. *One* row for producers. But what happens if the show isn't sold out? We still pay everyone. Sure, there's money to be made. The producers of *Hamilton* aren't worried about too much anymore. But producing is not for the weak of heart, and very few shows make money."

"Then why do it?" I ask.

"Because I'm desperately and helplessly in love with theater."

"I feel it, too," I say.

"You better, because acting is also not for the weak. But you're special, I can tell."

"Thanks," I say, hoping that means he will ask me to star in his next show.

"Now, my new friend, should I produce this show?"

I'm not ready to give my verdict. "Can I tell you at the end?"

He smiles. "Sure, kid, you know where to find me."

The lights dim down. Here we go. I ready my hands on the armrest and let the roller coaster take me away. The second act introduces Wanda's love interest—a janitor at the shelter named Ralphie. He's a cis guy with big muscles and tattoos—a man's man. He's wrestling with his love for a trans woman and confides his feelings to a friend on a park bench. He can't believe he loves "a chick with a dick." Armrest grab. He doesn't want to be gay. He doesn't want people to know. There are jokes in the dialogue, and the playwright is clever enough to not direct them toward Wanda, or trans people, but it gets close. Then the characters decide that Ralphie should follow his heart even if it's for a "chick with a dick." A moment of friendship at the expense of the trans person. I shake my head in defeat.

Wanda isn't in much of the second act. I mistakenly let my

guard down until Fresco's girlfriend, Nikki, goes missing, and she blames Wanda. When they find out Nikki is dead, Fresco goes after Wanda. They circle each other as Fresco yells transphobic insult after insult. "All trans people will go to hell and burn," Fresco shouts.

I want to fight back. Punch something. Stand up and say SHUT UP. I want to defend Wanda and every trans person who's had to hear these words. Fresco takes out a knife and stabs Wanda. The lights go dark, and everything is quiet. Defeat fills me up. Why did it need to go this way?

Wanda doesn't die from the stabbing and gets transferred to an LGBT shelter in Queens. I think the writer wanted to give her a happy ending. The lights come up, and everyone is on their feet for a standing ovation, with the largest applause going to the actor playing Wanda.

We start the slow shuffle toward the exit. My body is weak from the roller coaster. My jaw is sore from clenching it the whole show. The producer checks his phone. He looks up at me. "So, should I buy this thing?"

I think about my answer. I know it doesn't really matter—he's not going to make his decision off mine—but I want to give him my honest opinion. And I don't want anyone else to feel like that ever again. "No," I say. My eyes get wet, but I wipe it away quick. "I'm trans, and sitting though that was like being stabbed one hundred times with words. So my answer is no."

* * *

I look out the window in my bedroom. It's great to see the street, but not so great to *hear* it. Day and night, there are car honks, trash trucks, and people disagreeing loudly. Late one night, I even heard a couple *agreeing* very loudly. The only sounds from my window in Pennsylvania were dogs barking and trains passing. On wild nights, a raccoon would knock over the trash cans.

My bedroom is tiny—I think it's meant to be an office. Aunt Lil turned the master bedroom on the second floor into an art studio, her bedroom is on the ground floor, and my room has enough space for a twin bed, a small desk, and a dresser. My aunt used to rent this room to artists, until someone left jars of pee under the bed. I jokingly promised her I would always empty my pee jars.

I stare at the pineapple lamp on my desk, trying to summon energy to do homework. I feel drained from the week, and that show—it should be called *Happiness Is for Other People but Not Trans People.* I think about writing a letter to the playwright about my experience but decide to waste time on my phone instead. Don't want to brag, but I now have fifty followers on Instagram. Awfully close to internet famous.

Anna texted a few times this weekend. Her friend wrote a play (of course she has a playwright friend), and she wanted me to be her date. I declined the invitation and told her I was hanging with my aunt. I needed time to think. I don't understand why she didn't tell me her dad was Mr. Daniels. Why is it a big deal? There must be more to the story. I want to talk to her about it, but I'm unsure how to bring it up.

I open Aunt Lil's old laptop. I have one assignment left—the paper about my super-objective for Mr. Daniels. Won't everybody say they want to be a famous actor? And how will he grade this paper? I want to act, not write papers about acting.

Aunt Lil knocks, then enters. "Hey, August, that better not be homework."

"No way," I say, happy to shut the computer.

Aunt Lil starts making my bed, which is pointless 'cause I'm going to sleep soon. I've noticed she gets fidgety when she needs to say something. "I spoke to your mom today. She says you haven't called?"

"Oh, I guess I got busy," I say.

"She misses you," Aunt Lil whispers.

"And I miss her, too." I miss her in the mornings while getting ready for school, when I need help, and when Aunt Lil cooks all vegetables. I miss her hugs.

"She asked if we could face chat her tonight. Can we do that now?"

"It's FaceTime," I say as panic washes over me. Mom can't see my face. Well, the face is unchanged, but she can't see my hair and my clothes. "She will be pissed if she sees my new look."

"No problemo," Aunt Lil announces, then heads to the closet and pulls down an Ikea blue bag from the shelf. She digs around and comes up with a bright pink ball cap in one hand and a pineapple beanie cap in the other. "What's your flavor?"

"Neither," I say.

"Good choice," she sings, and puts the pink cap on my head. Mom has seen me in ball caps; she doesn't love it—too masculine— but she's seen it. I catch a glance of myself in the mirror and detest what I see.

"I'm allergic to pink," I say, pulling the pineapple beanie on my head instead. That's how much I dislike pink.

Mom picks up on the first ring and I see her face, a little too close to the camera, against the backdrop of the brown leather chair in our living room. There's no doubt that Randy is next to her in the La-Z-Boy. Above them hangs a deer head from Randy's hunting trips. I never liked that deer head—I swear its eyes would follow me at night. "Hi, Mom," I say.

"Hi, honey. That's an interesting hat."

"Aunt Lil is teaching me the way of the pineapple."

Aunt Lil puts a hand on my shoulder and lowers her face into the camera. "Just trying to teach the finer things of life to him."

I watch Mom's face tighten. Aunt Lil's grip on my shoulder goes from loving to deep tissue massage. She knows what she said. "To her, of course."

"Mom," I say, "did you get a haircut?"

"Oh, yes, thanks for noticing. Randy didn't," she says.

"You look great. And how is Trish?" I ask. Aunt Lil gives me a look and mouths, "Trish?" I shrug. She's been Mom's hairdresser my whole life.

"Always up to trouble," she says with a laugh. Trish is single and ready to mingle. Mom always loves her bad dating stories. "But enough about Trish; how's your school?"

"It's a great school, Mom. The classes are tough—I do homework on the weekends now," I brag.

"Now that's impressive," Mom says. Aunt Lil gets up and straightens things in the room, listening but staying out of the way.

"And," I continue, "the acting classes are going to change my life. If I can keep up."

"When you want something, you don't give up."

"Are you talking about the Easter Concert?" I ask, evoking one of our inside jokes.

The phone shakes as she laughs. "You didn't leave Pastor Tim alone until he let you sing the solo."

I went a little overboard in convincing him. If I had to go to church, and I had to participate in the Easter Concert, then I was going to get the solo. "I knew I was the best one for the job."

"And you were amazing," she confirms. "I get teary thinking about it."

Mom loved anytime I was acting or singing, but especially loved when I was acting or singing about Jesus. *"And He walks with me,"* I sing now. *"And He talks with me, and He tells me I am His own."* I repeat the lines as she hums along. For this scene, I am my mother's daughter. I will do anything to stay in New York and go to SPA. Aunt Lil dances and almost cracks me up, but I stay focused. When we sing the last note, Mom and I smile at each other.

"Miss you, baby girl," she says sweetly.

My body cringes at *baby girl*, but my face remains composed. "Miss you, too, Mom."

"Aunt Lil treating you okay?" she asks.

"She's making me eat the grossest things," I admit.

Aunt Lil leans against me, getting her face in the camera. "They're called vegetables. Did you not have them in Pennsylvania?"

"I tried my best," Mom says. "Say hi to Randy." As Mom passes the phone to him, my aunt gets out of the camera's range. Aunt Lil and Randy never got along.

A mustache takes up half the screen. "Hey, kiddo," he says.

"Hi, Randy," I say. And now I'm out of things to say to him.

"You behaving yourself? There's some weirdos in New York."

"I live with one," I try to joke.

"Don't I know it," Randy says. Aunt Lil rolls her eyes.

I can hear Fox News in the background. Randy and I never had much to discuss. I wish Mom hadn't passed him the phone. I'm struggling for the next thing to say. "How's work?"

"Same ol' every day. Liberals trying to mess up our taxes, but we stopped them."

"Thank god," I say sarcastically.

"Darn right," he agrees. "All right, kiddo, stay out of trouble. Your mom is worried about you. Bye." He hands the phone back before I can say bye.

"Mom, you don't have to worry; I'm here making our dreams come true."

"I know, but I'm still your mom. I love you so much, sweetie."

"I love you and miss you," I say, then hang up the phone. Even though my parents don't accept me and possibly want to send me to conversion therapy, I can't help but love my mom and want her to love me and not her version of me.

Aunt Lil sits back down on the bed. "Damn liberals and their damn taxes," she says, mocking Randy. She does a dramatic face-palm. "I forgot to ask about the show! How was it?"

"Happiness is not seeing that show," I say.

"Ouch."

I softly kick the desk leg, trying to put into words what's in my head. "There was a transgender character. She was a prostitute, addicted to drugs, and stabbed."

"So not a comedy?" Aunt Lil jokes.

I shake my head. "Lots of scenes with the main character yelling the most transphobic and awful things at the trans character. The worst words, Auntie. I still feel upset about it."

She puts her hand on my shoulder. "Oh, honey, I'm sorry. Off-Broadway can be more edgy. Are you feeling okay?"

"I don't understand why the trans character can't be the funny best friend or hero or love interest."

"The play took place in the nineties?" she asks. I nod. "It's possible that the writer wanted to stay true to the reality of that time. Even though it's hard, maybe we need to see those stories to understand trans history and create empathy and understanding?"

"I guess so," I say, but it doesn't make me feel better.

"I'm hitting the hay. Good night, kiddo," she says in her Randy voice, and walks out.

Once the coast is clear, I open my computer again. Aunt Lil is right—it's important for people to understand the history and struggle of being transgender. And it's great when there's a transgender character onstage, even if they are being bullied and hurt, but those aren't the parts I want to play. I don't want to stay in my lane.

MY SUPER-OBJECTIVE by August Greene

My super-objective is to play iconic male and female characters on Broadway stages. Roles like Sweeney Todd, Glinda, Evan Hansen. Characters usually only played by cisgender actors. A Jersey Boy, Pippin, Roxie Hart. I want to move the audience, make them feel things, think about things, and leave the theater changed. I want to be a star.

FIVE

2:36 P.M.

Between Improv and Audition Technique, I pay a visit to the gender-neutral bathroom on the first floor. There's the boys' dressing room in the basement, but I can't bring myself to go inside. I feel like I don't belong. I get up to the doors, panic, and retreat. I don't want to make anyone uncomfortable. I don't want to make anything awkward. I've been in several men's bathrooms, but that's easier—no one knew me in there. In the boys' dressing room, they will know I'm transgender. It's easier to use the gender-neutral bathroom and wear the dress code for drama classes—a black T-shirt and jeans—to school every day.

I head back to the basement and submerge myself in the crowd of people. Anna warned me that the lunchroom was socially stressful—and it can be—but I think the basement is the real popularity contest. Since every drama class takes place down here, it's like a five-minute party in between each class—which sounds fun but can be intimidating to the new kid with a limited social circle. Anna usually finds me—I swear she has a tracking device. And I'm trying to make friends but don't seem to be connecting.

When I walk into Audition Technique, the chairs are pushed against the wall and everyone is sitting on the floor facing the stage. I find a spot with a good view and lean against my backpack. A deep breath takes more concentration now that my binder has shrunk. (Aunt Lil "sends" the laundry out and it comes back folded and smelling so clean—another reason New York is a magical place—but they shrank my binder. I will hand-wash going forward.) I'm having trouble taking a full breath when I'm seated, especially on the floor.

I check Insta—I'm up to sixty-five followers. Only one hundred and seventy million or so away from Kim Kardashian. Not a great following. Not a great look. I need to do something about that. I take a couple of selfies, but the angle is wrong. Not flattering enough to post.

Ms. Ramos enters the room with a big smile. She's a fast-talking ball of energy, speed-walking around the room, always acting things out using accents and celebrity impersonations. There's a chaotic energy to her teaching, but it keeps me interested. Today is no exception for the Ms. Ramos Show. She begins the class with a full review of the latest jukebox musical to hit Broadway. "Did there need to be an entire musical about the Goo Goo Dolls?" she asks rhetorically.

Jukebox musicals tell a story through preexisting popular music. My favorite jukebox musicals are *Jersey Boys, Mamma Mia!*, and *American Idiot*. Ms. Ramos strums her air guitar and does a high kick. "Now give me a musical about Blondie. That's my kind of show." She plays more air guitar and sings, *"I'm gonna get ya, get ya, get ya, get ya."*

Whatever Ms. Ramos drinks or smokes before class, I want some.

"Today," she says, settling into a stool in front of the class, "we will start working on our cold reads. The curveball of the audition process." She swings an imaginary baseball bat. "And I'll throw a curveball by inviting a special guest to help."

A special guest? I sit up straight, hoping it's someone famous.

"As you know, I was the swing for *Evita* on Broadway. And made it onstage three times, even singing 'Don't Cry for Me, Argentina' for a former vice president." Ms. Ramos smiles proudly. She mentions this at least once a class.

"Well, today we have the director of *Evita* and other Broadway shows. Class, please welcome Evan Lancaster!" She claps enthusiastically and we join in. An older man with a bald head and a big Hollywood smile enters the room. He's wearing a black jacket, shiny blue jeans, and a white shirt. I've never heard of him, but I'm almost as excited as Ms. Ramos. A real Broadway director is here in the room.

"Hello, friends," he says, with a deep voice that could be on the radio. "I'm happy to be here with you today. As a former student of SPA, I know how important these years are for you. I learned so much, and having SPA on my résumé opened a few doors for me. But it was the friendships I made here that meant everything to me." He pauses and looks around the room. I think he actually misses this place.

"Show of hands, who here will be pursuing acting as their profession?"

Every hand goes up.

"Congratulations," he announces, "you have chosen the profession with the lowest success rate." Hands begin to lower. "Ninety percent unemployment rate, average income of seven thousand dollars, and a two percent success rate. Not great numbers," he says, shaking his head. "Your seat in this class improves those odds. Casting directors will take note of which school you attended, alumni will help, and you're learning from great teachers." He smiles at Ms. Ramos, who blushes.

"But the real factor that will separate you from the rest is your willingness to put in the work. You have to put in the work. You'll find that shortcuts are mostly dead ends. And you'll have to sacrifice. Don't worry, there's still time to turn back and pursue something a little less risky, like the stock market, perhaps." Mr. Lancaster looks around for a reaction to his joke, but we're all too stunned by his words to laugh.

"Don't mean to scare anyone, but I want to ground you. You can be a great actor. You can be in that two percent. But you'll need to be humble and hardworking and hungry."

"Do you hear that?" Ms. Ramos asks. We all say some version of yes. "Today, Mr. Lancaster has kindly offered to critique your cold reads!"

My stomach turns over with nerves. This is not how I imagined my first audition with a Broadway director. The class gets fidgety—they are as nervous as me.

"No pressure, kids," Ms. Ramos says, possibly sensing our worry. "We know this won't be perfect. Just do your best."

Mr. Lancaster sits on the stool, so calm and collected, as Ms. Ramos hands pages to a guy and girl. They walk up to the stage and begin the scene. It starts slow and choppy, but I'm amazed at how quickly they adapt. The scene works, and we clap loudly. They bow and wait for notes.

"Not bad, you two," Mr. Lancaster says with a thumbs-up. "The scene started bumpy. Be careful of pauses. Let your words flow and follow your instincts."

Students write this advice down as Ms. Ramos hands out more scripts. Three new actors get up and do a scene on a train—all bouncing up and down like it's a very shaky ride. It's hilarious— the class cracks up. "Fantastic," Mr. Lancaster says. "You were all present and playing with each other. The casting directors like to see that in an actor."

"Yazmin," Ms. Ramos says, "game to try a cold reading of a monologue?"

And there she is—Yazmin Guzman. She's in three of my drama classes and US History. We haven't spoken since the first day, but

I can feel the beginnings of a crush. She takes a script from Ms. Ramos on her way to the stage. Her hair is curly today (some days it's straight), she's wearing a baggy shirt and leggings (sometimes she wears jeans and sweaters), and she has a couple of scrunchies around her wrist (always). She has that pretty and tough thing, with strong eyebrows that define her face and bring out her eyes.

She clears her throat and pushes the hair behind her ear. "What am I doing here?"

The class watches as she finds her footing in the monologue. I hang on her every word. Yazmin acts self-assured and closed off, but onstage, there's a vulnerable openness. There's something different about her delivery, and something different about her. I look around—the class is caught up, too. Whatever it is, she's got it. She could be in the two percent.

After she finishes, her friends yell "Yes, Yaz" as the class claps. She smiles and my heart races.

"That was wonderful, Yazmin," Mr. Lancaster says. "But I'd like to see you make slightly bigger choices. Take more risks."

"That's all I do," Yaz jokes.

"Stay up here for one more," he suggests.

"I'll find you a scene partner," Ms. Ramos says, stepping over and around us as she makes her way through the room. "Not you," she says, patting someone on the head like it's a game of duck, duck, goose. "Not you, or you . . ." *Not me not me not me.* "Not you, not you." She stops by me. *Please not me. Please not me.* "You," she says to me. "Would you join her onstage?"

I get to my feet and take the script, my hand shaking as I try to scan the lines and walk to the stage. My foot gets wrapped up in a backpack strap, almost tripping me up. The script is about two con artists, I think. The couple hate each other—I think. I'm having trouble breathing. There's no spit in my mouth. A panic attack is nearing.

Once I'm onstage, I say, "Hold on, I need a second."

I know this looks silly—and the snickers confirm it—but I turn my back on the audience and shut my eyes. Focus on a breath. I just need one. I'm in a battle with my binder and no one has any clue what's happening. I loosen my shoulders and get air in my lungs. Relief washes over me. I turn around, all eyes on me. "I'm ready."

"Wonderful, August," Ms. Ramos says. "You had us all on the edge of our seats!"

Yazmin has the first line. She goes small, and I decide to go big. I look up and nearly yell: "I cry all night because of you." The class laughs at my strong and wrong choice. Yazmin goes bigger, meeting my energy. We make eye contact, but I get nervous and look away. I continue the angry-guy act even though the words are about forgiveness and love. It makes no sense, but I'm committed, and I carry it out until the end. The class laughs each time I say something, so I keep it up, even angrily saying, "I don't want to lose you."

"Very interesting choices," Mr. Lancaster says. "You two didn't connect as scene partners. The audience can tell." I walk offstage feeling mortified. I try to smile at Yazmin, but she doesn't look my way. Several more groups go onstage, then the bell rings, ending the school day. Everyone claps for Mr. Lancaster, then heads out. Some students wait to talk to the director, but I want to forget this class happened. I walk into the hallway expecting Anna to be waiting for me. She loves our after-school walks to the subway.

"Hello, Mr. Greene," I hear from behind me.

I turn on my heel, facing Mr. Daniels. "Hello, sir," I say.

"Could I get a word with you?"

"Of course," I say, immediately running out of breath again. I'd like to cut myself out of this binder. I find a deep breath while we quietly walk to his office. My mind races trying to figure out what he wants to talk about.

He opens the door for me. "Come in; this will just take a minute."

His office is mostly bookshelves full of leather-bound hardcover books. A globe by the window. Old Broadway posters framed. He's so elegant with his elbow patches and globes. Mr. Daniels sits down behind his desk, and I take the chair facing him.

"I wanted to check in with you, August. How was your first week here at our fine school?"

Mr. Daniels seems relaxed. Maybe he just wants to chat. I loosen up a little. "The homework is as overwhelming as promised," I admit.

Mr. Daniels says, "Yes, it's no easy task. We ask more from our students because we know they are capable."

"Who needs sleep?" I joke, but Mr. Daniels isn't amused.

"Mr. Greene, when you auditioned, I saw a spark. And I knew we could turn that spark into a flame. But I've been surprised by your attitude in class. I don't see you taking notes. You make jokes. I worry you aren't taking this seriously."

"Is this about my scene with Tess?" I ask, ready to explain.

He shakes his head. "This is about you."

I feel like I've been kicked in the heart. I hate that he thinks that. The class clown is an easy role. I didn't think it would lead to this. "Mr. Daniels, I promise I'm taking this seriously. Please believe me. This is all I've ever wanted."

"I don't believe it yet. Please don't make me regret my selection for this spot."

"You won't," I say.

"I need to see more from you, August."

"You will."

I think of Anna and the day we spent together after the audition. The long hug. She went home that night and talked to her dad. He was probably on the fence about me until Anna put her foot down and demanded that I get the spot. Mr. Daniels—probably smoking a pipe and reading the paper—wanted to avoid an argument with his persistent daughter and agreed to it. Or worse, Mr. Daniels was going to pass on me, but Anna swore she'd quit acting or stop cleaning the toilet.

Mr. Daniels picks a piece of lint off his turtleneck. "I understand that this must be quite an adjustment from Pennsylvania. And making new friends is important. But within these walls, respect goes further than a laugh. You should think about that approach."

"I will," I say, letting the feeling of defeat really soak in.

"And there's a counselor at this school," he says. "If you need someone to talk to."

My head gets hot. "I'm fine. But thank you."

Mr. Daniels stands up. "Very well. I'm looking forward to your monologue later this week."

"As am I," I lie. I haven't picked a monologue to perform yet.

As soon as I step outside Mr. Daniels's office, I deflate like a popped balloon. I give my binder a yank, trying to loosen it up. I'm glad the hallway is empty—no witnesses to my walk of shame. I exit the building, into the sunshine, and head toward the subway completely in my head about Mr. Daniels. I should have asked him if Anna is the reason I'm here. I just want to know. He doesn't like my Funny Guy routine. He expects more of me. I need to get serious. I need to play the part of Serious Student.

My thoughts are disrupted by a sharp whistle. Yazmin waves from across the street. I look behind me for someone else—she can't possibly be trying to get my attention—but no one is there. Her wave turns into a "come here" movement. Is this really happening? And now?

I cross the street and try to forget about Mr. Daniels. I stop in front of Yazmin. Put my hands in my jeans pockets. "That's quite a whistle," I say.

"Keeps me safe."

"I believe it."

"I guess we don't connect as scene partners," she says.

As if I needed another reason to feel terrible about today. "I'm sorry, Yazmin. I got nervous, made a choice, and went with it. Strong and wrong, right?"

"More like loud and dumb," she says, smiling.

"Can you forgive me?" I ask.

She laughs. "I'll think about it."

For Yazmin, I can be the Playful Guy. I put one hand on my heart and the other in the air. "Please, Yazmin, find it in your heart to forgive me."

"You're hard to figure out," Yazmin says.

"How so?"

She shrugs. "This mysterious cute boy shows up in class one day out of nowhere?"

"I prefer International Man of Mystery," I joke.

She laughs again. "But do you have what it takes to be at SPA?"

"I know I do," I say.

"Prove it."

"Gladly."

She looks around, then grabs my arm, and we walk in the direction of the bus stop. Yaz sits down on the bench, near two older ladies, and slumps down. I have no idea what's going on. "I can't believe you cheated on me," she says, loud enough for the women to hear. They both look at me. I look at her and she's got wild eyes. "With my best friend!"

I hear a small gasp from one of the women. We are doing a scene for an audience of two. "You gave me no choice," I say, then raise my hands up, "when you cheated on me with MY BROTHER."

I peek at the women, both watching. Yazmin takes my hand. "I couldn't handle it anymore. You telling me what to wear and what to eat. You can't control me."

"You signed the contract," I say calmly.

Yazmin almost laughs but stops herself. She gets up and yells, "I didn't read the fine print!" We both walk off and hold our laughs inside until we cross the street. Then we laugh for a solid minute, reliving the scene and imagining what the ladies thought. It's the kind of laugh that leaves you feeling spent in a good way. "I needed that," I say.

"Well, I'm still not convinced," she says, walking over to a man drinking coffee. We pretend we robbed a bank and fight over how to spend the money. The man doesn't seem fazed and ignores us, but it's still hilarious.

"One more?" I ask, then tilt my head in the direction of an older man reading a book on the steps of a building. The Playful Guy has an idea.

"Hell yes," she says. We sit down on a step near the man.

"How long have we been dating?" I ask, starting the scene.

"Nine days," she says.

I stand up. "And they have been the best nine days of my life."

"It's been all right," she says, flipping her hair.

"And you have changed my life," I say, then reach down and grab her hand. I can see the man looking at us from the corner of my eye. "I brought you here, to the place we met nine days ago."

I kneel on the step and hold up an imaginary ring. "Yazmin, will you marry me?"

The man is staring with his mouth open, and a couple of other people have stopped to watch. As I wait on bended knee, Yazmin doesn't move. Hard to know which way she will go. She covers her mouth and starts nodding. "You will?" I scream.

"Yes, of course." She gets on her feet as people start clapping. She hugs me and says, "Maybe we should kiss?"

My cheeks get hot. "That director said you should take more risks," I say.

She smiles and lets go of me. "Nice try," she says, and heads down the steps. I follow her—I want to hang out all night. I'm finally connecting with someone.

We turn a corner and she stops. "There's my ride," she says.

"You drive?" I ask, looking around for her car.

"Not quite," she says, pointing to a red car across the street. "That's my boyfriend. He goes to school in Jersey."

"Oh," I say, stunned. A boyfriend?

Yazmin throws me a peace sign. "See you tomorrow."

I wave and smile, wishing I were that guy in the car. I try to get a look at him but can't see. I'm both crushing and crushed. I head toward the subway, hands in my pockets, reliving the time with Yazmin in my head. Thinking about her face when I fake proposed to her. I cross the street and run right into Meena, my stage manager friend from lunch.

"Did you just propose to Yazmin Guzman?" she asks.

I look back at the scene of the incident. "Oh, that?" I don't know how to explain. "We were practicing a scene from class," I lie.

I can tell she doesn't believe me by the face she's making. "I thought you and Anna were talking?"

"We're just friends," I say.

"Does Anna know that?"

I shrug. "I haven't really gotten around to telling her."

She laughs. "Maybe you should."

"I looked at your Insta today. I like your food celebrities. My favorite is Chris Pine-apple."

"Thanks," she says, smiling. "I'm really proud of today's post: Corn-teney Cox. And I don't care what Anna says, I would rather be me and have no followers than be some fake version of myself."

"You don't have to be a fake version of yourself," I offer.

"And you don't either," she says. "Now if you'll excuse me, I'm late for my crystal knitting group at Starbucks."

"Crystal knitting?" I ask.

"Yeah, we knit cozies for our crystals. See you," she says, taking off.

I watch Meena cross the street. I admire her for being so self-assured. She knows what she likes, and doesn't care what people think. Before getting on the subway, I walk through Times Square and snap selfies in front of Broadway signs. I take about a hundred pictures to get the right one, then spend the subway ride home writing a caption for my post.

SIX

Thursday, September 19

11:50 A.M.

I made the mistake of telling the lunch table that I was nervous about messing up my monologue. This confession has sparked a retelling of everyone's most embarrassing stage moments.

"Remember when we did *Singin' in the Rain*?" Juliet asks.

"With no rain," Meena adds.

"I'm proud of my rain work," Anna says, pretending to shield her hair from rain.

"August," Jack says. Their hair has gone from pink to green. "Are you ready for the most embarrassing story of them all?"

"Does your hair change weekly?" I ask.

"I'm a mood ring, baby. I can't hide my feelings. Anna, would you like to start the story?"

Anna crosses her arms. "No, and let the record show that it was Meena's fault."

"How many times do I need to apologize?" Meena asks,

heavy on the dramatics.

"Who knows, and to be honest, I'm having trouble believing you're actually sorry anymore."

"And I apologize for that," Meena says with an eye roll.

"Anyways, it was the freshman showcase," Anna says.

Jack cuts in, "Everybody is there. You've seen the theater, August? It's like a thousand hundred seats."

"One thousand and twenty-three seats," Meena corrects them.

"Thank you, Meena," Jack says, not loving the interruption. "Every seat was filled that night. Even the seniors show up to freshman showcase. Seriously, you would not want to do anything embarrassing in front of that kind of crowd."

"Yes, everyone was there. Thank you for making it clear," Anna says.

"No problem, girl," they say.

Anna picks up the story from there. "I have two minutes in the middle of the first act to use the bathroom. Nerves do crazy things to my bladder. As usual, I run offstage to the bathroom, pull down my tights, and *let it goooo,*" she sings like the Disney song. "But little did I know, *someone* forgot to do her job."

"That's me," Meena admits. "I was on the sound board and didn't turn her mic off. The entire audience heard her pee. And for that, I—"

"Apologize," Juliet and Jack say together, then high-five.

"And the whole audience hears *pppppptsssssssssss,*" Jack says.

"It gets worse. I had no clue that this went down, so I run back onstage, hit my mark, and say, 'What did I miss?'"

"The crowd laughed so hard they almost pissed themselves," Jacks adds, laughing so much they almost piss themself.

Anna shakes her head. "Lucky for me, I have a great therapist."

Juliet hugs Anna and everyone laughs. Jack does a little dance, singing *ppppstttttt*. Meena tries to apologize across the table. Look at my new friends, so full of life. These are my people. I have found my people.

The realization that I'll be giving my monologue hits me again. My stomach turns, and nerves run through my body. I need to impress. The monologues started yesterday. Anna was first. She was awesome—gracefully slipping into Val Clarke from *A Chorus Line*. The last line had everyone on their feet: *So I said fuck you, Radio City and the Rockettes! I'm gonna make it on Broadway!*

The other monologues were smartly picked and performed. People got creative. A guy did a monologue from *Deadpool*. A girl reenacted her grandma's will. As weird as it all sounds, it worked. A good monologue is meant to show your range, your ability to take on a character, and your emotional delivery. It's like a short story. After seeing everyone yesterday, I started second-guessing my selection. But I've rehearsed and I'm ready. I need to trust myself.

Juliet leans over. "August, how are you?"

"Good," I say. Juliet checks on me often. It's sweet. "Just wondering, for a friend," I say with a smile. "If you like someone, when do you tell them you're trans?"

Juliet nods in the direction of Anna. "I think she knows."

I ignore her assumption. "Do you talk to them about it? Before anything happens?"

She shrugs. "It's different every time. I'll bring it up casually in conversation if I think my crush might not know."

"Like how's the pizza, I'm transgender?" I joke.

Juliet laughs. "Well," she says. "I'll say something like, did you hear the new messed-up thing the government is doing to trans people? Or, I'll just say, you know I'm trans, right?"

I'm afraid to ask the next question, but I do anyway. "Has anyone ended it when they found out?"

"Once," she says darkly.

"When you . . ." I trail off as Yazmin walks by, carrying a tray and walking with the most handsome guy I've seen at this school—and there're a lot of good-looking people here. He's African American, tall and built—muscles visible under his baggy shirt. He says something and Yaz laughs loudly, covering her mouth with her hoodie sleeve.

"Who is that with Yazmin?" I ask Juliet.

"Elijah Covington," she says. "He's a big deal."

"Does he live in Jersey? Does he drive a car?" I ask, wondering if that's her boyfriend.

Juliet looks at me, confused. "Those are oddly specific questions?"

"I swear I've seen him before," I say.

Yazmin's eyes find mine, causing time to stop and everything else to go blurry until it's just our eyes. It lasts one second, but the sparks could jump-start a car. Two days ago, I followed Yazmin on Insta—or at least I requested to follow her private profile. She has nearly a thousand followers. I wonder what she'll think of my eighty. As of ten minutes ago when I last checked, she had not followed back.

"Earth to August," Juliet says.

"Sorry, sorry. Very distracted by this monologue. I've never felt this kind of pressure before."

Juliet laughs. "August, that's so cute. Please don't be offended," she says, then turns to the table. "August is still feeling the pressure."

Huge laugh from Jack and Anna. Meena smiles. "This school breaks you down to build you up," Anna says.

"And then it breaks you again, just for fun," Jack adds.

I get up and put on my backpack. "I can't wait for that. But for now, the actor must prepare."

Anna pinches my elbow. "You've got this, Augustus."

"Break every leg in the room," Jack says, then the table cheers as I walk off.

I pace around the hallways on the first floor with my earbuds in, music cranked. I took Mr. Daniels's verbal kick in the butt seriously. I've been playing the role of the Serious Student by sitting in the front row, taking notes (never done that before), and not joking around.

The bell rings. It's time to meet my fate. I've prepared as much as possible without overdoing it and coming off too practiced. It should feel fresh. This monologue especially needs to be raw—and that's hard to fake. I find a desk in the front row. My lunch buds can laugh at me all they want, but the pressure is undeniable. I want to prove that I deserve to be at this school. A few weeks ago, I didn't know the School of Performing Arts existed, and now I can't imagine my life without it. I'm on my path, and I can't mess this up.

Mr. Daniels enters (two minutes late) and settles into his chair. "The first day of monologues set a high bar. I look forward to more today." He scans a sheet on his desk. "Timothy? Are you ready?"

After about five monologues, Mr. Daniels looks up from his sheet with a big smile. "August, please step up to the stage. *Mr. Greeeeeeeene,*" he sings.

As I take the stage, Mr. Daniels flips to a fresh page in his notebook. "And what will you be performing for us today?"

I straighten up my spine and stand as tall as possible. I lift my chin up. "I'll be doing a scene from *Full Metal Jacket.*"

The class looks confused. They probably don't know the movie. It's from the 80s, and it's about marines training under the hand of a spiteful commander. I wanted to pick something to show just how serious I am. "This should be good," Mr. Daniels says while scribbling in his notebook.

I am the Soldier. I'm in boot camp, preparing to go to war. I would die for my country, even though I haven't lived yet. I believe in what I'm doing, and what the marines are training me to be.

I turn around and slam my feet together. I hold my arm down by my side like it's cupping the bottom of a rifle. I put my other arm across my chest, gripping my imaginary weapon. I need to command the room. I focus my eyes on a poster on the far wall.

"THIS IS MY RIFLE. THERE ARE MANY LIKE IT, BUT

THIS IS MINE," I begin, loud enough to wake up the room. I keep every muscle in my body tight. I am at attention. I'm headed to war. "MY RIFLE IS MY BEST FRIEND. IT IS MY LIFE." I keep my voice steady and loud. Barking, almost. My words speed up. I remain still, using my eyes to convey the emotion. "WITHOUT ME, MY RIFLE IS USELESS. WITHOUT MY RIFLE, I AM USELESS." I'm hitting the loudest I can go. There's a good chance other classes can hear me.

I stop. The room is silent. Extra silent in comparison to me. I steady my voice. "BEFORE GOD I SWEAR THIS CREED: MY RIFLE AND MYSELF ARE THE DEFENDERS OF MY COUNTRY. . . ."

When I'm done, I drop the rifle and lower my head.

There's one clap, then more. It lasts a few seconds. There have only been a couple of monologues receiving applause. And now, mine is one of them. I look up, smile, and walk back to my seat feeling like I won.

"Well done, August," Mr. Daniels says.

The last four people go. All good performances. No claps. My mind races at what it all means. As soon as the bell rings, Anna is at my desk. "Holy shit, August. What the hell was that? It was awesome. The whole army thing. So smart. Such great commentary on transgender people not being able to serve in the military. Seriously, dude, you gave me chills."

My jaw drops. "That wasn't the point of my monologue. Is that what everyone thinks?" I ask, losing my cool.

"Don't know. Got to jet."

I remain seated as the room empties out. Even Mr. Daniels has vacated. Did my acting earn the applause? Or was it my unintentional political statement? My shoulders drop. There's no way to know. Before taking off, I check my phone. My heart stops. Yazmin followed me back. And sent me a message.

NotYourYaz: Hey august, that monologue was dope. Wanna go to a party on Saturday night?

5:54 P.M.

By the time I get home, I have twenty new followers, pushing me over a hundred. I guess my monologue got people talking. I can hear music coming from Aunt Lil's art studio. "Hello?" I say.

"We're in my studio," she yells from upstairs. "Come up."

"Promise we're decent," Davina calls out. They laugh. I drop my bag and head upstairs. Aunt Lil's art studio is huge, with all the trappings: cups filled with brushes, cloth tarp on the ground with colorful splatters, a bookcase filled with art books, and canvases everywhere—some mid-paint, some finished, and others wrapped up in brown paper leaning against the wall.

My aunt's painting has a style. She uses bright colors surrounded in darkness. There's a large one on the wall with a woman wearing a fancy dress, smoking a cigarette, and holding a drink. Behind her is a scary man, probably the devil. Same with a painting on the floor of a queen, wearing lots of diamonds but standing in a burnt field. I'm unsettled by her paintings. And surprised not to see a single pineapple. "Don't you dare tell your mom," Aunt Lil says, handing me a glass of champagne. "But tonight, we're celebrating."

I've never had champagne. Only beer. And alcohol at parties, but I've never been drunk. "What are we celebrating?"

Davina puts her arm around Aunt Lil. "Your aunt sold a painting today for an embarrassing amount of money."

"A semi-embarrassing amount of money."

I take my first sip of champagne. It's bitter, sweet, and removes all the spit from my mouth. "Congrats," I say, having no idea what a semi-embarrassing amount of money is. "Aunt Lil, your paintings are amazing."

"Oh, stop," she says, then takes a drink. "I mean, I have my moments."

Davina removes her wool blazer and slips off her shoes. She must work in an office. "Now you can take me on that cruise you've been promising."

"Actually," Aunt Lil says with a huge smile, pulling out folded papers from her apron, "I might have booked the jazz cruise for next summer."

"No way," Davina says, on her feet and hugging Aunt Lil. They are nose to nose, looking in each other's eyes. "Thank you, baby," she says, then they kiss. It's such a sweet moment. My parents never showed affection. Never went on cruises.

They continue to kiss, and I feel awkward. "Should I leave?" I offer.

"No," Davina says, then laughs. They are so cute together. "I'll head downstairs and get dinner ready."

"How did you know you were a painter?" I ask my aunt when it's just us.

"I don't think of myself as a painter, I suppose." She takes off her apron. That means the workday is over. "I'm an artist. I need to show the world what I see, and my medium is the canvas. Just like yours is the stage."

I nod to a painting with a cute cartoon baby swimming in a pool of motor oil. "So that's how you see the world?"

"Sometimes."

I love my aunt. Her sense of humor lightens things up. "Did you paint when you were in school?" I ask.

"Started in middle school. No, it was high school. That was a long time ago."

"Before the internet."

"Before computers. Maybe before calculators. I'm ancient history. But I'll never forget what painting gave me when I was your age."

"Not many friends," I say, feeling loose. I like champagne.

"An escape, wise guy." She puts her glass down by a brush can. "And a way to express my feelings. My teen years were confusing. I was alone carrying around this secret. And felt wrong for getting crushes on my friends."

I shake my head. I know all those feelings.

"Art class was my safe space, as you kids call it. The teacher let me work after school. And sometimes before. I needed a place to be myself and work through my feelings." She takes a drink of champagne. "There I go blabbing away again. August, how are you?"

"Everything is so good," I say. But there's been something I've needed to ask my aunt, and now seems like the best time. "I wear binders."

She tilts her head. "You wear school supplies?"

"No," I say with a laugh, imagining taping binders full of paper to myself and heading out into the world. "It's a chest compression binder. To keep my chest flat and looking manly." I flex to prove my point. "It's like a really tight shirt. My binder is from Point of Pride, a nonprofit organization that donates binders to those who can't afford them, or like me, whose mom would never allow them to buy one. And most of the binders are donated from trans guys after their top surgery."

"That's magnificent," she says. "I'll donate to them tonight."

"That's great," I say. "But this binder never fit exactly right, and now I wear it ten hours a day. And I'm having trouble breathing. I hate to ask this—you do so much for me—but could I borrow money to buy some good ones?"

"Oh, honey, I love you," Aunt Lil says. "I hate thinking about your organs getting smooshed together. I wish you didn't have to wear those, but I understand. I'll donate to you any day." She searches around her desk and hands me a credit card. "Buy a couple binders. Good ones. And anything else you need."

"Thank you," I say, fighting back tears.

"Do you know why I love pineapples so much?"

I haven't thought about it. "Because they are tart and sweet?"

"Just like me," she says, laughing. "No—a long time ago, a sea captain would spear one into his yard to let his friends know they were welcome in his house. Pineapples became a symbol for hospitality. I want everyone to feel welcome in my house. Especially my family. You're my family, and I'm taking care of you now. But when you're a famous actor, I expect a house in the Hamptons. Deal?"

I curl my toes together in my shoes—that's my trick to fight off tears. I have no idea why my aunt is so loving and giving. No idea why I'm so lucky. "Deal," I say, and give her a big hug.

"I love you, August. You're going to do great things. I believe in you."

"Sometimes I feel like I don't deserve to be here," I admit.

"You, my boy," she says, then boops my nose, "deserve it more than anyone else."

I nod, wishing I could believe her. An offensive smell, sour and rotten, hits my nose and derails our moment. "Did you just fart?" I ask.

Her nose wiggles as she smells. "That's dinner. We're having seitan."

"*Satan?*" I say back

"Seitan is wheat gluten that tastes like steak."

"Is it pronounced 'Satan' because that's who created it as punishment for our sins?"

Aunt Lil shrugs. "Ketchup helps."

SEVEN

Saturday, September 21

7:46 P.M.

I should be home right now. I should be studying, or sleeping, or taking some time to myself. Everything has been moving so fast, I haven't had time to think. But how could I pass up an invitation to a party from Yazmin? When I told Anna about the party, she freaked out. According to her, Riley isn't the best actor, but he's popular. She swore the "VIPs of SPA" would be at the party. How could I miss that? And even if I don't meet cool people, I can get pictures and look like a cool person. I'm typically shy at parties unless I know the people, but that won't get me noticed. Tonight, I will play the role of the Party Guy.

I invited Anna to the party—didn't feel like I had a choice after telling her about it—but she might have taken it the wrong way. I realize now, as we eat dinner, that she might think this is a date.

"Thanks for inviting me out, Augustus," Anna says with a big smile.

"No problem."

"I've never been to Riley's, but I hear his parents are super rich. Like, they own a hedge fund rich. My god, this matzo ball soup is too salty."

Maybe she doesn't think this is a date. I've never been on a date, so I wouldn't really know what one feels like. But she's acting flirty. "How's your burger?" she asks.

"Good," I say with my mouth half full. "My aunt is vegan—it's a struggle."

She looks around at the diner, then claps her hands together. "This is such a cute first date."

Yes, this was a mistake.

I like Anna. But I don't *like* like Anna. I don't think of her at night. Or get nervous when she looks at me in class. All those things happen for Yazmin. Too bad she's with someone.

Anna steals a fry. "How do you know Riley anyways? How did *you* find out about this party before *me*?"

I pop the collar on my button-up short-sleeved shirt—a score from the thrift store down the street from my aunt's place. I went shopping today—I needed a party shirt for the Party Guy. "Guess I'm more popular," I say.

She rolls her eyes playfully. "I guess so," she says. "But you did put people on notice with that monologue." She takes another fry, thinking. "It was just *so* smart. Everyone was talking about it yesterday."

"Everyone?" I ask with a slight crack in my voice. I'm up to two hundred followers—it's totally going to my head.

"Yeah, dude, you put yourself on the map."

I clear my throat. "Does everyone at school know I'm trans?"

Anna shrugs. "I'm sure not everyone. That's dramatic. But some people might. Does it matter?"

Sometimes I want people to know, but other times I'd rather keep it to myself. Being transgender felt like something to be ashamed of back in Pennsylvania. Something to hide. Something to never talk about. "I wanted the class to clap because I'm a good actor, not because I'm transgender."

"They liked both things. It was a good performance with social commentary." She does the chef's kiss.

"But how do they know?" I ask, unable to let it go.

Anna waves me off. "At SPA, your gender identity doesn't matter. It's just another thing—like you have brown hair, green eyes, and are also trans. It's the definition of no big deal."

She's so flippant about this. Does she understand it's not that easy to be trans, even in a liberal New York school? "My old town was different. I'm still adjusting, I guess."

"That reminds me," Anna says while mashing up a matzo ball with her spoon. "I think you should tell our lunch bunch the truth about your parents."

Real freaking ironic coming from Anna, who has yet to tell me that her dad is Mr. Daniels. My muscles tighten up, in defense of my lies and anger at hers. "They don't need to know," I say. "It changes nothing about me to know about my parents."

"I disagree," she says, then reaches across the table and puts her hand on mine. "Letting people know you isn't a bad thing. You don't have to keep your guard up all the time."

Her advice is probably sound, but I'm too busy thinking about why she won't tell me about her dad. I decided to wait for her to tell me about Mr. Daniels, but it's starting to annoy me. "I'll think about it," I lie.

We finish our meals, split the bill—I only had twenty dollars—and head into the night. I picked a diner close to the party, but not close enough considering how much it's raining. We walk under my four-dollar umbrella purchased from the bodega. It's a tiny umbrella, so we walk close, our bodies touching. This is becoming quite the unintentional date. Anna laces her arm into mine and we skip down the street, belting out the words from "Singin' in the Rain."

We enter the apartment lobby like wet puppies. The doorman holds the door while we shake off the rain and close the umbrella (which already broke).

"Who are you here to visit?" the doorman asks. He's wearing a suit and white gloves.

I shake the water out of my hair. "We're here for Riley's party. I'm August Greene."

"The infamous," Anna announces as the doorman scans the ledger. The lobby is marble madness—green marble floors with large swirls of white, and pearl marble pillars leading to the high ceilings. The walls? Also marble. The art looks expensive. The royal family could live here.

"Welcome to the one percent," Anna whispers to me.

"Ah, here you are." The doorman makes a note in his book. "Elevator to penthouse."

"The *fucking* penthouse," Anna loudly whispers. The doorman smiles at us. As soon as the elevator doors close, I ask, "Are all SPA parties like this?"

"Some," she says, "but this is a VIP party for sure. Tell me who invited you."

I don't want to upset Anna. Maybe she doesn't like Yazmin. I shrug as casually as possible. "Yaz told me about it."

Her mouth opens like it wanted to hit the floor. "No way."

"Way," I say, and look down.

Anna clears her throat. Or swallows the words she doesn't want to say. We both stay silent the entire ride up. The elevator stops and the doors slide open—not into the hallway, where we could have talked about it, but right into the apartment. Or penthouse, rather. The apartment is the entire floor of the building with floor-to-ceiling windows and full views of the city. "What the hell," I say, in disbelief that people live in apartments this nice.

"Hedge funds, man," Anna says, with the same wonderment.

The place is packed with people on couches, talking in groups, huddled up in the kitchen. Heads turn when we walk in, making me feel terribly self-conscious.

"You must be August," I hear from behind. I turn around to a shaggy-haired guy with perfect skin. "I'm Riley. Nice to meet you." He reaches for my hand. "Yazmin has said good things."

"And Anna," he says, and hugs her. "What a pleasant surprise."

"I'm part of August's glam squad," she says, leaning into me.

"Plenty of drinks in the kitchen for you," he says, and moves on to host other people. Anna grabs my arm and leads me into the kitchen. I'm uneasy and nervous, but I keep my limbs loose and my smile big. Tonight, I am the Party Guy. I will be outgoing and have a good time—or at least act like I am.

Anna gathers cups, vodka, and cranberry juice. "I'm making my favorite cocktail, the UTI."

"What? Why would you call it that?"

"Alcohol leads to sex, which can sometimes lead to urinary tract infections, which cranberry juice helps. It's full circle in one drink."

"It's just missing the sex," I say.

"August, that's so forward," she says, blushing. I keep accidentally making this a date. She hands me my drink. The cranberry is bitter and the alcohol burns, but it does relax me. Party Guy drinking.

"Why did Yazmin invite you?" Anna begins her interrogation. "How are you friends with her? This is all new information."

I shrug and take a drink. "She invited me after my monologue."

Anna thinks. "Did you know her dad is some famous music executive? She claims he helped create Selena Gomez."

"She didn't tell me," I admit. I try to imagine what it would be like to have a famous dad surrounded by famous people. Or to live in this big hedge-fund apartment. Or do anything that a typical SPA student does on a normal day. I wonder what Hugo would think of this party. I miss my best friend from back home, but I don't know if he would accept me like my new friends do.

"What did I tell you? You're on your way . . ." Anna keeps talking as I scan the room, in awe of the people who surround me. All good-looking. Stylish clothes. Much different from the parties in the woods at my old school. I spot Tess Montague in the corner talking to some girls. A few other people look familiar, and everyone looks cool.

"Anna Banana!" we hear from behind us.

"Elijah," she nearly shrieks, then throws her arms around the guy who was walking with Yazmin at lunch. His smile could bring about world peace. He's wearing a loose shirt, tight jeans, and Air Jordans. He *must* be in my morning classes—I know his face, but I still can't place him. Anna swings around, flipping her hair. "Elijah, meet August. He's new to SPA."

"I've seen you around, man, nice to meet you."

"Have we met?" I ask.

He laughs. "I get that a lot. Maybe this will help." He pretends to get into character, clears his throat, then says, "Hey, Mom! I need my Gushers!"

And then it clicks—he was the Gushers guy in a commercial that played for years. I had every line of the commercial memorized, and now I'm standing in front of the Gushers guy. "Holy shit," I manage to say. "You're the Gushers guy?"

"Oh yeah, sentenced to a life of being the Gushers guy, but that commercial is going to pay for my college next year."

"Did you decide where you're going?" Anna asks.

"Either NYU or USC," he says with a shrug, like he's picking between peanut butter and jelly.

"Wow," I say. Those are the top colleges for acting. I've done some research on this—dreaming of getting out of West Grove and studying theater. Then I would look up the tuition and my dreaming would end. "Does going to SPA help you get accepted?" I ask.

Anna and Elijah laugh. "Yes, August," Anna says. "It makes it easy."

"And there's a counselor who will help you with scholarships," Elijah says. I get excited. Maybe my dreams weren't as far-fetched as I thought.

Elijah puts his arm around Anna. "Catch me up, girl. We haven't talked in a minute. Is Demitri still a thing?"

She *shhhhh*s him. "New year, new me."

"Well"—he looks down—"Charles broke up with me over the summer."

"That sounds awful," I say, ready to be in the conversation. I want to be friends with the Gushers guy.

Anna waves it off. "Charles was not worthy of sharing the same air as you."

"I miss his air. But it's time to move on. Maybe tonight," he says, eyeing the room.

As they continue to catch up, I look for Yazmin. My curfew is midnight, and Aunt Lil was serious about not being late. Anna refills my drink. "Come on, Augustus, let's go make ourselves seen."

The three of us head into the living room and take over an L-shaped couch. Elijah tells a story about the fall musical when he was a junior that makes me laugh until my stomach hurts. Does being famous make him funnier? For sure.

"Out with it, Anna, what's the fall musical this year?" Elijah asks.

"You did not hear this from me," she says, then grabs his knee. "*Grease!* One of my favorites!"

Elijah raises his hands. "Stooooop," he says. "It's time for a Black Danny Zuko. I'm the one that I want, baby."

"And I'm trying something different this year," Anna brags.

"So not understudy?"

"I'm going to the other side of the table and assistant directing."

"That's so brave," Elijah says. "What about you, August?"

"What's the fall musical?" I ask. They both laugh like I should've heard about it in Pennsylvania.

"Only the biggest show of the year for SPA," Anna says. "Three nights in Theater One, all sold out. The sets are huge, the band plays—it's like one step away from Broadway."

The thought of being on that stage in front of a thousand people overwhelms me. I have questions, but before I can ask, a guy sits down on the couch. He's wearing a black turtleneck like Steve Jobs. His messy short hair is the "preoccupied with my art" look.

"Hi, Elijah," he says quietly. "Anna."

"Duncan!" they both say.

"Duncan Stanford is the most talented cello player," Anna explains to me loud enough for him to hear. "After graduation, he'll probably just carry his cello down the street to Lincoln Center."

"Wouldn't that be grand," he says with a British accent.

Anna and Elijah perk up like a celebrity joined us. This guy must be the real deal. "Nice to meet you," I say.

"Same," he says.

"How's the orchestra life?" Anna asks Duncan.

"No complaints. Deciding on colleges. And dealing with freshmen acting like they're the best things since Beethoven."

Anna and Elijah laugh. At a Beethoven joke? They worship him. It's making me feel a little forgotten over here. Time to put on the Party Guy. "Most people in my old town think Beethoven is a dog movie," I say.

"It's not the worst dog movie," Duncan says. "But the ending was a little heavy-handed."

"Heavy-pawed?" I ask.

"Yes, mate." Duncan laughs.

Anna leans closer to Duncan. "We didn't see you all summer, Duncan. Were you busy writing a concerto?"

"Not quite," he says, then runs his hand through his messy hair. "I was back home in London playing with the symphony. It was incredible."

"No doubt," Anna says.

Elijah puts his arm around Duncan. "When will you have time for us to fall in love?"

"I could start tonight," he says to Elijah, but looks at Anna. Only I catch it.

"I could start right now," Elijah kids.

I've never met a British person. My number of firsts continues to grow every day. Everything about Duncan is sophisticated, even the words coming out of his mouth. I've tried on British accents in class sometimes, but I sound like a fool compared to his smooth talk.

"Smile, please," Anna says, snapping a picture of the four of us and immediately posting it. We talk more and finish our drinks. I grab my phone to check the time and notice I have a bunch of notifications.

"Fifty people just followed me," I say, stunned, my heart beating fast.

"You're welcome," Elijah says. "I shared the photo."

"Elijah has like twenty thousand followers," Anna says proudly.

"Lots of Gushers fans out there," he admits.

"This party needs some life," Anna says, looking around.

"It's a little stiff," Duncan agrees.

My belly is warm from the vodka. I feel the need to dance. I have courage I shouldn't. I have fifty new followers. I can bring life to this party.

And then I see Yazmin. By the piano. Talking to someone. Hair up in a high bun.

Now there's more at stake. Party Guy needs to do something big.

I see the answer in the corner of the room. "I can wake this party up," I say, then walk over to the speaker, hoping it is what I think it is. There's a microphone and a folder on top—just waiting for me. Jackpot—this is a karaoke machine. I flip through the pages of the songbook and land on a winner. Party Guy is about to get this party started. I type in number 112. Lucky number 112.

The song starts and the words appear on the huge TV behind me. I don't need them. I turn to everyone. All eyes on me. *"Five hundred twenty-five thousand six hundred minutes,"* I sing, beginning one of my favorite songs from *Rent*. I push through the awkwardness like Party Guy would and gain momentum up to the chorus. People are watching. Some nodding with the beat. Anna and the guys have come closer to cheer me on.

"Sing along," I yell into the microphone. Everyone joins in, *"How about love, how about love,"* and I put the microphone near Anna. She belts high with her arm around me. The guys give her some backup. By the end of the song, everyone is singing and dancing.

Anna grabs the microphone and starts flipping the pages of the songbook as the party gets louder. Mission accomplished. I head to the bathroom and get plenty of high fives and fist bumps along the way. One girl hugs me. I feel like I could do anything. Maybe that's the vodka talking.

The bathroom is fancy and modern—there's even a bidet. I can't believe I'm at a party in New York City. Meeting people achieving their dreams. I'm so far behind the Duncans and Elijahs of the world, but it feels like I'm on my way. I spend extra time looking in the mirror and smiling at myself. August in the bathroom.

When I come out, someone is waiting for me in the hallway. Yazmin leans against the wall, arms crossed. I smile. She smiles. It's just us now. "Nice job on the mic," she says.

"I'm just getting warmed up." Party Guy flirting. The lights are dim, and my heart is beating so fast I can hear it in my ears.

"Want to join me for a smoke?" she asks, nodding in the direction of sliding doors leading to the balcony.

"I'm down."

I slide the door open and follow her out. The city looks big out here, like it could swallow me up. The balcony overlooks Central Park, but it's too dark to see. It's chilly out—the cold air feels good on my face. Fall is coming, pushing summer out of the way. Yazmin hugs herself, trying to warm up. I take off my leather jacket and put it over her shoulders. "What a gentleman," she says.

"I try," I say. "Does your boyfriend give you his coat?"

Her eyebrows go up. "Someone jealous?"

"Not at all," I say. Party Guy is all confidence.

"We broke up last night. We'd been fighting."

Well, this changes everything. I stand up straight. "I'm sorry," I lie—I'm actually not sorry.

She leans back on the ledge and pulls a vape pen out of her pocket. "Want a hit?"

"That's pot?" I ask.

She laughs. "Legal stuff from California."

Yaz coaches me through using the pen. I inhale, hold it, and feel my brain get light enough to float away. I've only smoked pot once with Hugo in the parking lot of our sophomore year dance. I had to wear this yellow dress and felt so uncomfortable. I was glad to have some escape. I breathe a cloud out and cough. I can hear someone singing Miley Cyrus in the living room. The city is alive around us with car horns and sirens. Strands of her hair dance in the wind. For no reason, I start laughing.

She laughs at my laugh. "What?"

"One day I'm in West Grove, Pennsylvania, and another I'm on top of the world. With you." She smiles but looks away. "I mean, you're here, too. Not *with* you."

"I get it," she says, looking at the bright lights. "This city is magic, but I grew up here. If you're always surrounded by magic, it's hard to appreciate it. I want to be new to everything."

The vodka and pot are partying in my brain and making me a little dizzy. "It's wild," I confirm.

"What's wild was your monologue the other day."

"Thanks," I say, blushing. I think of Juliet and her subtle ways of dropping being transgender into conversation. If this is something, I want Yazmin to know. This could be a good time. "Did you think it was good because I'm trans?"

She thinks, and I spiral. Is she processing that I'm trans? Did she know? Will this be over right now?

"I didn't think of that," she says. "Honestly, it was the steam coming off you. I felt the anger. The resentment of being forced to go die for your country. Your eyes did things."

My body lights up like I hit a high score on a game. "Cool," I say. She looks up at me and our eyes meet. It's happening too fast to be nervous.

"What's your favorite part of New York so far?" she asks.

I feel bold. Too bold. "You," I say.

"Boy, you're really going for it tonight."

"Well, I did propose to you," I remind her.

She bites her lip. "I do owe you a kiss, don't I?" She leans in. I lean in. Our lips meet, and it's perfect. She puts her arms around me. I want this to last forever.

"AUGUST," I hear someone yell. We stop kissing and I see Anna with her arms crossed. I let go of Yazmin and feel like I did something wrong.

"Anna," I say, but she's already turned around and walked off.

"What's her deal?" Yazmin asks.

"She kind of thought we were on a date tonight," I admit.

Yazmin hits her vape pen, thinking. I hate the quiet. It makes me nervous. I want to tell her how I'm feeling. I want to kiss again. I need to go after Anna but can't leave now.

"Yo, August," she finally says. "That kiss was nice. Fire, even. But Anna is a talker. Could you ask her not to tell anyone?"

My heart leaps off the balcony. "You're ashamed of kissing me?"

"No, I have a boyfriend."

"I thought you broke up?"

"But we'll probably get back together. And this school loves gossip."

I shake my head and swallow my feelings. "I need to go see Anna."

She hits her vape pen again. "Yeah, go deal with that."

The party somehow doubled in size in the ten minutes I was gone, and everyone seems ten times drunker. Someone is belting the lyrics of "Candy Store" from *Heathers: The Musical.* I see through the crowd that it's Tess. Of course it's Tess.

"Hey, buddy," Elijah slurs with one arm around Duncan and the other around me. "Where did you go-go?"

"I ruined everything," I admit.

"Oh, please. I like you, August. We're going to be best friends. Let's hang tomorrow and every day."

"Sounds good, but I've got to run," I say while searching the room for Anna. I don't see her, and I'm getting dangerously close to missing curfew. I compose a text to Anna while waiting for the elevator.

"Nice job on that monologue," someone says.

I look up from my phone and see Tess. "Thanks," I say cautiously while pressing the elevator button, hoping that speeds it up.

"Way to use your trans identity to carry your performance."

The elevator opens. I don't respond; I just get inside and push the button over and over. "What's next—" Her words get cut off by the doors shutting.

I ride the elevator down, wondering if coming here was a mistake. I should have stayed home. I'll call Anna once I'm on the train. Or text her. FaceTime. I'll figure it out. I push open the front door and almost trip over Anna, sitting on the top step hugging her knees.

She looks back, sees me. "I'm not waiting for you. I'm waiting for my car."

I sit down and accept that I'm missing curfew. I'll be punished however Aunt Lil sees fit, which will probably be eating meatless things for a month. "How many minutes?" I ask.

She checks her phone. "App says two."

It looks like she might be crying. The weight of my guilt hits me hard. "I'm sorry, Anna. It's not you, it's me."

"Don't feed me that clichéd bullshit," she says.

"Anna, I'm sorry. I can't lose you as a friend."

"You lied to me, August," she says.

Now I'm mad at Anna for lying about her dad. And Yazmin for having a boyfriend. Mad at Tess for not leaving me alone. And my parents and their stupid church. "You lied to me, Anna. Who is your dad, Anna? Who is he? Could he be, I don't know, our teacher?"

She recoils. "You knew?"

"Tess told me," I admit. "But I was waiting for you to tell me."

Anna checks her phone again. "I didn't tell you on the day of your audition because I didn't want you to like me for that."

"And I don't," I say.

"Right, you just don't like me."

"I do like you. As a friend. You're my best friend here."

"That's not what I wanted." She shakes her head. "I regret what I told my dad."

I knew it. "What did you tell your dad?"

"It doesn't matter. My car is here. Bye, August. Good luck without me."

I get home an hour later. Aunt Lil is waiting for me on the couch. She's in a pajama dress and cross-stitching with NPR on low.

"You're late," she whispers to not wake Davina.

"I'm sorry, Auntie," I say, my body slumped. I avoid getting near her in case I smell like vodka.

"You're really giving me a taste of this parenting thing, aren't you, son?"

"I had a bad night."

"This is your warning," she says. "But don't do that again."

I barely get my pants off before crashing into bed. I roll myself up in the bedspread. I'm utterly defeated by the truth of how I got into the school. It was Aunt Lil. It was Anna. It was never me. I didn't earn my spot.

EIGHT

Monday, September 23

11:58 A.M.

I'm the only one in the basement—everyone in class or lunch. I left the cafeteria five minutes early to slay the dragon of entering the boys' dressing room. I'm standing beside the double doors trying to will myself to go inside. The basement is empty, which means the dressing room will be empty. Sweat covers the back of my neck. If I get cast in *Grease*—even in the ensemble—I'll be in the dressing room. I need to do this now. Break the seal. Rip the Band-Aid. Now is the time. Go. Move your feet, August.

But I can't. No matter the logic, reasoning, or pep talks, I can't push through the intense feeling that I don't truly belong. I don't want the guys wondering if I should be in there, possibly feeling uncomfortable. A few guys enter and exit. I'm jealous of the casualness. Something insurmountable to me is second nature to them. How easy it must be for cis guys to exist in the world. The first bell rings, and I turn away from the dressing room, defeated. I have just enough time to go to the gender-neutral bathrooms upstairs. Boys' dressing room: 1. Me: 0.

Mr. Daniels walks into class two minutes late. "Students, my students," he says.

"Teacher, our teacher," we say back. This ritual started sometime last week as a joke. I check my phone before putting it away. Nothing from Yaz, but Elijah has texted often. At the party, he drunkenly announced that I'm his new best friend. I thought people didn't stick to their promises when drunk, but Elijah is not most people. I don't know why he's so excited to be my friend—he's a senior with thousands of followers. But I need a friend after getting dumped by Anna, who is sitting in the front row, probably planning my demise. Mr. Daniels locates his notebook and pulls out a piece of paper. "An announcement before we begin: the fall musical will be"—he pauses for dramatics—"*Grease!*"

The class starts buzzing with excitement and opinions. "Auditions will be held this Thursday. Please sign up on the web page." He looks up and smiles. "Yours truly will be directing this year."

The class claps politely. "Thank you, but your applause will not increase your chances of getting a role." The clapping dies down. "Now, we've been studying the different methods of acting. You'll discover which methods help you access characters through many years of perfecting your craft, but it's imperative to know them. I can guarantee you will be asked by directors, and even some teachers," he says with a wink, "to work a method during a rehearsal."

As Mr. Daniels talks, my mind drifts to *Grease*. When I wasn't wallowing in my despair over the party or doing homework yesterday, I was thinking about which role I would audition for.

"August," Mr. Daniels says, snapping me back to reality. "Could you come up front?"

On my way up to the stage, I try to remember what he was talking about. The fear of getting in front of the class has disappeared. We've now seen each other perform—good, bad, and ugly—and we are over it.

"Take this," Mr. Daniels says, handing me a piece of paper. "Give it a quick read and apply any acting method. I'll give you a moment."

He turns his attention to the class and regales them with a story about something, who knows, I'm not listening. While skimming the monologue, I search for the character. I'm an aging man, maybe a grandpa, looking for my lost dog. At the end, I realize the dog has been dead for years. I'm forgetting things, then mourning over and over when I remember they died.

I clear my throat. "I'm ready," I say, even though I'm not ready.

"Very well," Mr. Daniels says. I spot Anna in the front row, not even looking at me. Yazmin is watching me, smiling, making me instantly nervous. I look back down, take a breath, and get started. I am Grandpa; my mind is foggy. Things don't make sense. I loosen my body, confuse my mind, and begin. I talk slow and take pauses like a man searching for his next thought. I really nail the ending. The realization surprises people.

"Nicely done, August," Mr. Daniels says after I finish. "Hard to tell which method you were evoking for this exercise. Let me guess. Chekhov?"

"No, sir," I say, not even knowing that one.

"Strasberg method?" he asks.

I hesitate. The truth is, none. For me, it's not about being in the moment, or repetition of words, or using my own experiences or feelings. I have my own method. I step into the character, like putting on a mask. I can be Party Guy, or Serious Student, or Old Man with Dead Dog. Offstage and onstage, it's all the same. But I can't tell Mr. Daniels that.

"Yes," I say finally. "Strasberg."

"I knew it," he says, acting victorious. "Tell us, what experience did you tap into?"

I hesitate, searching for a lie. "My dog died a couple years ago. I was so sad," I say, giving puppy-dog eyes.

"Well, it worked. Good job, son," he says. I take my seat feeling good.

5:25 P.M.

At Riley's party, Elijah made me swear on a stack of Playbills that I would come with him to Underage Open Mic Night at Haswell Green's, a bar in Times Square popular with actors on Broadway and Off-Broadway. Every Monday night, they open at five and host an open mic for teens. It's cool to be in a bar—even if it's not serving alcohol and smells like the inside of a beer bottle.

Elijah told me the whole school shows up—which I didn't

believe—but it turns out he was right. People are in the booths drinking sodas and eating fries, or standing around the pool table, or gathered in front of the small stage in the back. This night is well documented—everyone has their phone out taking selfies, group photos, and videos. One of the twins Anna introduced me to on the first day (the "twiple threat") is onstage, strangling the mic stand, and belting at least two keys away from the right one.

Elijah finds me hiding at the bar and hands me a red plastic cup filled with soda. "What Tiffany is doing to 'Defying Gravity' should be outlawed." He covers his ears as Tiffany hits the high notes at the end.

"She is defying my ears right now," I kid.

Elijah hops up on a barstool, sipping on his Coke. "Take a drink," he demands.

I take a sip and my tongue burns. "Yuck."

"Yuck? Excuse me, that's the finest four-dollar whiskey."

"Thanks?" I offer.

"Are you going to grace the stage tonight?" he asks, raising his eyebrows.

"I don't think so," I say, getting nervous at the thought of being up there.

"I'm telling you, August, Amber DeJesus went viral from a video someone posted of her singing here, and now she's doing sponsored ads for laxative tea. Adam Long got his agent from this, and one time, I got a kiss from Richie Valentine. Anything can happen."

"Maybe next week?"

"Listen to me," he says, adjusting an imaginary bow tie, "I'm a senior."

"I listen to you because you're the Gushers guy," I say.

"Did you sign up for an audition spot?" he asks, avoiding any conversations about Gushers.

"I did," I say.

Elijah puts his arms around me. "Your first audition at SPA."

"Virgin right here."

He claps. "Allow me to lay things out for you. Or maybe Anna told you?"

"She did not," I confirm. She won't even look at me anymore.

"There's definitely politics to the casting of an SPA musical," he begins, and I take a big drink of my soda. "Lead roles like Danny and Sandy go to seniors unless there's an exceptional junior. Never an underclassman. The ensemble is filled with juniors and the occasional stand-out freshman or sophomore. Speaking roles go to the seniors mostly, but there's room. I've had speaking roles since sophomore year, but I'm me." He flashes a smile. Elijah has the confidence thing down.

"And you're going for Danny?" I ask.

"Oh yeah," he says in full Danny Zuko voice. "Hey, they won't know what hit them," he says, sounding more like a drunk John Travolta.

"Tell me more, tell me more," I joke.

"Soon," he says, dropping the impression. "But first, who are you going for?"

I haven't told anyone yet. I'm worried about the reaction. But Elijah seems like a safe audience. "I'm going for Rizzo," I admit.

"Rizzo," he says, his mouth remaining open. "Rizzo. Rizzo?" His brain can't understand it. "Why Rizzo?"

I don't want to lie to my friend. "It's my dream part," I say.

He scoffs. "Your dream role is Rizzo?"

"She's on the list."

"You're weird," he says with a laugh.

"You wanted to be my friend."

"I like you because you're weird," he says, then finishes his drink. "To be honest, this Rizzo thing will improve your odds. There's no sure-thing senior girl for any role but Sandy. Kelsey Whitton was born to play Sandy. That leaves Rizzo up for grabs. But you're going to piss off some girls."

"I will?" I ask, alarmed. I don't want to piss off anyone.

"Possibly, but I support you auditioning for any role you want," he says with the smile that makes everyone like him. "But I do wish you were my Kenickie."

"Who, me?" I ask, attempting the John Travolta accent. "I'll be your Kenickie in real life."

Elijah looks around. "So, I can trust you with my secrets?"

"Obviously," I say, pumped to hear secrets.

"Guess who had a make-out session in between parked cars after the party this weekend? *Me! Me! Meeeeee!*" he sings.

"With who?" I ask.

Elijah smiles big. "Here's a hint. He's a British cello master—"

"Duncan?"

"Bingo, baby. Can you believe it?"

"No, actually," I accidentally say. "I thought he was into Anna. Guess I read it wrong."

"You read it half wrong, my friend." He shoots me a smile. "He's pan."

"Pan?"

Elijah smiles. "Pansexual means into a person regardless of gender."

"I knew that," I lie.

"But he's not out about dating guys. He thinks it will hurt his career."

Elijah is about to divulge more but gets distracted. Maybe he spotted someone? "Actually," he says, not looking at me, "I'll be back, and we'll do a duet."

"No thanks," I say, but he's already disappeared into the crowd.

I'm headed toward the bathroom but stop to watch a girl with dirty-blonde hair walk onstage. She's beautiful in a chill, hippie way—wearing yellow-tinted aviator glasses, high-waisted jeans, and an acoustic guitar across her chest. There's already clapping and hollering—she must be a favorite. After centering herself in front of the microphone, she gives the guitar a strum.

"Hey, guys," she says in a small voice. The crowd cheers, and many people have their phones above their head, recording. "I'm Maggie Ridge, and I'm going to do an original. That cool with you?"

The crowd claps loudly; there are even a few yells. Maggie appears nervous and uncomfortable to be in the spotlight. "Cool. This one's called 'Too Much,'" she says, then starts strumming and creating a melodic, catchy tune. As the song picks up, she becomes more assured and open. It's a simple song about how things start good but become too much. Her words all make sense, beautiful in their simplicity, and they have heart. When she gets to the bridge, people are clapping along. The song ends, and the crowd goes wild.

I clap until I can no longer ignore my bladder and head down to the bathrooms in the basement. After using a dirty toilet in a small, smelly stall and washing my hands, I emerge from the men's room wiping my wet hands on my jeans. "Excuse me," I hear from behind me. The voice sounds familiar. I turn and see the girl who was just onstage.

"I'm sorry," I say.

She laughs. "Do you even know what you did?"

"No, but I could tell I should apologize."

Her shirt reads NIRVANA. I couldn't see it before because her guitar was in the way. "You pushed that door open with no regard for the shy girl hiding in the basement."

She's playing with me. I can be the Flirt. "Can I hide with you?"

"I guess," she says. "I like to get away after performing. Since there's no backstage, I come here. I can't deal with people talking to me about my music. Especially my own songs."

"So, this probably isn't the best time to tell you that your song was amazing?"

She smiles. Shrugs. "*Amazing* is a big word."

I lean against the wall. It's sticky. We're standing in a small basement filled with empty kegs, surrounded by the smell of pee, but I don't care. "I love when music makes me feel things. Your music did that, Maggie." I smile, proud I remembered her name. I like playing the role of the Flirt.

She blushes. "I came down here to avoid that, but thank you."

"I'm August," I say.

We shake hands and there's a charge of static between our palms. "Did you feel that?" I ask.

"I did."

"What if we're soul mates?" I ask with a smile.

"And this is our meet-cute, right here, in the basement?"

"You going to write a song about it?"

"What rhymes with urine?"

I laugh. She laughs. Soul mates.

"You go to SPA?" I ask.

"Yes, I'm in the New Music program."

"Cool," I say, having no idea what that means. "I'm drama."

"Are you drama or do you *do* drama?"

"Both," I flirt.

"Tell me, August, is it dangerous for girls to have crushes on actors? Aren't they always acting?"

This is loaded. Is she talking about me? Or another person? I take a drag of my imaginary cigarette and let out an imaginary puff. "Danger is my middle name."

She takes my imaginary cigarette and drops it on the floor. "I don't like smokers. And I don't trust actors," she says, stepping on my nonexistent cigarette.

"Both are bad for your health," I agree.

"I should probably head up and see my friends."

"Me too," I say—though I'd rather stay here with her.

We walk up the stairs together, and when we get to the top, Maggie turns to me and says, "Want to come with?"

I can tell she's a little nervous asking. Like how she was nervous before playing music. I'm about to say yes when I hear, "Hey, August."

I know that voice. It's Yazmin. "Hey," I say.

She looks around, bored. "Didn't know you were here."

"Same," I say.

"I'm going to head over to my friends," Maggie says.

Shit, I forgot about Maggie.

"Okay," I say, feeling torn between her and Yaz. "Nice to meet you."

"Having fun?" Yaz asks, texting on her phone.

I shrug but she doesn't see. "It's cool, I guess," I say.

"Look." She points back at the stage. Elijah walks on and adjusts the mic stand.

"Hello, New York!" he screams, too loudly. I would cheer, but Yazmin has rested her head on my shoulder and I'm not moving an inch. Thankfully, Elijah forgot about our duet. Instead, he's decided to tackle "Rose's Turn" from *Gypsy*. There are laughs among the audience as he sings, *"Here she is, boys"* while high kicking. Everyone is on their feet by the time he goes full tilt into the ending. *"Everything's coming up roses!"*

Yaz bites her lip. "Did you talk to Anna? About not saying anything?"

"Sure," I lie. "All good."

"Thank you," she says, then hugs me, like a reward. "I got back with my boyfriend. I didn't want any drama. I got to jet. See you around?"

"Absolutely," I say, but in a super casual way.

Once she's left, I head in the direction of Elijah.

NINE

11:21 A.M.

My audition is tomorrow. Twenty-eight hours until I'm standing in front of SPA's theater and music teachers. I should be more excited? Scared? Panicked? All those things. Instead, I'm focused on my unexpected lunch invitation from Yazmin.

I close my locker and nearly run over Juliet. "Hey," I say with a crack in my voice from the surprise.

"Hello, August. We miss you at lunch. Did our camp stories drive you away?"

"Just taking some me time," I say. It didn't feel right to sit at the table with Anna and her friends after what happened on Saturday. I didn't want to make it weird. Or weirder.

"And how long will this little tiff between you and Anna last?"

I shrug. "No clue. She won't even look in my direction."

"That's Anna," Juliet concedes. "She wears her heart on her

sleeve, even when she's wearing something sleeveless. And she likes you."

I nod. "I like her, too. Just not like that."

"Mmmm-hmmm," Juliet says.

"What?" I say innocently.

"Anna told us about what went down on the balcony, Romeo."

"She really did tell you everything."

"You know Anna," she says, then snaps her fingers and claps awkwardly. "Am I doing it right?"

"That's your hand jive?"

"Needs practice," she admits, then gives up butchering it any further. "Can't believe the prestigious School of Performing Arts is putting on something as pedestrian as *Grease*."

I don't care if it makes me nerdy to love *Grease*. I correctly jive my hands and say, "It's a classic."

"No, what you're doing is iconic."

I stop. "What's that?"

"Rumor is you're going for Rizzo?"

I look at her. "How did you know?"

She rolls her eyes. "Guess who."

Of course, Anna is telling people. But how did she know? "I am," I confirm, curious what Juliet thinks about my choice.

"Pegged you as more of a Kenickie. Or Danny."

"Elijah will get Danny—no reason to try."

"I suppose." She taps her feet together. "Are you auditioning for a female part as some kind of gender statement?"

"No," I say flatly.

"My bad," she says. "Don't want to overstep, but you identify as male and present as male—why play a female role?"

Rizzo is a great role. She's a strong character with a killer solo, but that's not why I'm auditioning for the part. The real reason is my mom. And Randy, I guess. They are planning on coming to see me in *Grease*. More correctly, they are coming to see their daughter in the show, and their daughter would play Rizzo. They can't know I'm August. They can't know I've socially transitioned. If they find out, they will take me back to Pennsylvania. Or send me to conversion therapy.

I want to tell Juliet—if anyone would understand, it would be her. I wonder what she would say. Would she dissuade me or support me? Her family is supportive, and mine is not. She might tell people, too. It's not worth risking. "Elijah said it was my best shot at a lead role," I say. "Plus, I've presented female all my life, and the only roles I played at my old school were female."

Juliet thinks. "So maybe you're scared to go for male roles?"

"No," I say, "I'm good at them, too."

"And it doesn't bother you to present female? You don't feel uncomfortable?"

I shake my head. "When it comes to the stage, I'm not interested in playing trans characters. I want to be the trans actor playing all the great male and female characters, including Rizzo."

"Rizzo is a bad bitch," she concedes. "August, you can always talk to me. That's why I came here. You don't have to go through this alone."

I lean over and nudge her. "Thank you," I say.

She picks at the polish on her nail. "I heard something else. Should I tell you?"

"Do I have a choice?"

Juliet shrugs. "Anna will be the reader during the audition."

That's not good news. Anna—the person who hates me most—will be in the room (judging me) and reading the lines with me (sabotaging me). "That's not going to help my focus."

Juliet waves me off. "You just need to kiss and make up."

I tilt my head. "She's pissed."

"Well, maybe not kiss. But I know she'll forgive you."

"Did she tell you we fought about her dad?" I ask.

Juliet stops fidgeting with her nail and looks up. "Actually, no."

Relief floods over me. At least she isn't telling everyone that I'm a fraud who flirted my way into the school. "Thanks for finding me," I say to Juliet.

"No matter what happens between you and Anna, we'll be friends."

"I'm glad," I say, then we hug. I'm happy to have Juliet as a friend. I can be more myself with her than anyone else, even if I don't tell her the whole truth.

"Want to get lunch?" she asks. "I could skip the lunchroom today."

"I'd love that, but I have something," I say, backing away. That something is a lunch date. With Yazmin Guzman. I woke up to something unusual: a text from Yaz. Even more unusual, she asked me to lunch. I nearly leaped out of bed and have been counting the minutes until now. My thoughts are crowded with

Yaz. Will she like this shirt? Did they break up again? Is she thinking about me? I walk up to the fifth floor like she instructed. Yaz wants to have lunch with me but doesn't want to do it under the scrutiny of the cafeteria. I spot her on a bench, looking at her phone. "Auggie!" she yells.

"Auggie?" I repeat, walking to her.

"You don't like? That's my new name for you. Auggie," she repeats.

Auggie is a kid's name. Is that how she sees me?

"I don't *love* it," I say, being honest.

"You'll *love* it when I say it. Now sit," she demands, patting the bench. She reaches into her turtle backpack and pulls out a foil ball. "I want to tell you something about me. Something I don't tell most people."

"Okay," I say, my heart beating fast.

"My family is from the Dominican Republic. My parents were born here, but my abuela, my grandmother, was born there. She lives with us and made these tamales."

Yaz picks off the tape holding the foil together with her long, bright green fingernail. The smell of corn and chicken hits my nose and wakes my stomach up. I watch as she peels the shell off and takes a bite. I do the same and the spice burns my nose, but the sweetness cools down my mouth. I want this moment to last forever.

"My family's not rich like Riley's, not even close," she says.

I nod, thinking of the hedge-fund penthouse. "Same. I can't imagine living like that," I admit.

She unpeels another tamale. "But I will be someday. I'll be rich and famous. And buy my family a big house."

"Can I ask you a question?"

She leans back, resting her head against the wall. "Of course."

"I heard your dad was some record producer," I say.

She pauses, thinking. Finally, she says, "He's not."

"Why lie?" I ask.

"Because people at this school like rich people with powerful parents. They get all hot and bothered in proximity to fame or power or whatever. So I lied. But I'm trusting you with my secret now."

"I won't tell anyone," I say, wondering if I should tell her mine.

"Thanks, Auggie."

I sit back and think. We both walk around with lies to protect our image. Yazmin Guzman is opening up to me. Her attention feels intoxicating.

"Auggie," she says in a cute voice. I still loathe Auggie, but do love hearing her say it. "Can I ask something?"

"Sure," I say, on guard about what she's about to ask.

She moves closer. "Can you not audition for Rizzo?"

I recoil. To the end of the bench. I didn't expect that. "Chill," she says, moving closer to me again. "Let me explain."

I drop my shoulders and try to relax. She continues, "I want to be Rizzo." She puts her arm around me. "And you could be my Kenickie."

The temptation is so real, but my parents would not approve.

"What do you say?" She's close enough to kiss me. "Will you be my Kenickie?"

"I'll think about it," I say.

"You do that," she says, getting up and putting her backpack on. "I'm out. Talk later?"

"Talk later," I say. She leaves me holding the tamales.

5:15 P.M.

The subway from SPA to Brooklyn takes about forty-five minutes. There's only a small body of water between Brooklyn and Manhattan, but the two boroughs can seem like two different worlds. Brooklyn is calmer and slower—and cooler. Better thrift stores. Less-crowded sidewalks. Everyone looks so low-key hip without trying, even parents pushing strollers.

I walk down a paved sidewalk covered in fallen yellow and brown leaves and think about the audition. And Yaz. Kenickie would be the perfect role for me, and Yaz would be my Rizzo. Maybe I should go for it. I could think of something to tell my parents, but they might not believe me. To stay here, to pursue my dream, I need to be the daughter my parents expect me to be. But Yaz really got in my head.

I'm looking forward to a quiet night. I need time to decide what to do; I need time to prepare for my audition. When I walk in the door, I expect to see Aunt Lil, and maybe Davina, making dinner and drinking wine. Instead, there's a handful of people crowded around the kitchen table. Some standing, some seated, and everyone with a drink in their hand.

"August! Is that you?" my aunt calls out when she hears the door. "Everyone, my nephew is here!" She navigates around the bodies and chairs—wineglass in hand—and puts her arm around me. Her cheeks are flushed from the wine. "This is August!"

Several variations of "Hello, August" come my way from the group. They smile at me with pinkish teeth, slightly stained from the red wine.

"What's going on here?" I ask.

"It's my turn to host the Park Slope feminist book club. I told you about this last week!"

How could I have forgotten? I would have stayed out longer. "What's the book?"

Davina holds it up. "*Bad Feminist* by Roxane Gay!"

"Have you read it, August?" someone asks.

"No," I admit.

"Neither did I," a woman wearing a leather vest says. "Come hang out anyway."

I drop my bag and enter the feminist book club. I sit in the chair by the leather-vested funny lady. "I'm Ginger," she says, her voice deep and scratchy.

"Watch out for Ginger," Aunt Lil warns.

"Who, me? I'm harmless!" Ginger says with her hands up. "Your auntie here, she's a real damp cloth, right?"

"She runs a tight ship," I joke.

"And how is life at the School of Performing Arts?"

"Stressful. But amazing. You know so much about me," I say,

giving my aunt a playful look. "And I know nothing about you."

"What!" Ginger yells. "Lil doesn't talk about us endlessly?"

I shake my head. "Not even once."

"Oh my god." Ginger fakes disgust. "What about Davina?"

"She talks about you even less."

The table laughs. It feels good. Ginger says, "Well, sir, I own a bar in Brooklyn. You should come by." She looks at Lil. "When you're of age, of course. And this is my best half, Celeste."

"Hi, August," Celeste says. "I'm an artist like your aunt, but not as good."

"That's ridiculous," Aunt Lil says.

"How about," Celeste tries again, "not as celebrated."

Aunt Lil considers it. "That's fair."

"Yet!" Ginger says, then gives her a kiss on the cheek. Celeste is younger and more feminine than Ginger, and they make a good-looking couple.

"I'm Terry," says a quiet white woman with gray hair and a welcoming smile. "I work in book publishing."

An African American woman waves at me. Her shaved head accentuates her sharp cheekbones. She could be a model. "I'm Judy. I work as a nurse at Callen-Lorde, an LGBTQ health-care center. It's a terrific resource for transgender people. You could start your hormone therapy there."

Aunt Lil jumps in. "He needs to be eighteen."

Judy waves her off. "He just needs a parent's consent."

"I'm afraid I don't have that," I say.

"I'm sorry, sweetie," she says. "But you could start therapy. It's good to talk to someone."

"He could? I didn't know that," Aunt Lil says. "August, would you?"

I have enough to do. I need to stay focused on acting. "Maybe during summer break?"

Aunt Lil frowns. "We can talk later," she says.

A plate of brownies has been tempting me since I sat down. I'm guessing they are void of dairy or even sugar, but I'll take my chances. I reach for one as the conversations pick up around me. Right before taking a bite, I hear, "Don't eat that!"

I drop the brownie on the table. All eyes on me. Aunt Lil says, "Your mom would kill me if you had that. It's a special brownie."

"Full of pot," Ginger jokes.

The room giggles, waiting for my response. "Just a bite?" I ask.

They laugh. And Lil takes the brownie from me playfully, then takes a bite herself. "In one year and two months," she says.

The conversations get going again. These ladies know how to party. Ginger scoots her chair toward me. "So, stud, I'm from Harrisburg, pretty close to your hometown. Fellow Pennsyl-suck-ian. It wasn't a great place to grow up a baby dyke."

Celeste cuts in, "That's why we all come to New York. To bloom."

"Look at me," Ginger announces. "I bloomed into this sexy butch dyke."

"I still have some blooming to do," I admit.

"I'm guessing both transitions, gender and geography, must be hard to process. Are you adjusting?"

"Honestly," I say—because why not be honest—"my life is such a blur of acting classes, regular classes, homework. And tomorrow, I have my first audition. I don't have time to process anything. I'm just surviving."

"I can imagine," Celeste says. Her eyes are sweet and understanding.

Ginger gives my knee a shake. "What's the audition?"

Aunt Lil comes over and leans against the table, wineglass in hand, to listen. "*Grease*," I say.

Ginger starts clapping loudly, getting the attention of the room. "No shit. My lesbian theater group in college did a parody of *Grease* called *Lube*. It was a hit!"

"I don't want to know how the hand jive went," Aunt Lil jokes.

"Who are you auditioning for, August?" Terry asks.

I look around, wondering what they will think. "I'm actually going for Betty Rizzo," I say, even though I might be going for Kenickie. Jury's still out. The group is quiet for a second. Taking it in? Are they going to judge me? They are feminists. They might have a problem with me playing a female part. "Why Rizzo?" Ginger asks.

I look at Aunt Lil, who gives me a nod. "'Cause my parents are coming up for the show. And they think I'm still living as a girl, and if they know the truth, I might have to go to conversion therapy."

I look down at the floor, ashamed. But it does feel good to finally be honest. Janet the nurse nods. "When I was in high school, my family wouldn't allow me to date girls."

"What did you do?" I ask.

She laughs to herself. "I had a best friend and she could spend the night. That worked out nicely, actually."

"I think," Ginger begins, "I can speak for the table and assure you that keeping a part of yourself private to protect yourself and keep safe is something we have all done."

"My girlfriend is so wise," Celeste says.

"Do you have a girlfriend or boyfriend?" Judy asks me.

My cheeks go red. "You're embarrassing him," my aunt says.

"There's a girl," I say proudly. "But it's complicated. She's awesome. When she walks into a room, I feel things."

"He's got it bad," Celeste says.

"Do not," I elegantly defend myself.

"What's complicated about it?" Davina asks. This is all news to Aunt Lil and Davina.

"She's got a boyfriend, but I think she likes me."

"The drama!" Ginger says.

I continue, "She asked me not to audition for Rizzo. She wants me to be her Kenickie."

"And not in her way," Janet adds.

"My turn to give advice," Celeste says. "August, your life has just begun. There will be more . . ." She trails off, realizing she doesn't know her name.

"Yazmin."

"Oh, what a nice name. But there will be more Yazmins. Does that help?"

"It does," I lie.

Celeste and Ginger high-five, then kiss. "My hero," Celeste says. They are really enjoying bestowing the younger generation with wisdom.

I spend another hour with the book club. They tell me about the history of gay culture in New York, but the brownies must be working because the story gets derailed by tangents. I politely excuse myself, say goodbye to everyone, and head upstairs.

After everyone leaves, Aunt Lil peeks in my room. "Hey, kid, you asleep?"

"Not really," I admit. I'm lying in bed mindlessly scrolling on my phone and trying to decide between Rizzo and Kenickie. My parents and Yazmin.

"Come with me," she says, with a happy tone and slight slur.

I follow her down the hall to her studio. She bumps into the wall. Someone had a fun night. After searching around, she lifts a canvas onto an easel. The painting is a mess of brown and yellow splashed around wildly. Aunt Lil leans against a table. "What do you think?" she asks.

"Not your best work," I say, making my aunt cackle.

"Years ago, I fell for a girl named Angelina. She was a spicy firecracker from Italy. I thought she was the one. I was heels over head for her," she slurs.

"And you painted this for her?"

"No, this was my bottom. She drained me of my creative energy. No, I drained myself of my creative energy." She pauses, reflecting. Or maybe she forgot what she was saying. "Love can be good and beautiful, like me and Davina. But sometimes it can be a fever dream running hot and cold, leaving you with art that looks like someone took a poop on a canvas."

I nod at both her wisdom and the painting looking like crap. "So, I should audition for Rizzo?"

"If it was love, dear boy, you wouldn't have to make that choice."

That hits hard. I love my aunt. "Aunt Lil, if you love Davina, then why won't you put a ring on it? Or at least live together?"

"I'm set in my ways. New dogs and old tricks, right?"

"Sure," I say.

Aunt Lil tuns the light off and bumps her way out of the room. Before leaving, she turns back and smiles. "Don't let a crush distract you from your dreams. And also, don't mix red wine and tequila. Thank you and good night."

TEN

12:03 P.M.

Fifteen minutes until the audition. I'm taking a big loop around the block to calm my nerves. My first audition at West Grove was for *Jesus Christ Superstar*. An ambitious musical for a small theater group, but my old high school would go to great lengths to have Christian content. I wanted to play Jesus, but that wouldn't have gone over well with my parents. I settled for the only female role in the whole show, Mary Magdalene. When I got the part, Mom was so proud of me. It felt like she loved me more.

Playing Rizzo will make my mom proud. It's impossible for her to not overflow with love while watching me in front of a thousand people in the fancy theater. For my parents' love, and so they won't take me back to Pennsylvania, I'm auditioning for Rizzo. Even if it means Yaz will be done with me.

I have a couple of pre-audition rituals. "A couple" makes it

151

sound cute, but there are five things I need to do, or I won't get the part. All completely necessary to my success. First, I need to eat two bowls of cereal in the morning. Doesn't matter what cereal, just needs to be two. Aunt Lil didn't have any cereal in her house when I first arrived, so I had to buy Froot Loops special for the audition to the school. Second, must wear a black shirt. Easy 'cause that's my uniform anyways. Third, and this is when things get weird, listen to my playlist of whale sounds. Fourth, give five compliments. This is important—it helped me book *Mary Poppins* at summer camp. I've given four compliments today and need one more. Finally, take a walk before my audition. And that's what I'm doing now. While listening to my whale sounds.

As I cross the street to school, there's someone familiar sitting on the front steps, leaning against her guitar case, soaking up the sun. Maggie from the New Music program, who sings songs called "Too Much."

Turns out the New Music program is a big deal. Elijah said only ten people get into the group and they all end up famous. I watch Maggie from across the street. She's got on black jeans and a denim jacket. Green shirt underneath. Maggie looks chill. Calm. Opposite of me right now. I will match her energy. For her, I'll play Cool Guy.

I mess up my hair a little, smooth out my shirt, and cross the street. "Come here often?"

"Almost every day, actually," she says, her voice scratchy and soothing. "I'm waiting for my bandmates. We're going to rehearse."

"Your New Music bandmates?" I say, flexing my memory skills.

"Yes, we have a band called Nerd Cheese."

"Not really."

"It's memorable."

"So are you," I say coolly.

She smiles. "Auditions are today?"

"Yeah, mine is soon."

"Nervous?"

Cool Guy says, "Nah."

"I would be. I couldn't imagine the pressure. Especially at this school."

"I'm not worried."

"Really?" she asks. "That's suspicious."

I wave her off. "I do this all the time."

"So, you're not nervous?"

I sit down beside her. "I don't get nervous," I say, wondering if she can tell I'm completely lying.

"Oh man, I do. The first time I auditioned for a musical in middle school, I told them my name was Magoo."

I laugh. "You did theater?"

"Yeah, but acting wasn't my thing. I love playing music—that's all I want to do. But I get so nervous onstage. Why do you love acting?"

"Do you think dentists get asked the same question?" I ask.

She laughs. "They have an undeniable passion for teeth."

I run my hand through my hair. Stare off in the distance. "I like being in front of a crowd. I'm good at it."

She rolls her eyes. "Be real. For one minute?"

I take a dramatic breath. "There's nothing better than being onstage. In front of an audience. It's a feeling I get, like I'm fully present and seen—even if it's not me they see. I take words and create a person. Then I make the audience believe that person is real." I stop, frustrated to not have the best way to explain.

"You're cute."

"Who, me?" I ask innocently.

"Yes, exactly, you. When you drop the act and get all excited about theater, you're adorable."

I smile and maybe even blush a little. "Are you going to write a song about me?"

"I just might."

I remember my last ritual, one more compliment. "You know, your voice is something else. The only thing better is your smile."

Her turn to blush. "Thank you, August."

Even though I don't want to leave, I say, "I better get going."

"What's a less violent version of break legs?" she asks as I get up from the steps.

"Rub legs?" I suggest.

"Go in there and rub some legs."

"Thanks, Magoo," I say.

I take the stairs to the basement, my heart beating loud enough to echo in the stairwell. The nervous energy hits me as soon as I enter the hallway. The place is packed—small groups huddled up talking, others sitting alone, and a few preparing for their audition. Yazmin is standing in a group of girls. She spots me and heads over, her oversized bright yellow jacket hanging off her shoulders. "Hey, Auggie," she says, then hugs me. I see people looking. This feels weird and performative.

"How'd it go?" I ask. Her audition was before mine.

"Ugh, I feel like I could have done the song better."

"I'm sure you were great," I say.

She shrugs. "When are you going in?"

"August Greene," the audition proctor yells across the hallway.

"That's me."

"Wait," she says, grabbing my backpack straps. "Who are you going for?"

I like her. I like whatever we are doing. I want to keep this going for as long as possible. "It's a surprise," I say.

She smiles like she knows what that means. "Break legs, Auggie!"

The proctor writes on her clipboard and opens the door for me. I'm feeling all the emotions of my first audition, but this time it's not just Mr. Daniels and Anna; there are also five other teachers and someone behind the piano. I gulp. I literally gulp.

I set my backpack down on a desk and hear, "You're sure you signed up for the right audition?"

I find center stage and smile at the line of people behind a long table facing me. "Yes," I say with a shaky voice. "I'm here for Rizzo."

They look at each other, silently deciding if this is acceptable.

Do they have a rule book? Even if rules do exist, I doubt one is outlawing transgender people from playing both genders. "All right, August," Mr. Daniels says. "Let's see what you got."

The teacher in the middle says, "Anna will be reading with you."

"Great, thank you," I say. Anna smiles at me, but it feels fake. This would be the perfect time for her to get back at me. I need to connect with her to do this scene. I return the smile.

I shut my eyes. I'm Rizzo. A tough Italian girl, more mature than her classmates, has seen more and been through more. I talk down to everyone because I feel below them. A big heart protected by the thickest skin at Rydell High.

I open my eyes and nod at Anna. She reads her first line. It's a scene between Rizzo and the Pink Ladies. I pretend to chew gum and assert my dominance in the group. I throw attitude and make jokes. When I can, I let my soft side show.

When I finish, I see a couple of teachers nodding. Good sign.

Mr. Daniels says, "Nicely done, August." Good sign.

Anna rolls her eyes. Bad sign.

"You ready to sing?" the music teacher, Mr. Gonzales, asks.

I nod and the piano starts playing "There Are Worse Things I Could Do." I sing the chorus, releasing the raw pain of wanting a life different from your own. I let the feeling swell, and when I hit the last line—*But to cry in front of you, That's the worst thing I could do*—a tear runs down my cheek. When I finish, I see a couple of smiles. One person claps. Good sign. I've worked so hard to be here. I'm finished with my first audition at SPA.

"Thank you, August," Mr. Daniels says. "You are excused."

"Thank you for considering me. And thank you, Anna."

I head out the door and every eye in the hallway stares at me—trying to judge how my audition went. I feel a tap on my shoulder. I turn around and see Tess.

"Rizzo? Really, August?"

"How did you know?" I ask defensively.

"We all heard you sing, obviously," Tess says, like I should have known.

"Yes," I say, no way to lie. "I went for Rizzo."

"That is so unfair. What gives you the right?"

She stands with her arms crossed and her foot tapping. I should tell her that she has no right confronting me. I should tell her so many things. Instead, I shake my head and walk off.

ELEVEN

Friday, September 27

2:23 P.M.

The casting sheet for *Grease* will be posted on the corkboard in the basement "before the end of school today." That timeline is too vague for my nerves, which are wrecked from anticipation. Everyone is in the same boat—you can feel it in the air, see it on people's faces, and it's the only topic of conversation in the halls. There's no need to wait by the corkboard; someone will post a picture and it will be widely shared instantly.

Last night was torture. I had a pile of homework but couldn't concentrate on anything but *Grease*. Instead of writing a paper on World War II, I texted Elijah—who isn't worried at all—paced around my room replaying the audition in my head, texted more, looked at everyone's posts, then texted some more. I would hear gossip from Anna via Elijah. And I didn't hear anything from Yazmin. Bad sign.

I haven't paid attention at all today, but improv class is a welcome distraction. We're learning how to incorporate audience participation. Our teacher, Ms. Jackson, is the funniest person in the building. She worked at Upright Citizens Brigade and even tried out for *Saturday Night Live*.

There's a group onstage doing a scene when my pocket vibrates. There's only one reason I'm getting a text now. The casting sheet is up. I wiggle the phone out of my pocket, hands shaking, and keep it under my desk. I feel sick to my stomach. The class laughs, I have no idea at what, but I fake laugh with them so it seems like I'm listening. It's a text from Elijah. I scan the picture of the casting sheet and see:

RIZZO: August Greene.

There's my name. I'm in *Grease*. I'm Rizzo. I want to jump out of my desk and run around the room. My head feels like it's about to pop off. Instead, I drop my phone—the *thud thud thud* getting the attention of the entire class. Ms. Jackson clears her throat in a way that means *put that phone away*. When everyone turns back to the stage, I pick up my phone and hold it between my legs for the rest of the skit. We clap and the bell rings.

"That's it, gang," Ms. Jackson says. "I think there's something on the Theater Announcements wall you might want to check out."

Everyone gets up and heads out, some already checking their phones. I stay in my seat and read the names. Elijah as Danny, Kelsey Whitton as Sandy, Jamaal Jones as Kenickie, me as Rizzo.

Yazmin in the ensemble. I feel bad, but I need to do what's best for me.

I head out to the hall—walking as coolly as possible—and try to ignore everyone looking at me. I just put myself on the map of this school. I am the Infamous August Greene. I feel like I can do anything. Including something that I swore I would do. I head to the basement. People congratulate me and stare at me on the way—possibly in disbelief—but I keep walking. Not being rude, just determined.

I make my way across the entire basement, and without looking back, stopping, or second-guessing, I walk into the boys' dressing room. I get a little too empowered and push the double doors so hard they slap against the wall. I cross the threshold and enter with confidence.

I do belong here.

It's the same as the girls' dressing room—lockers, benches, bathroom stalls, sinks, and mirrors. The only difference is the urinals—which I won't be visiting. I laugh. Why was I so scared?

I hit the bathroom stall feeling like a king. I belong here. In this bathroom—and also this school. I'm a lead in the fall musical. I can't wait to post about this and rack up the likes and maybe new followers. I have proven myself, and no one can take that away. Not Anna. Not Tess. No one. I smile and laugh a little, feeling giddy. I can do anything I set my mind to doing.

Right as I flush, a group of guys walk in, talking loudly. I stand there frozen. Listening.

"Congrats, man. Everyone knew you were Danny," a guy says. That means Elijah is here.

"Thank you," Elijah says in his John Travolta voice. "I couldn't have done it without you."

"That's why I'm your Kenickie," the guy says. That must be Jamaal.

"But what's up with Rizzo?" another guy asks. I stop breathing. There's a small silence.

"That's my friend August," Elijah explains.

"Why did he try out for the girl part?"

I hear someone peeing. Someone washing their hands. "I don't know, man, he wanted to play Rizzo. He's trans. He plays both genders."

More silence. My fears flood the quiet. Finally, a guy says, "For real? That's cool, I guess."

"That's cool, I guess" is the best response I could hope for. Maybe it will be okay. I let out a breath.

Once the guys have left and the dressing room is empty again, I leave the stall, wash my hands, and head out. Mission accomplished. Level achieved. I hit the hallway thinking about how excited Mom will be to hear the news. I'll call her on the walk to the subway.

"You did it," I hear from behind. I turn around and see Anna. She's wearing a leopard-print blouse, white jeans, and red lipstick. And for the first time since the party, she's talking to me.

"I did it," I repeat.

"Anna—"

"August," she cuts in before I can apologize. "No hard feelings. I didn't read the room. Or whatever. It's water off a duck's back. We're going to be spending lots of time together with *Grease*, and I don't want bad vibes."

I ask the question that has crossed my mind more than I'll admit. "Did you convince your dad to accept me to this school?"

She looks around. Shrugs. "We talked that night. I told him what I thought."

I don't like that answer. I don't like it at all. There's zero clarity.

"We are all good now, Augustus." She gives me a hug. "Besides, I'm seeing someone new."

"Care to share?" I ask.

She crosses her arms. "How can I trust you?"

I hold out my pinkie. She wraps her pinkie in mine. Our eyes meet. "Okay. Remember Duncan? The cello player?"

Oh, I remember. And so does Elijah. This is conflicting information.

She continues, "He's sweetest boy in the world. It's still new, so we're keeping it quiet."

"Wow."

"I know."

"How long has this been going on?" I ask.

She does a quick twirl. "Couple days ago. At Haswell."

"I'm happy for you," I say. And I'm sad for Elijah. Does he know? Do I tell him?

"Thank you, Augustus. I'm happy for you, too. Don't know why you went for Rizzo, but I knew you'd land any role." She pinches my cheek. "You got something special."

"Thank you," I say. "Want to walk to the subway after school? Orange line?"

She smiles. "Can't today. I'm meeting you-know-who after his practice, but I'll text you later." She hugs me again and I'm happy to have my first SPA friend back. Even if she's dating the same guy as my second SPA friend.

Instead of heading to Audition Technique, I find a quiet hallway and call Mom. I want to tell Hugo—my friend from back home who got me into theater—but there would be too much to explain. After two rings, Mom picks up with her usual greeting. "Hi, sweet daughter," she says.

Those words send shock waves through my body. When I lived at home, I was used to it. But I push through. I am Mom's sweet daughter. My voice goes higher. "Hi, Mom, great news. Are you sitting down?"

"You got that part?"

"I got the part," I confirm.

"Honey, that's so great. How can I sit when I'm hopping up and down?"

She's happy. That feels good. "Don't hurt yourself, Mom."

"This is the best thing. The Lord has blessed you with a gift, and He's creating a path for more to see it."

She brings the holy spirit into everything. "The theater has a thousand seats," I brag.

"We knew this would be your path. Didn't we? I knew it the

first time I saw you onstage as Mary Magdalene."

"We did know. Thank you for letting me be here."

"Of course; I trust you and your aunt."

"Are you proud of me?" I ask, feeling small.

She laughs. "How could I not be? I'm so proud of my daughter."

I shut my eyes. I lied to my friends, ruined any chance with Yazmin, probably have Tess planning my death, all to hear that. That she's proud of her daughter.

And what will I have to do for her to be proud of her son?

ACT TWO: GREASE

TWELVE

Friday, October 11

5:35 P.M.

I'm trying to enjoy this moment. It's not every day that you stand in front of your first dressing room station at the School of Performing Arts. I know it's mine by the card taped to the mirror with my name in cursive. This is my station. This is my chair. I earned this spot. The two weeks of rehearsals leading up to this dressing room station were brutal. Rehearsals during school, after school, on weekends. I'm exhausted. I'm behind on homework. I'm having the best time of my life.

Over this two-week rehearsal process, I've really come into my own. Well, not exactly *my* own. Nobody is impressed by a newly transitioned guy with a family who doesn't accept him. I've come into my character. No more bit parts like Confident Guy and Party Guy. Now I am the Infamous August Greene, a student at the School of Performing Arts with talent and confidence, who's quick to the joke and flirty, and who doesn't have a lot of back-story.

The future is bright for the Infamous AG. Already booking a lead role at SPA, and the sky's the limit. Basically, I've become the social media version of myself. Fake it until you make it, right? I can act big and bold and confident until I *am* those things.

Tech rehearsal for *Grease* starts tomorrow. Tech week is when we move into the theater and the sets are put up, lights are programmed, sound is checked, costumes are finalized, and the band gets added. Something always goes wrong. Most things go wrong. And the only thing guaranteed about tech week is blood, sweat, and lots of tears.

I hear "Auuuugust" from the hallway. Meena is coming after me. I must be late for something. She wasn't kidding that first week of school: Meena is a hell of a stage manager. The devil doesn't wear Prada—she carries a clipboard. And does not suffer fools. "Everyone is waiting onstage. Where's your head?"

"Just taking in the scenery," I admit, then snap a picture of my station to post later. It's all about capturing the moments of tech and putting together a multiple-picture post with a sappy—yet humble—caption. My seven hundred followers will be inspired. I'm already writing the post in my head.

"Come on, mister," she says, pulling on my shirtsleeve. "You think you like this view, wait until you stand on the stage."

We walk fast, nearly running, down the hallway. Meena has been at every rehearsal and serves as the glue holding this ship together. I can't wait to see her flex her management skills all over this week. It's already obvious she takes pride in her walkie-talkie headset. "Found the missing greaser, be there now," she says into the mic. We arrive at the double doors leading to the stage and Meena stops. She looks at me and smiles. "You ready?"

"As I'll ever be," I say. I've seen Theater One, but not from the stage. She pushes the doors open and I step into the light. The stage is washed with bright spotlights, making it hard to see. A thousand empty seats face me—the fluorescent orange upholstery almost offensive to the eye. In one week, they'll be full. We have three shows. Wednesday, Thursday, and Friday. All sold out. My parents are coming on Friday night.

"Thanks for joining, August. Now we can begin," Mr. Daniels says. I walk over to the huddle of actors around our teacher and director.

Meena covers her walkie-talkie mic and whispers, "Eagle starting the speech."

"Actors, we have made it to the final stretch. Thank you for your hard work over the weeks," Mr. Daniels says. Everyone claps politely. He continues, "But this, as you know, will be a demanding week. I want you to get plenty of sleep, eat good meals, and take care of yourself. We don't want anyone getting sick. Well, maybe the understudies do," he jokes. People laugh nervously.

Mr. Daniels finds Meena. "Please regale everyone with the schedule."

She weaves through the people and takes her place beside Mr. Daniels. "Tech starts tomorrow. This week will be backbreaking, soul-crushing. Someone won't make it out—"

"Meena," Mr. Daniels cuts in. "The schedule will be fine for now."

"Right." She looks at her clipboard. "Actors have tomorrow off as the set and lights are put into place. Your call time on Sunday is ten. In the morning. Don't be late. We'll be doing a cue-to-cue for the lighting, sitzprobe, then a stumble-through."

My heart starts beating. Cue-to-cues are boring; it's just standing in place so they can move the lights and program the sound, then moving on to the next scene. But the sitzprobe—when we finally sing with the band—is the most exciting moment. Then the stumble through is a mess but helps us get our bearings. I'm now living for Sunday.

Mr. Daniels clears his throat. "The seats are empty now, but soon they will be full of people looking to get away from their problems, to be entertained, to escape from life for a couple of hours. *Grease* is pure entertainment. Can we give the audience some summer loving? Some beauty school dropout? Some fun? Can we give them that?"

Everyone yells in the affirmative.

"You've all worked hard, and I thank you for that. This week you must work harder, and that may sound impossible, but you can do it. Your discipline and focus will get you ahead in this business. Now, go home and get some rest. See you on Sunday."

Mr. Daniels walks offstage and Meena fast-walks behind him, whispering into her walkie-talkie.

Jamaal turns around and smiles. "Nobleman August," he says. "To Old John's or not to Old John's? That is the question."

Jamaal believes he was Shakespeare in a past life. This belief influences his speech, movements, and sense of importance. He's attractive and straight, a deadly combo in theater. I'm still deciding if the Shakespeare thing gets the attention of girls, or if they ignore it because he's so good-looking.

"When it comes to Old John's, the answer is always yes," I say, then we fist bump. When Jamaal isn't busy channeling his past life, he's a great Kenickie and probably the nicest guy I've ever met.

Before heading out, I take a picture of the empty seats—both for my montage post and to send to my mom. I text her the picture and say: SEE YOU IN SEVEN DAYS!

I'm acting like my parents' upcoming visit is exciting, but I'm more nervous about playing the role of their daughter than Rizzo. They are driving up on Friday for the last show and spending the night at a hotel in Times Square. For one night, I will play the role of their daughter. It's only a show and dinner after. As much as it hurts that they don't accept me, I do miss my mom. I can't wait to hug her after the show.

She writes back immediately: Can't wait to see you shine but not ready to see your short hair. ☹

An emoji? That's new. I didn't teach her that.

I called Mom last week and told her I was going to cut my hair short for my role. A perfect cover-up for having short hair— thank you, Rizzo. Mom fought against it—always preferring my hair long—and suggested a wig. I told her the director made me. When in doubt, blame the director. My hair has grown out a bit— my curls are the perfect length for Rizzo. After my parents leave, I'm going to a real barbershop and getting a haircut—a gift to myself for surviving both the musical and my parents' visit.

Jamaal and I wait outside the school for the rest of the cast. It's already dark out—the sun now sets before we get out of rehearsal. Fall is here, and without much notice, it became hoodie and leather-jacket weather. Soon it will be puffy-coat weather.

"Can you keep-eth a secret?" Jamaal asks. Sometimes sharing a soul with Shakespeare is just adding "eth" to the ends of words.

"I can try-eth," I say.

"I'm crushing on Yazmin hard."

My heart sinks. Yazmin ghosted me after the auditions. She's friendly to my face—which is good because we're in a show together—but no more texts, tamale lunches, or even eye contact. I've accepted that I ruined any chance with her by getting Rizzo, but I haven't stopped liking her. How do you unlike someone?

"Doesn't she have a boyfriend?" I ask, pretending not to know.

"She says they've been fighting. Anyway, I'm only looking for a showmance."

"Maybe Tess?" I offer.

"Her and Justin have something going."

"Oh," I say, stunned. I'm behind in my gossip. Anna is dropping the ball.

Jamaal hops off the wall and stands face-to-face with me. "Maybe you could talk to Yaz for me? See what you can find out?"

I almost laugh, but hold it in. I'm never having that conversation with her. "Sure," I say, wanting to be Jamaal's friend.

"Thanks, man," he says, then gives me a hug.

"Whoa, what's happening here?" Elijah yells, emerging from the school with the group behind him.

"We're hugging it out," Jamaal says. Elijah joins and the others do, too.

There's an unexplainable bonding that happens within a cast. We get so close during the show, like going through a war together. It's weird and hard to explain, but when the last performance is over, I miss the cast as much as I miss the show. The bond is so real. There are inside jokes, games, and drama unique to each show. And there's one thing that can end the bond: a showmance.

Showmances are a real thing. The whirlwind of the rehearsal and shows brings people together. Sometimes really closely. Showmances are micro-relationships that typically don't last longer than the final bow. Or after the closing party. I've never had a showmance, or even a showcrush. I've seen them not cause trouble, and I have seen them end the cast bond.

We walk in a tight—and loud—pack down Amsterdam Avenue toward Old John's. Elijah is telling me about something, but

I'm too busy thinking about what Jamaal asked me to do. I've packed up my feelings about Yaz and put them away, but this just brought them back.

As we pass by a bodega, Justin Sudds jumps out from behind the outdoor refrigerator. "GOT YOU," he yells while hitting Kelsey with a water gun.

"Dammit," she yells, playfully frustrated. Our cast is embroiled in a heated game of Assassins. During the lunch break during a long Saturday rehearsal, we walked to the dollar store and got brightly colored water guns. Everyone drew names for targets, and the only rule is you have to hit your target off school grounds. That means preparation, planning, and execution. People have gone to great lengths to hit their target. Waiting for hours outside apartments or gyms.

My target was Elijah, which was easy. Got him the next day. After rehearsal, I waited outside Starbucks and soaked his rusty orange shirt. We made a big, loud scene of it. People standing around were not amused by our antics. I haven't been hit yet. Whoever drew me hasn't made their move.

We pile into Old John's and crowd around the small hostess stand. The smell of bacon and burnt coffee hits my nose immediately. The diner is old-school retro with neon lights wrapping around the walls. The kind of place you might find off a highway in Pennsylvania. But with New York prices. "How many?" Connie, the hostess, asks.

I turn around and count. "Seven," I say proudly.

"Mr. Popularity over here," Connie says. After rehearsal, it's usually just me, Elijah, and Jamaal. Sometimes we have a special guest like Anna or Kelsey. But never seven.

"Actually," Jamaal says, "there's eight."

Yazmin weaves through the crowd and stands next to him.

"Eight it is," Connie sings, pulling a handful of menus from the rack. We follow her to our table. "What's the special occasion?"

"It's the night before tech week."

"Oh, hell week. I remember those times fondly, and not so fondly."

"You do?" I ask.

"Yes, dear boy," she says, maneuvering around a table of elderly people. "I used to be an actress. Turns out, I make more money at this gig."

I hate when people give up on their dream. I get scared I will someday, too. "You could still act," I suggest.

She lets out a guttural laugh. "I've retired. And this is your table, monsieur."

I take the seat at the head of the table. "Tonight, we will feast on the most expensive wines and meats," I say to everyone as they find a seat, pretending to be the king. Everyone laughs—they love the Infamous AG—and sits down. Anna and Elijah take the chairs by me.

Anna puts her napkin in her lap. "Did you hear about Justin and Tess?"

"Yes, actually," I answer. "You're failing me."

She acts offended. "As the director, it would be uncouth for me to gossip with the actors."

"You're the assistant director," I remind her.

"Watch this," she says, and turns to the table. "So, I heard there's going to be a workshop of a play at SPA before it goes to Broadway."

"Yeah," Kelsey says. "There's an article on Broadway World about it."

Anna looks at me. "Maybe I am losing my touch."

"Why SPA?" Tess asks.

Anna shrugs. "It's bigger than most Off-Broadway theaters."

"Didn't Julie Taymor workshop a Shakespeare play at SPA?" Kelsey asks.

"Did I hear-eth my name?" Jamaal sings.

"Yes, Jamaal," Anna says with a verbal eye roll. "They did one of your best works, *A Midsummer Night's Dream*, like five years ago, before it went to Broadway."

"My dad worked with Julie Taymor on a short film," Justin adds. He's got his famous dad's IMDb memorized and is ready to drop names whenever he can.

"Anyways," Anna continues, not liking to share the gossip spotlight, "the play is called *Conversion*. It's apparently a dark comedy about LGBT conversion therapy."

The back of my neck gets hot. I think about that envelope from Brand New Day. If I had stayed in Pennsylvania, I might be in conversion therapy now. Instead, I'm here. I'm safe.

"Joshua Downs is directing," Yaz says.

"Isn't that the hotshot director out of California?" Kelsey asks.

"Hot is right," Elijah confirms.

"Don't believe the hype," Anna says. "His last two shows have been total flops."

Justin laughs. "He's probably not happy about doing a workshop at a high school. My dad would have quit."

Yaz jumps in. "I heard the cast is top notch. Imagine that, Broadway stars just walking around our school. I'm flipping out."

I can't imagine it—I'm already starstruck by my classmates and their beginnings of fame.

"They aren't all from Broadway," Anna says, grabbing the attention back. "There's a star from some Nickelodeon show. Chris Caesar?"

"Holy shit," Tess says. "From *Caesar's World*? He was my first crush."

Anna continues, "And he's playing the . . ." She pauses, looking at me. "He's playing the part of a transgender boy."

"But he's cis?" Elijah protests, also looking at me.

Turns out, everyone else is looking at me, too. They want to clock the reaction from the official trans person in the room. Tess smiles at me. "August shouldn't have a problem. He believes the best person should get the part regardless of gender."

"This is different," Justin says, earning him a look of death from Tess.

Anna jumps in, ever coming to my defense. "August can play

any role he wants, but cis people shouldn't play the roles of trans people. It doesn't go both ways."

"That's a double standard," Tess says, acting like the star of *Legally Blonde*.

"There are very few transgender characters on Broadway, right, August?" Anna asks, giving her best Elle Woods.

Everyone looks at me. Do I hold all trans knowledge? "Yes," I confirm.

"So why should some little Nickelodeon shit get to play the part? A transgender actor should play the transgender part."

"I'm fine with it," I say, not knowing how I really feel about it. But the Infamous August Greene is laid-back and doesn't like to cause a stir. "Chris Caesar was probably the best person for the role for some reason."

"August, seriously?" Anna asks. I shrug. I don't know if I should be mad or sad or what. More than anything, I'm not surprised.

My favorite waitress, Jane, comes by to take our order. "The usual, hon?" she asks me, pen in hand.

"You know it," I say. My usual is a bacon and egg sandwich with a cup of coffee—helps with the late-night homework. Also, I love that I have a usual order.

"Where'd you find all these people?" she asks.

"This," Elijah says with an arm flare, "is the rest of the cast. We usually don't invite them."

"We usually wouldn't come," Anna jokes.

"Well, if your new friends aren't good tippers, they can't come back," Jane says with a wink, then moves on down the table.

"Guys," Anna says to me and Elijah. "I have some news for you."

Elijah puts down his spoon. "I'm ready."

If the news is about Duncan, I'm not ready. They are both still secretly dating him. I was torn on what to do—tell Elijah, or Anna, or tell them together (then run out of the room). Aunt Lil told me to mind my business. So that's what I did.

"August has known for a while, but I wanted to keep it quiet . . . ," she begins. I start to panic and stand up, accidentally pushing the table and nearly spilling the water glasses.

"Elijah, can you come outside with me?" I ask.

The entire table is looking at me. I smile at them. "Dude, what's up?" Elijah whispers.

"I'll explain outside," I say, then walk toward the door. Once outside, I start shivering. Should have grabbed my hoodie, but everything was moving too fast.

Elijah exits Old John's, laughing. "What's going on?"

"Look," I say. "I should have told you this before, but Anna has been seeing Duncan."

His mouth falls open. "My Duncan?"

"Your Duncan," I confirm. "I'm sorry I didn't tell you. I didn't know how."

Elijah leans against the trunk of a car, hugging himself. I watch as he processes what I told him. He claimed the Duncan thing was casual, but it's clear he caught feelings. "Duncan has been distant. I guess that's why." I'm relieved that he's not mad at me for not telling him sooner. "I thought it was the cello. I guess it was Anna."

"I didn't want you to hear it from her first."

"Thanks, man. I might have thrown up."

If that's true, I'm glad I pulled him out here. "You ready to head back?" I ask, hoping he says yes because it's cold out.

"No," he says, and buries his face in his hands. "I really like that guy. And now I have to hear Anna gush about him? How will I do that, August?"

I lean on the car beside him. "I understand," I say, trying to think of what to say. "You're an actor, so act."

He looks at me, slightly shocked. "You can do that?"

"Sure," I say, wondering why he's surprised. "Just like onstage, I can be whoever I need to be for the scene. It's working out for me."

"I can't do that, but you do you," he says.

THIRTEEN

7:45 P.M.

It's the night before the long tech day, and I should be home. Doing homework. Running my lines. Practicing songs and choreography. Instead, I'm standing on Broadway and Fiftieth Street, waiting for Elijah. I did homework all day—minus a small nap—and feel only a little behind. There's always downtime during tech week. I can knock some algebra out then.

But tonight, I need to show my friend a good time. He took the Anna-and-Duncan thing hard. I watched his face while Anna regaled us with the blow-by-blow of her and Duncan's budding romance. They aren't serious, but serious enough for Anna to brag. Elijah stayed strong, didn't tell Anna about him and Duncan, and shed no tears into his western omelet. That's a success in my book.

I texted Elijah this morning and told him I had a surprise for tonight. I went to TodayTix in search of a show cheap enough to not make my aunt's head explode when she gets her credit card bill. Broadway was out of the question—even the cheapest tickets were sixty bucks each. While scrolling through the Off-Broadway listings, I found a long-running show that sounded like the perfect night out to cheer up Elijah. And the price was right.

"Hey, bro," Elijah says, coming around the corner with a large coffee in hand.

"How you doing?" I ask.

He shrugs with his whole body. "I've been better. I really liked that guy. Oh, August, hold me," he says, throwing his arms around me. I've never seen Elijah down. Usually he's the brightest person in the room.

"I'm sorry, man."

"I'll never recover."

"Too bad you're in a city with no hot guys," I joke.

He pushes me. "But I liked that one."

I put my arm around him and head north. "Come on, we're going to be late."

"Wherever are we going?" he asks.

"Just trust me," I say, almost giddy for the surprise. We walk three blocks talking about the big tech day coming up tomorrow. Elijah has been through it at SPA, and he's not stressed. Good for him.

"Watch out for Mrs. Templeton," he warns. "She's in charge of costumes. Stay on her good side or you might have a costume malfunction, like a rip in the back of your pants."

"That didn't happen."

"Did so," Elijah says. "To this kid named Trip Fischer my freshman year. Also, get in good with the sound guy. He controls your levels, and you want to be heard. His name is Kenny and he collects what people think is too many Pokémon."

"I knew that," I say.

"You did?"

"Yeah," I lie. "Someone told me."

"Oh, I guess you don't need me." Elijah pretends to be hurt.

"No, I need you. I'm freaked out about this week."

"It's no big deal," he assures me. "Just too many hours and someone gets sick. Someone gets hurt. An actor has a breakdown. Typical tech-week stuff. Also, did you see Tess and Justin last night? God, get a room."

"I hope she's in love," I say. "Maybe she'll be nicer to me."

"Don't waste a minute on the haters." Elijah tosses his coffee cup into an overflowing trash can.

"Here we are," I say, pointing to the marquee.

He looks up. "*Naked Boys Singing*?"

"Thought this could take your mind off Duncan."

"Oh boy, will it," he says, hopping up and down and clapping. "Naked dudes are exactly what I need to see." He stops jumping and looks at me seriously. "Is this real?"

I looked up reviews that confirmed the show is, in fact, guys singing in their birthday suits. Couldn't find any videos online—probably due to the nudity. Hope Aunt Lil doesn't go through my internet searches. "I guess we'll find out."

"Oh yes we will, thank you," he says, then kisses my forehead. It feels good to help a friend. We go inside an old church that's now an Off-Broadway theater. I guess church-to-theater is a real thing in New York. The lobby is cramped with men and a couple of bachelorette parties wearing plastic penises all over their bodies. While Elijah runs to the bathroom, I pick up the tickets at the will-call window.

The grumpy old man behind the window looks at me. "You over eighteen?" he asks.

"I'm nineteen," I lie with a smile.

"Sure thing," he says, then winks. He hands me the tickets and tries to hold on too long. I back away and dash off looking for Elijah, trying to not spill drinks out of people's hands. This is not your typical Broadway crowd. They are younger, livelier, and wearing more plastic penises.

I find Elijah by the makeshift bar trying to make eyes with a group of guys nearby. "August, man, this is exactly what I needed," he says, then returns his attention to smiling at the guys. Having the cool senior as a friend is thrilling—it never gets old. I take a selfie of us under the *Naked Boys Singing* sign and post it. I hope Elijah shares it.

"Doors are now open," someone announces, and the mob starts funneling into the theater. I look around. It's a small and beat-up theater, probably fits a hundred people. We find our seats—the only seats I could afford—in the last row. The upholstery is ripped, with stuffing coming out. The fabric on the armrests is barely holding on. When we sit, our butts sink down to the floor.

Elijah smiles at me and says, "Ah, the charm of Off-Broadway."

"This is very far from Broadway," I say, pretending like I've seen more than one Broadway show.

"You know it's called Off-Broadway because of seating capacity?" Elijah asks. "Any theater under five hundred seats is Off-Broadway, and anything above is Broadway."

"I knew that," I say, even though I didn't, in fact, know that.

"You did?" he questions.

When it comes to theater, I feel behind, but too embarrassed to admit it. "Yes." I confirm my lie.

He tilts his head. "Are you doing that thing where you act in real life right now?"

He's referring our conversation last night. "No," I say.

"You sure?" he asks, flipping through his Playbill—which is two pages long.

I get frustrated that he doesn't believe me. I don't know how to respond.

"August," he says, "what's wrong with being the new guy at school? People appreciate fresh eyes. There's nothing wrong with it."

I don't like fresh eyes. The newbie isn't cool. I'm not interested in that role. "I don't want to be known as that."

"But you are like that. You are literally the new guy," he says.

"I still know tons about theater."

He gives me side-eye. "I can tell when you're acting. Don't get me wrong: you're a good actor. You should just keep it on the stage."

I look down at my Playbill. Does he hate me? I'm self-conscious and there's no pages to flip on this damn Playbill.

The lights go down and Elijah starts clapping. The whole crowd is rowdy, ready to see some skin. Eight men come onstage in various bathing suit and underwear combos. Elijah sits up straight, his hands gripping the torn-up armrests, with a smile as big as Broadway. The crowd gets on their feet, hollering at the men. Begging them to get naked. It's all in good fun. Like the title promises, the eight men onstage get completely naked by the end of the first song. Halfway through the third song, "The Bliss of Bris," Elijah leans over to me and whisper-yells in my ear, "I am living my best life. But if I ever think about auditioning for this show, please lock me in a basement."

"Will do," I say, laughing, as the men dance onstage with their dicks flapping around comically. I watch the oddly shaped things bounce around, all different sizes, some hairy and some not. Some circumcised and some not. When the guys do a kick line, I see too much.

I look down at my pants. Nothing in there. I feel like I was assembled wrong. Born missing a part. I'm afraid I'll never feel complete. Cis guys grab them so proudly. Talk about them. Send pics of them. Have sex with them. And I'll never know how any of that feels. I could never join *Naked Boys Singing*. I had no idea this show would bring me here. Theater always has a way of moving me, but this time it's in the wrong direction. I spend the rest of the show in my head, thinking about my missing part.

The final song brings everyone to their feet. Standing ovation. How could we not after the actors have revealed so much? Elijah is whistling loudly.

As the crowd finds their way to the exit, Elijah says, "Let's wait for the actors."

I look at my phone. Curfew is an hour and five minutes away. I'm already cutting it close. "Please," he begs. "Pretty pretty please?"

"I'm going to be late," I say.

He stops. "You have a curfew? Don't you live with your aunt?"

"It's the only rule."

"It'll take ten minutes," he promises. "I want an actor to sign my Playbill."

"Are you sure that's all you want from him?"

"A boy can dream," Elijah says, and we head outside to wait at the stage door—which for this Off-Broadway theater/soup kitchen is just the exit. Elijah stretches his back as we wait near a fire hydrant that's been spray-painted gold. He stops. Looks at me. "You're being weird. What's up?"

"I'm fine," I say.

"August, if we are going to be friends, you need to open up. I'll wear you down. You won't have a choice. So start talking." He pinches my cheek to show his commitment.

I'm too embarrassed to tell him about my gender dysphoria. "I'm exhausted," I say. Maybe it's the rehearsals, or school, or maybe it's carrying around my secrets. I just want to tell someone. So I take a deep breath and tell Elijah about my parents, the letter from the conversion therapy place, running away, and lying to my parents about transitioning. And I explain why I'm Rizzo. Why— despite the pressure from Tess and Yazmin—I had to audition for a girl part to not raise flags with my parents. And when I tell him all of this—which feels like one long monologue—I tell my friend most of my secrets.

After I finish talking, a funny thing happens. I feel lighter— like a weight has come off my shoulders, even if only temporarily, and I can stand up straight. I can tell by the way Elijah listened that he cares about me. That it's hard to hear. This is what I was worried about—my friends pitying me. "Don't feel sorry for me," I say.

"Sorry?" Elijah asks, taken back. "Dude, that broke my heart. I feel sad for you."

"And that's why I haven't told people at SPA. I don't want them to feel bad for me."

"I don't feel bad for you; I respect you more now. You ran away from home and came to New York. You're basically my hero. But what happens if your parents find out you transitioned?"

"I don't know. I have a plan, and if it works, they won't find out."

"Care to share?"

"They are coming in Friday for the last show, where they will watch their daughter play Rizzo. After the show, my aunt will escort them to a restaurant near the school, where I'll join them."

He shrugs. "That's not too bad."

"But," I continue, "when I meet them for dinner, I have to wear the clothes they know me in. A flowery shirt and skirt."

"No."

"I need to be their daughter."

"Oh, August, that's tough."

"I'm more nervous for that performance than *Grease*. If I get it wrong, if they find out I've transitioned, they will bring me home. Or to conversion therapy."

He puts his hand on my shoulder. "If you need help, I'm here for you."

"Thanks," I say. We look around and notice that everyone has left. "I think we missed the actors."

"Who cares," Elijah sings. "We had this little heart-to-heart—that's much better. I'll walk you to the subway."

I hate to ask, but I need to ask. "Could you not tell anyone?"

He pauses. "Of course."

Fast-forward an hour and thirty minutes later, I run all the way home from the subway stop, carefully turn the key, and quietly open the door. My aunt switches on the lamp beside the couch. "You're late," she says in an ominous voice.

"I'm sorry. The subway stopped—"

"You can't walk all over me, August. I gave you one rule and that's to be home on time," she slurs.

I put my hands up—she just needs to hear me—and say, "It was the subway—"

"August." Her hands are shaking. "You have to plan for those subways. This is the second time. What would your mom do?"

"Nothing," I lie.

"Why are you doing this to me?" she asks, then stands up, knocking a wine bottle off the coffee table. "Oh, shit."

I pick up the bottle. "It's empty," I say, to reassure her.

"Yeah, because I was waiting for you."

"I'm sorry, Auntie. It won't happen again."

"I've never been a parent. It's awful when your kid doesn't listen. You had me sitting here for an hour feeling bad about my entire childhood. Now go to your room," she says, wobbling in the darkness. I want to help her to her room, but she's not happy with me.

I head upstairs, wondering why she's so upset. And why she mentioned my mom—that's not like her. None of this is like her.

FOURTEEN

Sunday, October 13

8:33 A.M.

Today is officially hell day. Also known as "10 out of 12" because we're at the theater for twelve hours but only allowed to work ten of those hours. I'm feeling hopeful. I chew my cereal as softly as possible to not wake my aunt. She's usually up by now, but wine happened. She typically has a few glasses and goes to bed. But recently, she's been drinking more.

I set my bowl in the sink. I have an hour and twenty-seven minutes to get to school. Maybe even time to stop at Starbucks and stock up on caffeine for the long day ahead. The subway is on a Sunday schedule, but I planned for it. After last night, I'll never be late again.

"August," Aunt Lil moans, wearing a tattered yellow robe. "I'm hungover and I blame you."

I put my backpack on. "I accept all blame," I say with a smile.

"My head is split in two."

I clear my throat. "Last night, you asked what Mom would do."

"I did?"

"You don't remember?"

She shrugs.

"If I missed curfew, she would take away my phone and ground me for a month."

"A month?" Aunt Lil questions while beginning her coffee process. "Look, August, I'm not trying to be your mom. I'm not going to take away your phone and shut you in your room. But you need follow my rules. My liver needs it, too."

"Deal," I say.

"Now get out of here so I can suffer alone."

"Davina's not here?" I ask, surprised. They usually are at their peak happiest on Sunday morning. Always heading to a brunch and art galleries.

She stops grinding the coffee beans. "We had a little fight last night."

"Oh," I say, feeling responsible.

Aunt Lil senses my guilt. "Nothing to do with you and your tardy butt. Now get out of here. Scram!"

"Love you," I say, then run out the door. I will not be the late one.

9:59 A.M.

The actors—full of nervous energy and caffeine—sit onstage and watch Meena pace the floor holding her clipboard tightly to her chest. The all-powerful headset hugs her head and has been decorated with purple and yellow stickers. People are working on the sets and lights. There's a makeshift director's table in the middle of the audience where Mr. Daniels looks over some papers. Or just politely ignores us.

It's a minute before call time and two actors are missing: Justin Sudds and Beth from the ensemble. Who will be the late one? Meena is ready to jump. Beth walks in, leaving the honor to Justin, aka Tess's showmance. Every second that goes by leaves me more tense. The other actors feel it, too, but are also glad it's not them.

Every tech week, there's typically a moment when an actor messes up and gets lectured in front of everyone. The stage manager—and sometimes the director, depending on their temper—pounce on the sacrificial lamb to set the tone of tech week and make it serious. Up the importance. Heighten the drama. From the looks of Meena, the freak-out will come sooner rather than later. I lean over to Elijah and say, "I don't think Justin will survive this."

Elijah laughs. "I've seen her like this before. Meena is all bark, no bite."

Poor Justin runs in with a panicked look.

Meena stomps over, waving her clipboard. "Justin, you're late. Do you think there are special rules for you?"

"Sorry," he says, hands up.

"You're sorry? Just 'cause your dad is James Bond doesn't mean you can make up your own rules." She makes her star turn toward the cast. "Guys, tech week is no joke. We need you here on time, focused, and ready."

"Yes," Mr. Daniels says from the director's table. "Meena is right, we need to be our best selves this week."

"That's strike one," Meena says to Justin, staring daggers into him as he walks over to us.

And tech week has officially begun.

12:45 P.M.

We've been running the cue-to-cue for hours. It's more mentally exhausting than physically—we basically run each scene, making sure the sets and props are in place as the lighting cues are programmed and sound is mixed. Our job is to stand or sit quietly onstage, waiting to be told our next move. The set is behind schedule, the band is behind, and the lights and sounds are, you guessed it, behind. No matter what, every tech rehearsal runs late. If you're on time, there's probably something very wrong.

They are trying to run "Greased Lightnin'," but the car hasn't arrived from the prop shop. They're running the scene with wooden blocks in place of the car, and everyone is trying to stay calm and make it to lunch without anyone getting murdered.

While we are holding for a light change, Anna comes up to the actors in the audience. She's enjoying the role of assistant director—the small amount of power already gone to her head. She's wearing black jeans, black shirt, and a beret. "Think of it, guys," she says. "*Conversion* will be rehearsing in this theater next week. Broadway stars standing right here. How cool is that?"

It's so cool.

"Meena." Mr. Daniels's voice comes booming over the speakers. The director is in control of the God mic and rules from his wooden table in the audience. A clipped-on lamp reflects his serious face.

"Yes, boss," she says over the speakers. She also has a wooden table, farther back than Mr. Daniels, covered in a sound board, binders, and two laptops illuminating her face.

"Let's move on to scene twenty-three," Mr. Daniels says.

"All right gang, moving to 'There Are Worse Things I Could Do,' August to center."

I walk to the center of the stage as marked by bright green tape. This is where my solo song will begin. This is my moment. I look up at the rows of lights above me. I'm always a little afraid they might come crashing down and end the show (and my life). My old school had a row of about ten lights. There must be fifty up there, all shining on me.

"Cue forty-three," Meena says. The lights go dark onstage and the spotlight comes up on me. The light blinds me, warms me, and feels like home.

Mr. Daniels taught us about how they lit the stage before all these fancy lights were invented. Back in the 1800s, actors stood in the limelight—a bright light created by aiming a hot flame at a block of a mineral called lime from the theater's balcony. The system wasn't accurate, but the light would be brightest center stage, and that's why they call it standing in the limelight.

I step into my limelight.

This is my first time performing the song in front of everyone. Our acting classes and after-school rehearsals focused on dancing and group scenes. I had an hour session with our musical theater teacher, Mr. Gonzales, working the song. And I've rehearsed it about a million times in front of my mirror.

The music begins and I straighten my back, stick out my chest, and hold my prop—a notebook—close to my chest binder. I'm Rizzo. Dealing with big issues. Always feeling different from others. I start singing—*There are worse things I could do*—and channel the hopelessness of Rizzo. I put everything into the performance, pretending the theater is full. I imagine my mom in the audience and I'm singing to her. As the song ends, I step back into my limelight and hit the last note perfectly.

The actors clap loudly and yell my name. A tear finds its way out of my eye. I wipe it away, hoping no one saw. I'm overwhelmed by the song—it reveals Rizzo's heart and leaves me unsettled—but the tear came from standing in this light after so much darkness.

Mr. Daniels clears his throat over the mic. My heart pauses in fear of his notes. "Very nice, August." My heart starts again. "We need to work on a few things, but very nice."

"Thank you, August," Meena says. "That's lunch. One hour. Don't be late."

* * *

1:50 P.M.

After lunch, I took a walk to get some fresh air. Well, as fresh as you can get in New York. I'm almost back in the building when I nearly collide with Juliet.

"Hey," I say, feeling disoriented to see her at school on a Sunday.

"Hi there, August. Oh, right, this is the dreaded tech week. How's it going?"

"Meena has only lost her shit once."

"Only once?" she jokes. "Well, you still have another twenty hours, right?"

"Thirty hours? A lifetime?"

"I'm sure you're having fun," she says, switching her purse from one shoulder to the other. "Any showmances?"

"Tess and Justin."

"Too predictable," she says.

"Hey, Juliet," I say, getting shy. "You said I could ask you about transgender stuff?"

"Absolutely," she says, smiling.

"Do you ever think, I mean, when you think about . . ." I trail off and stall out. Talking about my body isn't natural to me. The words are more eloquent in my head. "I'm missing a part, and I wish I had that part, and I worry I won't feel complete without it," I say.

She puts a hand on my shoulder. "Oh, August, you sweet thing."

"Do you feel that way?"

She nods. "I do feel that way. Well, different than you, but the same. But not every trans person does. It varies from person to person."

I nod and feel relief that my friend has the same feelings. "I'm glad I'm not alone on this," I admit.

"August, you're never alone. Ever. But I think—"

"Oh my god, two of my favorite people!" Anna says as she walks up the steps with a tray of coffees. "What the hell are you doing here Juliet? It's Sunday!"

I forgot to ask that question. What *is* she doing here? I'm so wrapped up in me. "Yeah?" I add, eloquently.

"Oh, I use the studio on the weekend. Ms. Sanders gives me access."

"I can't believe you want to be at school on the weekend," Anna says, then turns to me. "August, we're going to be late. Let's jam."

"See you around," I say to Juliet, wishing we could talk more.

"Hey," she says to me, "let's talk this week about that recipe for chocolate chip cookies."

I laugh. I guess that's our code. "Sounds good."

"Oh my god, I want cookies," Anna says, turning to me. "I didn't know you baked. That's adorable."

2:35 P.M.

"You can look," Mrs. Templeton says.

I'm about to get my first look at myself in the Rizzo costume. High-waisted jeans, white Keds, and a tight pink sweater. Mrs.

Templeton wraps a bow around my head. "What do you think?" she asks, spinning me around to face the mirror.

"I look like Rizzo," I confirm. And then remind myself that it's just a costume. It's always shocking to see myself in girl clothes. This isn't me—I'm playing a character.

"Will you wear this?" she asks, holding a padded bra. "To give you some curves."

My heart sinks. After Elijah's warning, I want to stay on Mrs. Templeton's good side, but I don't want to wear that. "Do I have to?" I ask, in the nicest voice ever.

She frowns and thinks. "Nah," she says, and tosses the bra on a pile of clothes. "You look great without."

I hug Mrs. Templeton. "Thank you."

"Easy, kid, you'll squeeze the life out of me."

"Can I change here?" I ask.

She gives me a puzzled look. "You don't want to go back to your dressing room?"

I'm having stage fright. I don't want to change in front of the guys, don't want them to see my binder, and don't want to be dressed like a girl in front of them. "I'm just going to change here," I say.

"Sure thing, honey, I'll step out."

3:15 P.M.

Sitzprobe time—my favorite part of tech. Just watching the band ready their instruments is giving me life. This is our first time singing with live music and not recorded tracks. It can get messy introducing the vocals with the music—tempos go all over the place. But I can tell it will be completely magical to hear the voices and the music coming together with the acoustics of this grand theater.

Actors bounce nervously in their chairs. Elijah is sitting by me. Jamaal might be his Kenickie onstage, but I'm his Kenickie in real life. I'm squeezing honey out of a stolen packet from Starbucks in the hope that it will help my vocal cords.

"I can't wait for this," Anna says, hovering over my chair. "You guys have worked so hard, and now the music comes alive." She flips her hair and waves at someone. "And look at that hot cello player," she adds.

"I'd rather not," Elijah says, with a little too much attitude.

"I think I'm in love with Duncan," Anna whispers. Elijah grips his seat. I want to help him but don't know how. "We were meant to be together."

"Are you guys together?" I ask.

"Not yet. But we kissed. And I could just tell."

"How?" I ask.

"Just a feeling," she admits.

Elijah rolls his eyes. I give his foot a kick. He clears his throat. "Good for you, girl," he manages to say.

"You're sweet," she says, then heads back to her assistant director perch beside her dad.

Once she's gone, I say, "They've only kissed."

He shakes his head. "But she's in love."

I ask the question that needs to be asked. "Are you in love?"

He laughs. "I don't know. It doesn't matter. Duncan doesn't want to be pansexual, or bisexual, or anything but straight. Says it will hurt his career."

"Maybe you should move on," I suggest.

"You haven't kissed him," Elijah laments.

"Are we ready?" Mr. Daniels asks over the God mic.

"We are ready!" Meena echoes.

The music director waves her baton, setting the pace, and when "Summer Nights" begins, my heart matches the tempo.

5:39 P.M.

"Fifteen," Meena warns from the intercom.

"Thanks, fifteen," we all say back. The boys' dressing room is packed with guys changing, talking, eating, and looking at phones. Everyone's got a case of the sillies—symptoms include random outbursts of laughing, waves of euphoria, dancing, singing, and general backstage madness.

We're about to do our first stumble through and no one feels ready. A stumble through is just like it sounds—we literally stumble our way through the show by throwing on costumes, forgetting props, dropping lines, and not finding our light. It's a fantastic mess.

"Why aren't you getting in costume?" Jamaal asks, looking cool in his leather jacket and white shirt.

My high-waisted jeans and tight white shirt taunt me from the hanger. "In a few," I say, trying to delay the inevitable. I'm going to have to change from August to Rizzo soon. I just can't decide where to do it.

"If you don't wear this," Elijah says, tugging on my Pink Lady jacket, "I will."

"I'd look better in that leather jacket," I say to Elijah, who is fully Danny Zuko'ed.

"And I would look better in this," he says, putting the pink jacket on over his leather jacket and snapping a few pictures.

I can do this. I can change quickly. No one cares. I take off my pants and pull on the tight Rizzo jeans. I take off my shirt—feeling completely exposed with my binder on display to anyone watching—and pull the V-neck shirt over my head. Once in, I look around, expecting everyone to be staring at me, but instead, no one is looking. Not a single guy. I sit down in my chair and put my bow on. There's lipstick, but I'm not doing that until the show.

Elijah comes up behind me—I can see him in the mirror—and drapes the pink jacket around my shoulders. "You look so handsome, even in that," he says with a wink.

"Places," Meena sings over the intercom.

6:25 P.M.

At the end of the first act, during an energetic and scattered version of "We Go Together," a crash comes from the wings. It's so loud that we freeze mid-dance.

A loud "SHIT" follows the crash. Then crying.

"Who has eyes on Yazmin?" Meena yells over the mic.

"She's right here," a stagehand answers.

"It's Tess," Justin says, running offstage. Mr. Daniels is close behind. We take a knee and exchange looks of concern. Injuries are so scary in the theater.

"She fell on the stack of props," someone says from backstage. Last time I was backstage, it was cluttered with props and quick-change costumes. The theater is quiet. A girl in the ensemble is crying softly.

Elijah scoots over to me and whispers, "Bet she's faking it."

A few minutes later, Justin carries Tess onstage like she's a baby. "I'm okay, guys," she says in a weak voice. We all jump to our feet, clapping with relief. We cheer as Justin carries her into the audience toward the exit. Before they leave, she waves, like she's the queen.

Meena throws her clipboard down. "This is inexcusable, guys. Props are everywhere. Your castmate could've been seriously hurt. Do you even care?" She's about to cry. "We need to be better than this," she says, then stomps offstage.

"Has she snapped?" someone behind me asks.

Anna looks at me and I nod. Whenever someone freaks out, no matter how weird or irrational, their closest friends must chase after them. It's unspoken theater code. This is peak tech day drama.

We find Meena in the green room, lying on the couch with her head buried in the cushion. "Meena, baby," Anna says. "What's going on?"

She doesn't answer. Anna gives me the *say something* eyes. I clear my throat. "Hey, Meena, want to talk?" I ask.

Meena turns her face to me, her cheeks bright red from crying. "You wouldn't understand," she says.

I nod. "I could try."

She fishes a tissue out of her pocket and blows her nose. "Being the stage manager really sucks sometimes."

"I can imagine. You do so much," I say, always appreciating the stage manager and their hard work to make the actors look good.

"Why don't you invite me out after rehearsals?"

My heart sinks. We didn't tell her about Old John's on Friday night. "Meena, I'm so sorry," I say, feeling awful.

"And you," Meena says, looking at Anna. "You're too bossy. Talking down to me. You won't listen when I try to explain something."

"Calm down, Meena," Anna says.

"No way," she says, sitting up. "You do this every show, but it's ten times worse now that you're assistant director. You treat me like your assistant. No thank-you. No appreciation."

Anna shakes her head. "The cast always gets you flowers after the show?"

"You know what? At freshman showcase when everyone heard you pee? I didn't turn off your mic on purpose! You were so mean to me that day."

"Meena!" Anna yells.

I hold in a laugh. That's kind of funny. Another good reason to be nice to the crew. It's surprising to see Meena lose her shit. She's always so headstrong and secure. Maybe she's hiding her feelings and truths, just like me. There's no question that Anna and others are putting on an act, but I didn't expect it from Meena.

Anna sits on the floor beside the couch. "Meena, I'm a jerk. I'm sorry. The truth is, Dad made me take the assistant director position. He said I wouldn't get a part onstage. It was devastating. I've been thinking about going to business college."

"Be reasonable," Meena says sarcastically.

"I'm sorry that I'm bossy. It's the Aries in me. I'll work on it."

"I just want to be included. And thanked. Is that too much to ask for?"

Anna hugs her. "Not at all. I'm sorry, girl."

"I'm sorry," Meena says, "but not about the pee."

We all laugh. The room gets lighter. Meena gets up and puts her headset back on. "Can you not tell people why I got upset? Just say my parents are getting divorced."

"Sure, honey," Anna says.

9:12 P.M.

Elijah and I zombie-walk to the subway. We hardly speak—all the words have been spoken or sung. I'm ready to collapse. My legs are tired, my vocal cords are spent, my body is done. I want a long shower and a warm bed. I wish I had a teleportation device because sometimes taking the subway is such a bummer.

Elijah picks a greasy McDonald's bag off the ground and throws it in the trash. He's always trying to make the world better. "What *was* the deal with Meena?" he asks.

"Her parents are getting divorced," I say.

He shoots me a look. "Her parents have been divorced."

"She was hurt we didn't invite her to Old John's," I say, revealing part of the truth.

"Crap," he says.

We arrive at the subway station. "You coming?" I ask.

"Actually," Elijah says with a mischievous smile, "I'm going over to Duncan's place for a little hang."

I shake my head. "I think you like the drama."

"Who, me?" Elijah asks, smirking.

10:59 P.M.

After a long and hot shower—washing the day off—I'm headed to my room with two pepperoni slices from the pizzeria on our block. I wanted three, but Rizzo has tight costumes.

Aunt Lil's studio light is on. I thought she would be with Davina tonight. I peek in, expecting to see her painting, but it's a sadder scene. She's hunched over her table, empty wine bottle nearby, reading letters. She doesn't see me. I duck out to go eat my pizza in bed and think about how to help her.

FIFTEEN

Tuesday, October 15

4:50 P.M.

Tomorrow is opening night.

At this point, I'm no longer a human, more a walking, talking ball of nervous energy.

This is our last rehearsal, but I could use three more. I'm not confident about entries, exits, props, or blocking. Got to remember my quick changes, choreography, songs, lines . . . It's endless.

"Are you nervous?" Kelsey whispers. We're in the wings waiting for the next scene.

"Not at all," I say, because the Infamous AG wouldn't be nervous.

"Really?" she asks. "I'm practically about to die from nerves."

"You'll be great," I assure her.

She plays with her earring. "I really admire you, August. You walked into this school and fit right in. I would be a mess, and you just came in here like no problem. That's cool."

I look at Kelsey, surprised by her compliment. She's one of the most popular and talented seniors at this school. "Thank you," I say, and give her a hug.

"Are you ready, Mr. Greene?" Mr. Daniels asks over the speakers.

"Let's do this," I say, heading toward my limelight.

Meena cues the music. The band is rehearsing without the actors today—we stop and start too much, and it drives them nuts. I count the beats, then start singing. I love my Rizzo solo. It leaves me sad and empty, but the song is beautiful. There are worse things I could do than sing "There Are Worse Things I Could Do."

I go full out on the song, hitting all the notes, even flexing a little vibrato. My feet stop where they started as I hit the last *worse things you could*, and then I hold the last *do* until the music ends.

Once the music is over, the theater is silent. I look in the direction of Mr. Daniels in the audience, but the spotlight is too bright. I see the shape of him get up and walk down the steps toward the stage. The whole theater is quiet. Every eye on me and him.

He stands in front of me. "What's this song about, August?" he asks.

"Rizzo is thinking about the choices she's made and dealing with what people say about her."

Mr. Daniels nods. I unclench my palms, both sweaty. "Has

anyone talked about you behind your back?" he asks.

"Sure," I say. He's working the Strasberg method with me. I can play along.

"And how did that make you feel?" he asks.

I shift my weight. "Mad."

"And what they said, was it true?"

"Not really," I say, having no real example in mind.

"And how did that make you feel?"

"Like they had control."

Mr. Daniels gets excited. "And what did you do?"

I would obsess about it, but the Infamous August Greene wouldn't. "Eventually, I didn't care what they said because I know who I am."

"Perfect," Mr. Daniels says. "All those feelings of anger and control and acceptance. Use them. When you sing, think about those people saying things that upset you. See their faces in your mind. Understood?"

"Understood," I say, already knowing I won't.

"Meena, can you cue up the music?" he asks, heading back to his perch.

The music starts. I should just pretend to use the Strasberg method. But I'm feeling bold. I don't want him to take the credit for my work. "Actually, I have my own method."

Mr. Daniels turns around. The music cuts out. "What's that?" he asks, annoyed.

"I step into the character. I don't use my own experience or emotions. For me, it's like putting on a mask. I become the character," I say.

"So, you stay un-present and un-plugging into your own emotions?"

"I act," I say plainly. A couple of laughs escape from the wings.

"And what do you call this style?" he asks.

"The August method?"

Mr. Daniels grunts. "Someone please write a Wikipedia page immediately." Everyone laughs. "Son, your quote-unquote 'August method' might be working for you now, but it won't always work. Then what will you do?"

"It's worked so far," I say.

"Why waste your time at this school if you have it all figured out?"

"I came here to get better at my way of acting."

Mr. Daniels shakes his head, then turns toward the actors in the wings. "*Grease* is a light and fun musical, but the characters must feel real. There must be honesty in your acting. Otherwise, the audience will not connect with you. They will not care who put the bop in the bop shoo bop shoo bop."

Everyone nervously laughs.

"Meena, cue the music," Mr. Daniels says, returning to his director perch. "Mr. Greene, how about doing what I asked? Humor me, please."

I start singing like my life depends on it. I don't use my own experience, but I use my own anger. And when the song ends, I hit my note, and there's silence. "Nicely done, August," Mr. Daniels says, "I could feel the anger."

"Let's take ten and run the second act," Meena announces.

8:19 P.M.

I'm slow-walking home from the subway. I didn't know this level of exhaustion existed. And I still have homework to do.

I regret calling it the "August method." I should have kept my mouth shut, but I wanted to be honest about my process. And for that, I got my ass handed to me by Mr. Daniels. Elijah assured me it was no big deal and promised everyone would forget by tomorrow. The second act ran smoothly, but I was in my head. I was angry. I'm still angry. But not at Mr. Daniels. Oddly enough, I'm mad at my parents.

I stop at my favorite bodega, two blocks from Aunt Lil's, for a bacon-and-egg sandwich. No matter what time of day or night, breakfast is served at the bodega. While I wait for the sandwich, I scroll through my photo library and select a photo of me onstage in a silly pose. I post it with the caption: **The August Method.** I figure I'll get ahead of the joke by making it first. I have over a thousand followers. Mostly people from school after hearing about the casting of *Grease*.

When I get to the apartment, I try to be quiet—not knowing what to expect.

"That you?" I hear my aunt ask from the kitchen.

"No," I say in a deep voice. "It's the police."

"Come on and arrest me, then," she says. I set my bag down, hang up my coat, and bring my foil-wrapped sandwich to the kitchen—ready to hear a lecture on the evils of bacon.

"Hi, Auntie," I say, on my way to wash my hands. There are five empty wine bottles in the sink. "Did you drink all of these?" I ask, both scared and in awe.

She laughs. "I poured them down the drain in a dramatic gesture."

"I would have taken them," I kid. After drying my hands, I sit down at the table.

Aunt Lil clears her throat. "I've been struggling a bit. Don't know if you noticed?"

Oh, I noticed. The heavier drinking, sadder nights, no Davina. "Maybe a little," I say.

She takes off her glasses. Rubs her eyes. "Your mom's upcoming visit has been weighing on me. Does it weigh on you?"

"I'm worried they'll take me back to Pennsylvania," I answer. "Or worse."

"I hate that you have to play dress-up," she says. That's what Aunt Lil calls the dinner with my parents because I'll be wearing girl clothes.

"I hate it, too," I admit. "I appreciate you being there. An actor needs an audience."

Aunt Lil frowns. That's not a good sign. "August, this dinner has been bringing up all of my past crap. That's why I've been struggling."

Is she not going to go? I need her to be at the dinner. If she's there, I'm putting on a show for her. If she's not, it'll feel like one big lie. "It'll be fine. It's just acting," I say. "And I'm playing the role of my parents' daughter."

"I know, honey, and you'll nail it. But I'm not good at acting. I'm nervous about messing it up for you."

I get more desperate. "You can invite Davina," I say, then remember Mom doesn't know about her. "Is that why you two are fighting?" I ask.

"Not exactly. But she does think I should come out to my sister. The lying is tough on me. My parents never knew who I truly was, and that hurts. I've spent my life, like many queer people do, as two different people—the person my family knows and the person I am. I've not been honest with my family to keep them in my life, but also pushed them away so they don't find out my truth. Thinking about this dinner with your mom, it's surfaced all these feelings I'd tucked far away. Made me face them. And they're ugly. Like those two different people I am are fighting in my belly."

"And who will win?" I ask.

"I don't know," she says. "But once my sister knows the truth, she'll never talk to me again, and that'll hurt."

"If I understand any feeling, it's that one," I say.

"That's the problem—a child shouldn't have to understand this feeling. We should have fixed this problem by now. If you love someone, how could you not accept them for who they are? It truly boggles the mind."

I've caused my aunt pain. I'm messing up her life. I don't want to be a burden on her. "If you want me to move out, I can figure something out."

"Boy, you've lost your mind," Aunt Lil says, pinching my cheek. "I would never push my future Tony winner out into the cold."

"You still want to be in my acceptance speech, right?"

"Exactly," she says.

"Aunt Lil, I could really use you at this dinner. I need your help to make this work. More than anything, I want to stay here and keep going to SPA."

"Oh, dear love, I would never leave you. I will be there, and we will get through this together."

"Thank you, Aunt Lil. I love you."

"Love you more, muffin," she says, then gives me a hug.

I take my egg-and-bacon sandwich—probably cold now—and head to my room. Before I leave, I turn around and ask, "Why is Davina mad?"

She smiles. "She says I won't let her all the way in."

I look around at the pineapple statues, the pineapple-shaped bowls, pineapples dancing on the tablecloth. My aunt is the most welcoming, loving, and accepting person, and all she was taught as a kid was the opposite.

When I get to my room, there are twelve text messages—all from Anna and Elijah in our group chat.

ANNA: Guys, have you seen the news?
ELIJAH: About Pokémon on Ice?

ANNA: No. What? About Conversion play.

ANNA: People are pissed about that Nickelodeon star

ELIJAH: He couldn't help that Nickelodeon made him a star

ANNA: Lol. People aren't happy that a cisgender guy is playing the trans part

ANNA: Augustus? Where you at?

ANNA: There's going to be a protest at the school

ELIJAH: I'm there!

ANNA: You can't be—it's tomorrow night and you're onstage

ELIJAH: Dammit.

ANNA: Augustus?

I'm over this day.

And too exhausted to handle much more.

I don't know how to respond. Of course a transgender actor should be playing the transgender character—it's so obvious. But why don't I feel mad enough to protest? Why are cisgender people in my life more upset than me? Should I post online about it? Will people wonder why I haven't posted about it yet?

AUGUST: People are really upset?

ANNA: UH-HUH. The Broadway World message board is on fire.

AUGUST: Why?

ANNA: August, really? It's called REPRESENTATION. Trans people should represent themselves onstage. Why am I explaining this to you?

AUGUST: Do people only want to see transgender actors play trans characters?

ELIJAH: Not at all. Rizzo played by you, for example. . . .

AUGUST: I don't know any trans actors playing cisgender characters on Broadway. That's what we should be protesting.

ANNA: August, focus!

AUGUST: It's cool that people care so much

ANNA: I'm going to bed

SIXTEEN

8:55 P.M.

"Come on, man, your fans await," Elijah says, at the boys' dressing room door. Everyone is headed outside to go talk to parents and friends and admirers. The front of the school is the equivalent to the stage door on Broadway.

I wave him off. "I don't have fans."

"Oh, now we're acting humble?"

"I'll be there in two minutes, I swear," I say.

"Making them wait, total diva move," he jokes, and leaves.

I look at my face in the mirror, red from the makeup remover wipes, and smile. I did it. My first show at SPA is done. I performed in front of one thousand people. It scares me how right this moment feels. This is what I want forever. The stage. The audience. Acting. Being out there tonight felt like a dream come true and also just the beginning. But that's scary because if something goes wrong on Friday night, my parents could end this dream.

But right now, for this moment, I will live in this feeling. The show went by so fast—like a blur—almost like it didn't happen. My performance was solid minus a slight wobble when my foot slipped through the set piece during "Look at Me, I'm Sandra Dee." And I messed up a couple of dance moves in "Born to Hand Jive." But my solo brought the house down. The energy from the audience was electric. At the end of the show, they were on their feet as soon as we hit our last pose. And during the curtain call, when I took center stage for my bow, the crowd went nuts. The feeling was explosive, like a firecracker going off in my body.

Backstage after the show was an orgy of emotion. Everyone hugging. Crying. Lots of compliments. Even Tess hugged me. I thought it was an accident, but she said good job. If you ever want to catch actors at their nicest, try after a show.

"What are you doing?" Meena appears in the doorway, careful to never enter the boys' room. "Go outside and receive the praise you deserve."

"Soon," I say.

"You made magic happen on that stage, August. I wouldn't bullshit—the audience was on your side. Ugh, you were freaking great."

"Thanks," I say, blushing. "We're headed to Old John's. Want to join?"

She smiles. "Sounds good. I need waffles, or I'll die."

"Meet you outside?" I ask.

"Give me five," she says, disappearing to her duties.

Anna got a bunch of flowers, and we called Meena onstage during the curtain call. She took the flowers, and a bow.

I check my phone. Twenty new followers since I walked offstage. I'm up to twelve hundred. I got a big bump when an article came out on Playbill.com about SPA's diverse casting of an African American Danny Zuko and Kenickie, and a transgender Rizzo. I'd rather they write about my performance, but it was cool to see my headshot on the website. I'm worried about my parents seeing the article, but I don't think they know how to google things.

I throw on my backpack and head toward the exit. When I open the door, I'm swallowed up by a crowd of people gathered around. I thought a couple of people would wait around, but it seems like the entire theater is still here. I'm sheepish, but not the Infamous AG—he acts like he does this all the time. I hear "good job" and "nicely done" and "you're amazing." A girl asks me for a picture—the modern-day autograph—and we pose as her mom takes the photo. An older man asks me to sign his Playbill. My head fills up like a balloon from the praise. Is this what it feels like to be famous?

Someone taps me on the shoulder. "Hey, star," Maggie says, then hugs me.

"I didn't know you were here," I say. If I had time to have a crush, it would be on Maggie. I see her at school occasionally, but New Music and drama rarely cross paths. We could be the Romeo and Juliet of SPA, houses divided. Maggie's music is amazing—I've found more online, and even some YouTube videos of her singing in her bedroom and coffee shops. Not stalking, just researching.

"What did you think of the show?" I ask. For the record, if any actor asks that question, it really means: What did you think of me?

"I think that Rizzo stole the show. August, you're really . . ." She trails off, thinking of the word.

"Handsome?" I offer.

She smiles. "I was going to say exceptional."

I let the word *exceptional* bounce around in my head. I'll play it humble for Maggie. "I do my best," I say humbly.

"I'm into it," she says.

"Do you have other friends in the cast?"

She looks around. "I'm close with Justin, but I came to see you."

My body warms up. That's a good sign.

"The cast is going to Old John's. Want to come?" I ask Maggie.

"I should probably get home." She pushes her hair behind her ear. "Are you going to the closing party on Friday night?"

Justin Sudds is hosting the official *Grease* after-party at his famous dad's apartment. Everyone is pumped. Who wouldn't want to party in James Bond's apartment? It all sounds amazing, but I'll be at dinner with my parents putting on my second performance of the night as their daughter. "I can't," I say.

She looks confused. "You can't go to your show's closing party?"

"I have other plans. Family things."

"Oh," she says, looking disappointed. "Well, I'll be there."

"I'll try to make it," I lie. I want to be there more than anything, but this dinner has my future in the balance. It's mandatory atten-dance.

"I hope so." She hugs me and I don't want to let go. "I'll see you around," she says, then turns away and heads toward the subway. I watch her walk away, hoping she'll turn around. Before crossing the street, she does. And smiles. That's a very good sign.

I make my way through the crowd and find Elijah holding a bou-quet of flowers. "I want you to meet my parents," he says. I follow him over and say hello. His dad's in a nice suit and his mom is wearing a dress. They are as stylish as Elijah.

"You're so talented," his dad says with a kind smile.

"Well, your son is very talented, too."

"Don't we know it," his mom says, giving Elijah a hug. His dad joins in, and I stand there. It's clear they love their son unconditionally, and it makes me jealous. I wish my parents were accepting. Elijah's parents say goodbye to us and hug him again.

"Who's that?" I ask Elijah, pointing to the large group of peo-ple gathered across the street.

"That's the protest for the trans character in *Conversion*," he says.

There are about fifty people chanting, with posters reading TRANS RIGHTS and HIRE TRANS ACTORS and REPRE-SENTATION MATTERS.

Anna joins us, carrying an armful of flowers. "Look at that protest, August. There were so many more people earlier. I'm proud of them." She raises her arms above her head and yells, "I

STAND WITH YOU!"

I look at the protesters across the street and feel guilty. I should be over there. I should be on the front lines fighting for my transgender community. Elijah puts his hand on my shoulder. "If they fire Caesar, maybe they'll need a replacement?"

My heart speeds up. I can't think about it. Even if there was a remote possibility of that happening, my parents wouldn't allow it.

"Augustus," Anna says. "You were fantastic tonight. I cried. No joke. I've never cried during *Grease*."

"Thanks," I say, getting shy.

Elijah dramatically clears his throat.

Anna smiles at him. "Elijah, you're the king of Rydell High."

"But did I bring it?" he asks.

"Oh, it was brought," Anna says.

"Thank god. An agent came tonight to see me. So don't you dare lie to me."

"Are you kidding?" I jump in. "The audience couldn't get enough of you."

"Stop, you guys," Elijah says. "Or keep going."

After-show adrenaline is the best drug. I haven't done many drugs, but I can tell. The high makes me feel powerful—like I could do anything, full of energy, all mushy with emotion, and ready for more. I can talk to other castmates about the show and what went wrong and what went right all night. Mix in all this attention and compliments and I'm on top of the world.

Someone messes up my hair from behind. I turn around and see my lunch buddies, Jack and Juliet, hand jiving away. I didn't know they were at the show. I give Jack a huge hug. I haven't seen them much—they have been focused on their dance performance next week. "August, you literally took my breath away. Smile," they say, snapping a selfie to post. My follower count is going to explode this week.

Juliet takes my hand and twirls me around. "You were magnificent," she says.

I take a bow. "I'm so glad you were here."

"I wouldn't have missed it." Juliet waves her arm toward the protestors across the street. "Look at our community and allies coming together to fight the good fight."

"It's a beautiful thing," Jack agrees.

"Do you think it's fair that Chris Caesar will lose his job?" I ask.

Juliet fidgets with her earring. "I think it's fair to hire trans actors to play trans characters."

I nod. "I think that, too."

"Everyone, let's move out!" Anna yells, signaling to the actors it's time to say goodbye to our fans and head to Old John's.

Juliet and I say goodbye to Jack, who needs to go home, and walk toward Old John's. We walk behind the group so we can talk. "I wanted to finish our conversation from the other day," she says.

"About the chocolate chip cookies," I say, evoking our inside joke.

"Exactly. I've been thinking about what you said."

"You have?" I ask, honored.

"I have. You should have someone to talk to about these things. Even though we're the same age, I feel like your fairy transmother or something."

"That's nice," I say.

"Have you heard of gender dysphoria?"

"I have," I confirm. "It's the uncomfortable feelings I'm having around missing *that* body part, right?"

We cross the street. "Right. And everyone has a different level of discomfort. Each trans and nonbinary person is like a unique and beautiful snowflake. Some people are more comfortable in their body and don't need surgery or hormone therapy, and others do. No one way is right or wrong, and what you're feeling is your gender dysphoria."

"Today doesn't feel as bad as the other day. Can it change day to day?"

She laughs. "It can change hourly. But know this: It's okay to feel uncomfortable in your body. And it's okay to be mad at your body sometimes. I know how that feels."

"So maybe seeing a show called *Naked Boys Singing* could have thrown me?"

"It's possible," Juliet says.

"How do you deal with your gender dysphoria?" I ask.

"I talk to my therapist about my feelings. And I have a gender-affirming doctor to help align my body with my gender identity."

"That must be nice," I say. "The minute I stepped foot in New York, I become August and my life became busy. I haven't had time to think about, process, or accept much of anything. August was a role I jumped into when I got here. I could have used a couple more rehearsals."

Juliet looks at me, confused. "I thought you were out in Pennsylvania."

My heart drops. I hate when I forget a lie. There's no reason to lie to my friend who only wants to help. "My parents were not accepting of me being trans. They didn't let me transition. I think they were going to send me to conversion therapy. They don't know I'm August now. They still think I'm a girl."

We stop outside Old John's. "August, I'm so sorry. Why didn't you tell me earlier?"

I watch as my friends go into the restaurant. "I didn't know what you would think."

"Oh, August," Juliet says.

"August!" Elijah yells from the door. "Get your butt in here."

"You coming?" I ask Juliet.

"No, I'm going home. Have fun, and I hope you really celebrate. You deserve it," Juliet says, with a big smile.

"Fairy trans-sister. How about that?"

"I'll take it," she says.

Before I go in, I slip back into the Infamous August Greene.

SEVENTEEN

Friday, October 18

5:25 P.M.

How can this be the last show? Three performances are not enough considering the amount of work we put into getting it up. And now it's over, just like that? I'm ready to be in a Broadway show with eight performances a week and no closing date on the calendar. I'm dreading the show starting tonight, because then it will end and this will be over. *Grease* has been special. The cast bonding was the tightest and most real I've ever experienced. We'll still be in the same school and same classes, but it won't be the same. It never is.

I can't get properly in my feelings about the show ending because I'm worried sick about my parents' visit. Everything must go perfectly, or this won't just be my last show—it'll be my last day as a student here. I've played the role of their daughter for sixteen years. What's another night? Being a professional actor is my dream, and this is my path to achieve it. There can be no mistakes tonight, both onstage and especially off.

Two minutes before call time, I walk through the dressing room doors feeling nostalgic. The show isn't over, and I already miss it. The feeling is mutual—everyone hugging and exchanging handwritten cards with pieces of candy taped to the envelopes. A few cards wait for me on my workstation. I eat the candy while arranging my makeup but get distracted by my phone. That happens a lot now. I'm up to two thousand followers. There are more each time I check. Social media feels like a game, and for now, I'm scoring points.

There's also a text from Mom. My parents arrived in the city a couple of hours ago and checked into their hotel. She sent pictures of their small room in Times Square with a view of a brick wall. Aunt Lil is about to escort them to the theater. I wouldn't be able to pull this off without Aunt Lil. We spent an hour last night going over the details. This isn't easy for her, but she knows I need her.

I've thought about everything that could go wrong with my parents. Mom could talk to someone at the show. My exit plan could fail. Something could happen at dinner. To avoid the concession stand—which could be a hotbed for parent small talk—I had Aunt Lil pack snacks and water bottles. They don't do social media or the internet—so I'm not worried about that. I hope I didn't miss anything.

"August Greene," Meena says over the intercom. "Mr. Daniels would like to see you onstage."

My heart stops. What could this be? He's mad. He hates me. He hates my performance. He hates me and my performance. He's going to make me sit out the show. I walk down the hallway thinking up every worst-case scenario for this impromptu meeting. I enter from the wings and find Mr. Daniels sitting on the lip of the stage typing on his phone. "Hello, August," he says without looking up.

"Hello, Mr. Daniels," I say, trying to keep my voice steady and low.

"Come have a seat."

I walk across the stage and lower myself near him, our legs hanging over the stage. "How's it going?" I say, feeling the need say something.

"Fine, fine," he says, then drops his phone into his coat pocket. "Last show."

I nod. "I'm sad it's ending."

"Did your parents come up from Pennsylvania to see you?"

I straighten my spine. "They'll be here tonight."

"Well, they will be proud of you. August, you've done an excellent job as Rizzo."

"Thank you," I say, feeling immediate relief.

"And you know what will be in this theater after *Grease* ends?"

"Yes, I've heard all about *Conversion*," I say.

"Did you hear that Chris Caeser is no longer with the production?

"No," I say, my pulse quickening.

"No one has—it hasn't been announced. The producers listened to the demand for a transgender actor to play the role."

"That's surprising," I admit.

"Is it?" he asks. "There are some good producers out there." Mr. Daniels shifts his body so he's facing me. "August, the producer and casting agent are coming to the show tonight. They want to see you perform."

My hands fidget. "They are considering me for the part?"

He picks something off his sweater. "They might be. It would make a good story, hiring a trans actor from the very high school they'll be workshopping at."

I think of Mom. She won't let me be in that show. How would I keep it from her? This won't work. I can't do something like this, not now, not with my parents. "I don't have enough experience," I say.

"Says who?"

"Says me."

Mr. Daniels frowns. "I thought this would make you happy."

"I don't know how I feel about it."

"That's fair. And I do worry about you skipping steps in your actor's journey. There's so much for you to learn about your art and the business. Please don't take this harshly, but I'm not convinced you are ready."

Skip steps? Not ready? He doesn't know me, or what I've been through. "I think I'm ready," I say defiantly.

"Very well," he says. "Pressure is an interesting thing. Some actors can handle it, others cannot. The ability to act is only half the battle of being an actor. A great deal of your time will be spent in auditions, callbacks, rehearsals. And the strong, the ones who not only handle pressure but shine brighter because of it, those are the ones who make it."

"Mr. Daniels?" I say as he gets to his feet. "Why did you tell me they were coming?"

"You didn't want to know?" he asks.

"I don't know," I admit. Part of me thinks I would've been better not knowing. I have enough to deal with knowing my parents are in the audience. "Ignorance is bliss, right?"

"Is it really bliss, Mr. Greene? I wouldn't know."

I fast-walk back the dressing room—I'm behind schedule. I haven't even started my preshow rituals. As soon as I enter the dressing room, Elijah jumps in front of me. "What was that about?"

I know Elijah well enough to know he won't let up—I need to tell him something. "They fired the Nickelodeon star from *Conversion*," I blurt out, cutting to the chase to buy myself some time.

"HOLY SHIT," he says, way too loud. Everyone stops talking and looks over. Elijah smiles, and they return to their business. In whispered tones, he asks, "And they want to hire you? Are you going to be in a Joshua Downs play and make everyone insanely jealous?"

I whisper even softer, "They're sending people to come see the show."

"Who?" he asks.

"People."

"August."

"The producer and casting director."

"Holy shit," he says again, almost yelling.

"I don't want the part," I say, while trying to edge past Elijah to my changing station.

"You have lost your mind."

I shake my head. "I don't want to only play trans characters. There are too few of them to build a career. Name a trans character on Broadway."

"Hedwig," he says proudly.

"So, one?"

"Angel in *Rent*."

"Okay, two."

He thinks, gives up. "You. You could be on Broadway. Dude, do you understand what this means?"

I don't have time to understand what that means right now. "You can't tell anyone."

He frowns. "Jamaal?"

"No."

"Anna?"

"No way. I'm serious. I have to go. I'm behind," I say, not waiting for a response. I sit down at my station and look at myself in the mirror. No makeup on yet. I start readying my foundation. I hate wearing makeup, but it's acting.

As I settle into my routine, I think about pressure. I'm feeling it now. Getting a chance to be in a workshop that could go to Broadway would be big-time. But my parents would never let it happen. The minute they found out, I wouldn't be playing a trans boy in conversion therapy, I'd *be* a trans boy in conversion therapy.

Jamaal slides his chair over. "Hey, August," he says, checking himself out in my mirror. "You ready for this after-party?"

"Can't wait," I say. I didn't tell the cast I wasn't going to the party. I'll just make up an excuse on the group text tomorrow. My phone dings. A text from my aunt. It's a picture of my parents in front of the school. They are here.

"All right, gang, for the last time," Meena's voice booms from the intercom. "Five minutes to places!"

"Thanks, five," we all yell, then cheer and holler. Guys bang on the counters. The energy is up, up, up. Closing night is always magical. No one is nervous about their lines or entrances; we're all ready to enjoy our last time. The last show is like a bunch of little painful deaths. When each scene or song ends, you know it's the last time. Twenty sad little goodbyes.

We take our places in the wings, ready to hit the stage. Lots of smiles, hand-holding, and hugging. Everyone is celebrating like it's over, but to me, this is the only performance that matters. Seating is first come, first served, so I have no idea where my parents are, but all that matters is that Mom is out there. The most important audience of all.

The lights go dark, our cue to take the stage in first position.

My heart is beating hard. The crowd is going nuts—double the energy of the other nights. Lots of whistles, people screaming their friends' names, and an airhorn goes off.

I find my chair on stage left, shut my eyes, and take a deep breath.

The music starts, the lights get bright, and the show begins.

8:59 P.M.

The dressing room is empty. Everyone is outside getting love from their friends and family. I can hear the crew breaking down the sets as quick as they can. The show is done, *Grease* is over, and now I need to give the performance of my life. I can barely zip my backpack—filled with things from my changing station and my next costume.

I take the stairs up to the gender-neutral bathroom to change. Less of a chance someone will walk in here and question my outfit. I briefly considered changing outside in between cars, but it's too cold and I don't want to explain myself to the cops. I need to be quick—Aunt Lil is escorting my parents to the restaurant, but I don't want to leave them alone too long. I put on a blouse with tiny yellow flowers and a long blue-jean skirt—the exact outfit I left Pennsylvania wearing. I borrowed my aunt's long trench coat to hide my costume as much as possible.

Before leaving the restroom, I stop at the full-length mirror, open my coat, and look at my body. The old me—here for an encore performance. I reach into my pocket—almost forgot the last touch—and pull out a pink barrette. I put it on and frown at myself in the mirror.

I am my mother's daughter. I love my parents and theater and Jesus—in that order. Insecure, uncomfortable, unsure, and confused. I pretend to be a girl because my parents have given me no choice. They have imprisoned me in this identity because they can't accept my reality.

I feel a panic attack coming on. I remind myself that I have escaped. I just need to play this role for a couple of hours. Not days, months, or years. Just appetizer, dinner, and dessert. I take a deep breath and exit the bathroom.

I fast-walk down Amsterdam Avenue to Olympic Flame Diner, about five blocks from the school. I needed a nearby restaurant that nobody from SPA would be at. Elijah told me the Olympic Flame is the hangout for Juilliard. The odds of anyone coming here at this time of night are low.

Before going inside, I check my phone. Forty new followers and texts from Elijah and Juliet wishing me luck. It makes things easier knowing that they are thinking about me. I wish I could be at the after-party celebrating with the cast. I wish I could be anywhere other than here.

I walk inside and spot Mom across the diner. I wave and walk past the hostess, careful to carry myself like a girl. I missed my mom's smile. Big as ever. Her arms open and I walk directly into them. There's nothing better than Mom's hug. So comforting and warm, like home. The smell of her floral perfume makes me miss her more. She rubs my back as she hugs me, and I'm sure we are making a scene.

She lets go of me, but keeps her hands on my shoulders and looks at me. Or my hair, rather. It's the perfect length for Rizzo. Masculine when styled, feminine when wrapped up with a bow. Or with a dumb pink barrette. Her eyes tear up. "I'm so happy to see you," she says.

"Me too," I say, tearing up, too.

"Can I get a hug?" Randy says, putting his arm around me. He's a bigger guy—football player in high school, fried food eater the rest of his life. "You're a real star now," he says.

As my parents take their seats across the table, I sit down next to Aunt Lil and try to gauge her mood. "Having fun?"

She leans over and whispers, "I picked the wrong time to stop drinking."

I give her a half hug. "We can do this."

"You look . . ." She searches for the right words. "Like shit."

I laugh, loud.

"What's so funny?" Mom asks while putting her napkin in her lap. Her hair is the same—curly locks to her shoulders. She wore one of her fancy dresses—blue with white trim made of felt material they stopped making dresses with decades ago. Mom doesn't spend money on clothes.

"You know Aunt Lil," I say. "She's always got something funny to say."

Mom nods. "Lil, you should have invited Davina."

I look at my aunt, stunned. Did she tell them about her partner?

"Oh yeah," Aunt Lil says, fidgeting with her silverware. "I mentioned Davina earlier, you know, my art dealer who comes over for dinner occasionally."

I nod, agreeing to the story. I need to settle into the scene. I need to call on my improv skills and stay focused. "It's so good to see you," I say to my parents. "I miss you."

Mom reaches across and holds my hand. "Miss you more, sweetie."

Randy takes a drink from his beer bottle. Like Mom, he dressed up in his Sunday finest. Mustard-yellow button-up shirt with his brown suit. "What an impressive school," Randy says, foam from his beer hanging on his mustache. He wipes it away. "That theater must have had a thousand people."

"Can you believe it?" I ask.

Mom smiles. "We knew we'd see you in big theaters."

"You've got talent," Randy says, beaming.

"I can tell you have improved. It's clear," Mom adds.

"Oh, definitely," he says.

"We're proud of you," Mom says.

It's raining compliments, and I let the words wash over me. Their admiring looks fill me with love that I've missed more than I realized. I rearrange my silverware, not knowing how to respond. "Thanks," I say. "Means so much for you to see the school. For you to know that I'm doing okay."

"Okay?" Aunt Lil questions. "Kid, you're thriving."

"But, Audrey, can you explain something?" Mom says, picking her purse up from the floor and digging through it. She pulls out the Playbill and hands it to me. "Look what they put your name as." She points at my bio. "A. Greene?"

I had anticipated this question and made sure my bio was ambiguous and empty of pronouns. But there was no way to hide my name. I went with "A. Greene" but knew that would raise questions. "That was my mistake," I say. "I thought the cast was putting an initial as their first name. Turns out, they didn't."

"It's your name. Such an important detail," Mom says.

"Make a call, honey," Randy says. That's his famous line. Whenever something was happening at my school or church, Randy suggested she call someone to complain.

"That's not needed," I say. "The show is over."

While the waiter refills our water glasses, I scan the room for anyone from school. There's an older couple. Some families. And a group of kids, but they don't look familiar. I lucked out.

"I can't believe you live in this city," Mom says. "I tell everyone at church about it."

"Oh yeah," Randy says, biting into a pickle. Where did he get pickles? "Bragging all the time about her daughter in the big city."

Each time my parents misgender or deadname me, my aunt shifts in her chair, uncomfortable. I look at her and smile—hoping she knows I'm fine.

"Any boyfriends?" Mom asks. A usual question for her.

"No time for anything like that," I say.

"How about you, Lil? Got any boyfriends you want us to meet?"

"No time for anything like that," she repeats.

Mom shakes her head. "Both of you, too focused on art and acting." She smiles at Randy. He somehow has another pickle. "You need to make room in your heart for love, too."

I want to change the subject. I wrote out and memorized a list of conversation-starters for these moments. "Hey, Mom, how's church?"

"Oh, the same. Keeping me busy. Don't want to toot my horn, but I've been elected leader of the Moms' Bible Study."

"Congrats," I say.

Mom gets shy. "It's just thirty or so moms. I'm happy to be in service."

New York is a religious place—so many different religions and places of worship. But no one talks about it at school. At least not like they did back home. And as far as I know, I haven't met another Evangelical Christian.

"I should remember this," Mom says. "What church do you two go to here?"

"Uh," I say, looking at Aunt Lil.

"Uh," she says back to me.

"Oh!" I nearly shout, happy to come up with an acceptable answer. "We watch an online service!"

"That's wonderful," Mom says, smiling, her eyes wide and

bright blue. I've never seen her this happy. I want to live in this moment forever.

"Guess what," Randy says. "We're thinking about staying in New York another day."

Mom claps excitedly. "We want to see more of your city. And you. Would you like that, honey?"

"I would," I say, mostly telling the truth. But I have no other girl outfits. I'll need to improvise. Maybe go to a thrift store in the morning.

Mom looks at Aunt Lil. "Would that be all right with you?"

"Of course," she says with a really big (and really fake) smile.

"August?" I hear from behind me. I shut my eyes and pray someone is yelling about their favorite summer month. "August!" I hear again.

I watch Mom's eyes moving between whoever just ruined my life and me. I turn around and see Sandra Dee herself, Kelsey Whitton, and her parents. "Hey," I say, then stand up and hug her while my mind goes into overdrive figuring out how to get out of this situation.

"What the hell are you wearing?" Kelsey asks loudly.

"Are these your parents?" I ask, attempting to avoid the question.

"Yes, they are." She presents them proudly. "Dad makes us come to this diner even though the baklava tastes like wet paper bags." She looks at me and shakes her head. "Is that a barrette in your hair? August. What's up?"

I turn and present my parents to them. "This is my family," I say, hoping Kelsey can figure out to keep her mouth shut.

"Nice to meet you," she says to my family.

"You were Rizzo," I hear from behind Kelsey.

I look at her mom. "Yes," I confirm.

"You were fantastic, sweetie."

"Thanks," I say, wishing I had an eject button from this moment.

Kelsey's mom walks over to my mom. "You must be so proud."

Kelsey follows her mom. "August has only been at SPA for two months. He's a star!"

I sit back down. No one at my table is responding. Finally, Aunt Lil says, "We are so proud of our star. Now if you will excuse us, we are going to get back to dinner."

"Of course," Kelsey's mom says, then heads back to the front of the diner.

Kelsey looks at me again. Puts her hand on my shoulder. "We are going to talk about that outfit," she says, then walks off.

I hear every little sound of the restaurant. Knives scraping on plates. An old man laughing. A chair moving. No one at the table is talking. Mom's face looks distressed. Randy is sitting back in his chair, arms crossed, face red.

"August?" Mom asks, her voice shaky.

"We asked one thing of you," Randy says. "To not come up here and pretend to be a boy."

I feel my aunt's hand squeeze my knee. It's time to come clean.

I sit up straight, tighten my muscles to handle the emotional blowback, and say, "My name is August."

"Your name is Audrey," Mom says, a little too loud.

"And I'm transgender," I say, pushing back tears.

Randy shifts in his chair. "We let you come here, and we asked one thing."

Mom points at Aunt Lil. "You lied to me, too. You are responsible for this behavior. She's confused and you're allowing her to act that way."

"Mom, Randy, whether you believe it or not, I'm transgender," I say, my voice steady and low.

Mom waves me off. "I'm not listening. Pastor Tim told you this was a sickness."

Sickness. The word makes my skin crawl. My stomach upset.

"Tammie," Aunt Lil says. "Your child is talented. Smart. Kind and loving. And a boy. A transgender boy who needs your support. Look how much he's grown."

"Stop it. She's a girl," Mom says, not hearing anything.

"No, HE isn't," Aunt Lil shoots back. She hesitates. Thinking about something, she says, "And I'm a lesbian."

We all look at Aunt Lil, shocked. At the perfectly wrong time, our food is delivered by our waiter, who's trying to balance every plate on one tray. We all sit in awkward silence as the plates are put in front of us. Aunt Lil takes a big drink of water, probably wishing it were wine. I watch Mom's face, wound tight, as she tries to process everything. My heart sinks when I realize my life in New York is over. As the last plate is set down, the waiter asks, "Are we good?"

We are definitely not good.

"Yes," says Aunt Lil, the only one able to form words. Once the waiter is gone, she continues, "I'm gay, and I've always been. I didn't tell you because I didn't want to lose you. You're my sister. My family. And Davina isn't my art dealer, she's my girlfriend. Well, she was. Long story."

Mom wipes tears away. "I can't be here. I need to leave. Randy?"

Aunt Lil leans forward, frantic. "I realize this isn't the best way to tell you these things, but you're going to lose both of us if you can't accept who we are."

"That's enough from you," Randy says, helping Mom up. Hate boils in his eyes. It's scary to see this side of him.

We watch my parents walk out of the diner.

Aunt Lil looks at me. "I think that went well."

I laugh, because it's easier than crying. Aunt Lil waves down the waiter and asks to get my parents' meals packed up to go. "I can't believe you came out to them," I say.

"I couldn't carry it around anymore. I needed her to know my truth."

"How do you feel?"

"Better than I thought I would. Like a weight has been lifted."

I look down, wishing I felt the same. "Guess I'll be going back to Pennsylvania in the morning."

"You don't know that," she says, eating her salad.

I'm wearing a blouse, a skirt, and a goddamn barrette. "The lengths I will go to for them to love me. I wish they would try to understand me."

"They will someday. And if they don't, that's their loss."

"I don't feel that way," I say.

"Look at me, my boy," Aunt Lil says. "Look at what you have done for me."

"Made you come out to your sister and break up with your girlfriend?"

"August, my dear, I have watched you become a better person every day. All that you risk to live authentically, as hard as you have worked, and how bad you want it. I admire that. You've made me want to be a better person. No, not better, that's boring. You've made me want to be more me."

I shake my head, unable to process. I manage to get out a quiet "Thank you."

"Should we go home and eat all the ice cream in Brooklyn?"

"I think I should go to the after-party. My last hurrah before conversion therapy."

"August, I will not let that happen."

"I wish you had control over it," I say.

"Maybe I do? That's a tomorrow problem. Have fun at your party. I'm going to Davina's to win her back. Don't know if I can." Aunt Lil signs the bill and stacks up the to-go containers. "But at least I'll be bringing food."

"See you later. Midnight on the dot?"

"You can be late tonight. I won't wait up."

We stand up and hug. I see Kelsey sitting with her family—smiling and laughing. She has no idea how lucky she is. Aunt Lil leaves, and I head to the bathroom to take this ridiculous costume off my body. If this is my last night here, I'm going to go out with a bang.

10:05 P.M.

THE AFTER-PARTY

My car pulls up in front of a very tall building. Two doormen wait under the awning wearing suits and caps. The building is about a mile away from school—at the bottom of Central Park. The lobby makes my first rich-person party at Riley's look cheap. Being hedge-fund rich is one thing, being famous rich is another. Everything in the lobby looks expensive—the doors, the art, the couches. There's a massive fish tank and even the fish look wealthy. As I'm waiting for the doorman to find my name on the list, a man walks by, headed to the elevators with two bodyguards following behind him. I try to get a look but can't see his face.

The doorman finds my name and sends me on my way to the penthouse. The elevator is all mirrors—impossible not to check myself out and take a quick selfie. I have plenty of time—there are forty-four floors between the ground floor and the penthouse. I broaden my shoulders and try to smile, but it's not convincing. Will this be my last night as August?

I know what'll go down with my parents. I can picture it now. My phone will ring early tomorrow. Mom will tell me to pack my things and say goodbye to Aunt Lil. They'll check out of the hotel and pick me up. The drive will be quiet. Painful. I'll be leaving behind my dreams. I can't think about it. Maybe they'll take me directly to Brand New Day. Maybe they'll need a few days to arrange it. If they take me home, I'll make a plan. Run away, or something.

The elevator dings, opening into the living room. My mouth drops open. The apartment is the definition of extra. Really classy, but also over-the-top. The place is filled with oversized furniture, massive paintings, and lots of windows revealing unreal views of the city. There's an Oscar statuette in a glass box surrounded by movie posters of Justin's dad. The place is packed with people talking, drinking, dancing. They all seem as starstruck as I am by the opportunity to party in a famous person's apartment.

"Your coat, sir?" asks a man wearing a white button-up and black tie.

I take off my trench coat and hang it on his arm. "Thanks," I say, wondering if I'm supposed to tip him.

"Enjoy the party," he says.

I plan on enjoying myself like there's no tomorrow. Before I make it to the kitchen for a drink, another man in black tie approaches balancing a tray of drinks. "Champagne?" he asks.

"Don't mind if I do," I say, settling into the rich life with ease. I drink the whole thing. The bubbles burn my throat and all the way down to my stomach. I wipe my mouth and ask, "Can I have another?"

"Of course," he says.

I put the empty glass back on the tray. I don't know if that's what you're supposed to do, but there are no rules tonight. I take another glass and walk in the direction of the living room. Elijah is really going for it on the dance floor. I sip my drink and wait for him to see me.

He spots me mid-head-whip. "Oh my god, August!" He navigates around people—bumping into them—and then jumps over the couch. "My dude!"

We bear hug. I'm going to miss Elijah the most. No, Aunt Lil first. Him second.

"Why are you here?" he asks, his voice slurred.

"It didn't go well," I say, holding back tears.

"Shit, dude, want to talk about it?"

"Not really. Tonight, I just want to have fun. Can we do that?"

"Hell yes, we can. I haven't had the best night," he says, pointing his head toward the corner, where Anna is sitting close to Duncan on a love seat (how fitting). "They keep kissing. Kissing, August. Kissing. It's disgusting. I hate watching."

"So stop watching."

"I can't do that."

"You're torturing yourself. Why are you doing this?"

He stomps a little, playfully. "I like him. He's Duncan Stanford and he's going to be a famous cello player." He finishes his White Claw, crumples the can, and sets it down on a table. "And because I don't want her to have him."

"There it is," I say, watching another black-tie guy pick up the can and disappear into the crowd.

"What can I say? White Claw brings the truth out—it's the law of the Claw."

"Can I be straight with you?" I ask.

"I'm gay, but I can play straight?" he jokes.

"You should use the White Claw honesty and tell Anna the truth. Or end it with him." I hesitate, wondering how much more to say. But tonight is my grand finale, and I owe it to Anna to say something. "This love triangle is going to really hurt her. Have you thought of that?"

He scoffs. "I'm not lying to her."

"Not telling her is lying to her," I say.

"And you're one to talk?"

I look down, ashamed. "It's different. But yes, I'm telling you from experience that this will not end well."

"It went that bad tonight?"

"Worse than bad. Kelsey showed up and blew my cover."

"Kelsey saw you wearing that outfit?"

I never showed Elijah what I was going to wear, just told him about it. "Afraid so."

"Shit," he says. "Shit, shit, shit."

"I don't want to think about it, really. Matter of fact, I need another drink. Want to head to the kitchen?"

Elijah finds the beat. "Get your drink, my boy." His dancing gets bigger. "The dance floor's calling my name."

I do the rounds and make sure to talk to everyone from the

cast and crew. I hug them like it's the last one. Give them compliments like I'll never see them again. And say goodbye like it might be forever.

Meena is having the time of her life—dancing with some band people. "Hey," I say to her, trying to dance beside her. "I think you're the coolest person in the room."

She stops dancing. "How drunk are you?"

I shake my head. "I just wanted you to know."

"Drink some water," she says, then gets back to dancing.

Justin and Tess are holding court with people circling them. What would it be like to be Justin, even for a day, and live in this place with a famous dad? He must have it so easy. Not a worry in the world.

When I get to the kitchen, there's a black-tie girl tending bar. I ask for a beer—too nervous to order a drink. I twist off the bottle top and hear, "Hey." I turn around to find Yazmin holding a pink water gun. She squirts me a couple of times in the chest. "Got you."

Assassins. Of course. Yazmin drew my name. "You got me," I say, putting my hands up.

"Do I?"

"Not anymore," I say, earning another squirt from her water gun. She's wearing a shiny black dress with her hair in a tight bun. "You look incredible."

"Who, me?" She spins around. "Auggie, no joke, your Rizzo was amazing. They were right to cast you. You blew me away."

I lean against the counter. "I'm sorry I didn't go for Kenickie," I say. After everything that happened tonight, maybe I should have.

Yaz waves me off. "No, you do you. This whole thing made me realize I want to focus on TV and movies."

I nod. "I could see that."

"My boyfriend thinks that will be the best move."

I wait for jealousy to wash over me, but it doesn't. Maybe because my parents will be taking me back tomorrow. Or maybe I'm over my crush. "I'm glad we are friends," I say, smiling.

She nods. "Me too, Auggie. You're a cool guy."

"And you're really special. I know you'll buy that house for your family someday."

"You're so sweet," she says, then hugs me.

Elijah appears behind us. "There you are," he says, out of breath. "Come dance with me. I demand it!"

I look at Yaz. "Go do that," she says.

"Bye, Yaz," I say, acknowledging this might be my last time to see her. Elijah nearly drags me back into the living room. I've never really danced at a party, but tonight, I go for it. I move around, somewhere near the beat, as the champagne makes everything feel all right. My arms feel light, this moment feels light, I have so much darkness ahead, but this moment is all light.

I dance until my hair feels a bit sweaty. I leave Elijah in the middle of a dance-off with Jamaal. I find a couch and check my email, wondering if there will be something about *Conversion*. Or maybe the producers will call? I wish Mr. Daniels had never told me. When I'm forced home tomorrow, I would have had no idea.

Now I'll always wonder what could have happened. I was right—ignorance is bliss.

"August?"

I look up and see Maggie. She's wearing a black turtleneck with a gold chain and jeans. Her hair is parted in the middle. "Hey," I say.

"You made it after all. Your family thing end early?"

I pocket my phone. "You could say that. And I wanted to see you."

"Me?" she asks, blushing a little.

"Want to have a seat?" I ask, extending my hand to the sofa.

"I'm actually heading home. I need to be up early. I work at a guitar shop on the weekends."

"Oh, just in case you needed to be any cooler," I joke, trying to hide that I'm completely bummed she's leaving. Maybe if I tell her this is my last night here, she'll stay.

"Maybe you'd like to walk me home?"

I look around. The party is dwindling down. "It would be an honor."

Maggie takes my hand and we walk directly to the elevator, unseen by most people—too busy dancing, and singing, and making out. I spot Elijah talking and gesturing excitedly. The black-tie guy hands me my trench coat, which gets a laugh from Maggie. I snap a few pictures of us in the mirrored elevator. They will be good memories of my time in New York.

It's cold but not freezing. It's hand-in-your-pocket weather but not time for gloves. "You live close?"

"No, I'm making you walk me to Brooklyn," she jokes.

"I would," I say. "But I also live there."

We pass by a man walking three dogs the size of small horses. Maggie tells me about her mom, who works on Wall Street, and her cat that sleeps in her guitar case. She tells me about growing up in New York, and I could listen to her talk forever. "Want to play a game?" I suggest.

"Sure," she says.

"Quick-fire questions. I ask, you answer," I say, borrowing Anna's game.

"I'm ready."

I think fast. "Favorite color?"

She laughs. "Are we ten years old?"

"Okay, dream college?"

"Smith."

Never heard of it. "Dream stage to play on?"

"Grand Ole Opry in Nashville."

"Do you like me?" I ask, feeling bold.

Maggie stops walking. Looks at me. "I don't know."

"What do you not know?" I ask.

"You're always putting a little act on. I promise it's cute, but I see through it."

"What do you see?" I ask, curious.

She thinks. "I see a nice guy with a good heart. But he's also good at acting. Always putting on a show."

"I'm not putting on a show," I say.

"I like you without the show."

"I like you, too."

"Then drop the act."

"I'm an actor—this is who I am."

We walk in silence. I like Maggie. I feel good around her. I want to tell her everything, but what does it matter now? This is my last night here. I don't want her feeling sorry for me.

She stops. "This is me."

I look up at the building, six stories high and old-fashioned, a very New York apartment building. A shiver moves through my body.

"August, when you're ready to be real, give me a call."

I watch her walk up the stoop steps and unlock the door, hoping she will look back. When she doesn't, I feel cold and alone.

EIGHTEEN

Saturday, October 19

8:10 A.M.

Panic and regret hit as soon as I open my eyes. Yesterday rushes back to me. I should have picked a different restaurant. My stomach turns and my head throbs from the champagne. Today is not going to be a good day.

I need water. Lots of it. Aunt Lil is at the kitchen table, sipping coffee while reading the newspaper. "Good morning, sweet boy. How was your night?"

"I said my goodbyes."

"This isn't the end."

"Did you make up with Davina?" I ask, pouring a glass of water.

Aunt Lil shushes me and whispers, "She's sleeping."

I'm happy they made up. She starts collecting her things like she's leaving. "You going somewhere?" I ask.

Aunt Lil exhales loudly. "I can't stop thinking about last night. I've decided that our conversation with your parents isn't done. We need to go up to Times Square, knock on their hotel door, and demand to talk to them."

"Go there? They will force me back to Pennsylvania."

She grabs her keys off the hook. "If they want you to go back with them, then we'll deal with that. But for now, let's show up. Maybe they are enjoying the free hotel buffet or whatever. We need to talk to them. We can convince them."

I'm unsure about this approach. My parents aren't big on confrontation. But my aunt is so confident. Hope creeps in. I won't be alone. No more lies. Everything on the table. "I'll go change," I say, and head upstairs.

Minutes later, with my hair messy and no shower, wearing a black hoodie and blue jeans, I get into my aunt's truck. "Why aren't we taking the subway?" My aunt usually doesn't drive in the city.

"I'm too nervous. I need to keep my hands busy and mind distracted."

"This sounds dangerous," I say, buckling up.

As we cross the Brooklyn Bridge, she tells me stories of her first years in New York. I'm not really listening, too busy running scenarios of how this will go down. The closer we get, the more tense I become. It's almost nine; Mom will be up and about. Maybe we can catch her in the lobby and talk alone. That could help our case.

We descend into the underbelly of the hotel's parking garage. It's dark. Empty. Aunt Lil kills the engine and doesn't move. "August, are we making a mistake?"

I look at her, surprised. "I don't know. You're the adult here."

"I've been avoiding this confrontation all my life," she says.

"I've tried to have this confrontation and failed," I admit.

"This is a fool's errand, and we are two fools. I've lived too long scared of my sister knowing I'm a lesbian. I've kept her in my life by keeping her out of my life. She loves her version of me, not the real me. And I have paid for it without even realizing."

"You're brave," I say.

Aunt Lil smiles big. "I learned it by watching you."

"I don't feel brave," I admit.

"Bravery isn't not being afraid—it's doing what you need to despite the fear. So, let's put brave pants on and go."

"You've always been my favorite aunt."

She laughs. Pinches my cheek. "Mark my words, they will not take you to conversion therapy. I'll sell all my paintings to pay for lawyers."

I nod and get out of the car wearing my invisible brave pants.

The hotel lobby is packed with tourists. I scan the crowd looking for Mom's curly hair. Or Randy's mustache. Aunt Lil talks to a man behind the concierge desk. His head is down, typing away on a computer. Her movements get more animated. A minute later, she puts her hands on my shoulders. "They checked out last night."

"Last night?"

My mind swirls. They left without saying *come back*, or *stay here*, or even *goodbye*. My body goes limp. Aunt Lil tightens her grip on me. "Do you need to sit down?" she asks. "You're going pale."

I haven't eaten, the champagne is punishing me, and my parents left. "I thought they would see me onstage and be so proud that they would accept me," I confess, and realize how irrational it sounds.

"I wish it was that easy."

"I disgust them," I say, my stomach in knots.

Aunt Lil grunts. "They disgust me."

"They never want to see me again."

"Good," she says. "They don't deserve to see you again."

Then it hits me. As much as it hurts that they left, this is the best outcome. They aren't going to take me back to West Grove. No more Mom using my deadname. No more Randy being Randy. I can stay here and go to school. I can play any role I want. "Actually, I'm glad they are gone. I'm free!"

"You're not upset?" Aunt Lil asks, surprised.

Before I can answer, my phone vibrates. Is that Mom? I pull out the phone, nervous. "Unknown number," I say, showing Aunt Lil.

"Could it be your mom?"

"Maybe I won't answer."

"Up to you."

I accept the call—for better or worse. "Hello," I say.

"August Greene?"

"Yes?"

"Hi, I'm Rosalyn. Sorry to bother you on a Saturday. Are you busy?"

"Who is it?" Aunt Lil whispers.

"I'm not busy," I say into the phone.

"Wonderful. I'm the casting agent from *Conversion*, the show doing a workshop at your school," she says. My heart beats so hard I feel it in my ears. "I'll get right to the point; there's a role that needs to be filled quickly. We heard about you and went to see *Grease* last night. And you, my friend, really stood out. Your Rizzo was fantastic."

"Thanks," I say.

"Would you be available to audition for the role of Ajax? The director couldn't attend last night, but we've told him about you. I know this is short notice, but we're working on a tight timeline. Could you come to the school today for an audition?"

I look at my aunt, stunned. "I'm actually close. I could be there soon."

"That'd be great. I guess this was meant to be. Thirty minutes?"

"Or less. Or thirty if that's better for you." Oh god, I need to get off this phone.

"Great. We're in Theater Two. No monologue, we'll have sides for you. See you soon. Thanks, babe," she says, then hangs up.

"August," Aunt Lil says. "Can you please explain what the hell is happening?"

"On the way there?" I ask, heading to the parking garage.

Twenty-five minutes later, I'm sitting outside Theater Two. Trying to get out of abandoned-by-parents mode and into audition mode. On the phone, Rosalyn said it was meant to be, and maybe she's right. My parents wouldn't have allowed me to be in this play, and now they're gone. The door opens, and a lady comes out. She's wearing black tights and an oversized sweater. "August?"

"That's me," I say, getting up from the bench.

"Hi, sweetie. I'm Rosalyn. Thanks for making it so quick. Do you live near here?"

Probably not a great idea to tell her what I was just doing. "I was having breakfast with my aunt," I lie.

"Sounds nice," she says. "Here's the sides. I'll come get you in a few."

She leaves me with two pages and a bunch of nerves. I scan the words, trying to figure out the character. The scene is a back-and-forth with a counselor during a group therapy session. My reading is interrupted by footsteps coming down the hall. A man approaches with a scruffy beard and a man bun on top of his head. Bulky sweater and big boots. Like a big, stylish bear. He looks at me as he nears, chewing on a toothpick. He says nothing as he enters the theater. That must be Joshua Downs.

Shortly after that, Rosalyn peeks her head out the door. "You ready, babe?"

I get on my feet. "As I'll ever be," I say, following her to the stage. I find center and let the limelight warm me.

"Everyone, this is August Greene," Rosalyn announces as she takes her seat in the audience among a row of five serious-looking faces.

"Hello, August. I'm Joshua Downs. The director of this show." A toothpick rests at the edge of his mouth.

"We saw August in *Grease* last night," Rosalyn says. "He was a spectacular Rizzo."

"Rizzo?" Joshua asks. "Why Rizzo?"

"Because she's a great character," I say, my voice shaky.

"But you're a guy? Why play a girl part?"

Is this an audition or an interrogation? I steady myself. "That's the role I wanted. I can play both genders."

Joshua looks at the older man to his right. "This guy can play Rizzo, but Caesar can't play Ajax? This world makes no sense anymore." He leans back with his arms crossed.

"All right, August," Rosalyn says, "I'll be reading the part of Cheryl, the counselor. We know you haven't read the script and don't know much about Ajax, but show us what you got."

I look down at the pages and collect myself. I am Ajax, a trans guy forced into conversion therapy by his parents. I'm too tough to show emotion. My edges are rough and I'm ready to fight. More than anything, I don't want to be in conversion therapy.

"Ajax," Rosalyn says, beginning the scene. "You've been quiet today. Care to share?"

I look away. Snarl my lip. Let hate and pain well up in my

chest. "Not really in the mood to talk, I guess."

"The point of this group is to share your feelings," she says.

I look at Rosalyn with untrusting eyes. "The point of the group is to brainwash."

She sits up in her chair, meeting my energy. "You know that's not true."

"You don't know shit about me, lady," I yell, pointing at her. "My family didn't put me in here to get better—they put me in here to die."

"Your family loves you."

"Loves me?" I spit, my face reeling from the offense. I spread out my arms, the script gripped tightly in my hand. "Is this what love looks like?"

"This is what *real* love looks like," Rosalyn says. "We will help you find the right way to live as God intended."

"You're wrong, ma'am," I say as a tear—just one tear—falls from my eye and runs down my cheek. I pause and let the theater get quiet. My eyes search the room. "I'm going to die in here."

The silence lingers for what feels like forever. "Well done," the man beside Joshua says.

Rosalyn smiles. "Yes, we do appreciate you coming in today, babe."

"August," Joshua says. We lock eyes and he smiles. "Why should we give this role to you?"

I straighten up. "Because I can do it," I say.

He tilts his head. "How do you know that? How are you even qualified?"

Rosalyn cuts in, "August, you don't need to answer. My apologies, but Joshua is still a little upset about having to replace Caesar."

"A little?" he asks with a laugh.

"No, its fine," I say. "I'm qualified because I'm attending the School of Performing Arts. And I'm qualified because I'm transgender. And that's who should be playing the part."

A woman says, "We agree with you."

"And," I say to Joshua directly, "I watched a bootleg of your production of *Othello* in Central Park two years ago. It was the best Shakespeare I've seen. It would be an honor to work with you."

Joshua nods and grumbles, "That's one of my favorite shows, too."

"Have a good day, August," Rosalyn says, meaning get out of here while I'm ahead.

ACT THREE: CONVERSION

NINETEEN

11:45 A.M.

My friends look at me like I'm famous. Or an alien.

Other people in the lunchroom are looking, too. News travels fast.

"Then what did you say?" Anna asks, her complete focus on me. I love my lunch crew, and I really love being the center of attention.

"I told him I was qualified because I'm a student here, and transgender." I take a bite of my sandwich. Really hold the suspense. "And that he would regret not hiring me for the part," I say, embellishing the story for dramatics. They laugh. The table is eating up this story.

"What did you think of Joshua Downs?" Anna asks. "Total egomaniac?"

I can't tell them the truth. I like the way they are looking at me. Today, I feel seen by everyone. I don't want to lose that by revealing how mean the famous director was to me. "He's not happy about losing Caesar."

"No shit," Anna cuts in. "He's been pretty public about his feelings online."

"Digital hate crimes," Jack adds.

"How did they offer you the part?" Meena asks.

I got the call yesterday—too early, but I acted awake. Rosalyn made the offer and told me to call her back with my decision by the end of the day. Aunt Lil and I had a long talk about taking the part. She was concerned about the character. I convinced her I would be fine. No way in the world I would turn down this opportunity. This is my path. Getting the part of Ajax is my star turn. When I walk into a room, people will point and mention it. I called Rosalyn back and accepted the offer.

"The casting director, her name is Rosalyn—"

"Rosalyn Perez?" Anna asks, always knowing someone in the industry. "Did she call you babe?"

"Yes, she did, babe," I say, then everyone laughs. It wasn't even that funny. "She called yesterday morning and offered me the part on a probationary contract. I don't really understand it, but they are finding me an agent to handle it."

"Hell yes, August," Meena says. "They are going to *find* you an agent. When does that ever happen?"

I shrug, knowing it's cool, but playing it off.

"Someone found *me* an agent," Elijah says casually.

"Who? Your mom?" Anna asks.

"Yes, but still," he says. Elijah usually eats lunch with seniors, but I guess he wanted to hear about my audition.

"Did you celebrate the offer yesterday?" Meena asks.

"You could say that." I keep it vague because I spent the entire day in bed. I needed a day to decompress after my parents' visit, the audition, and closing *Grease*. I'm no stranger to the post-show blues. There's no avoiding the sadness after your show closes. So much energy and time put into something, so many ups and downs, bonding with the cast, and memories. I did find enough energy to post my *Grease* montage of pictures, from first rehearsal to closing party, with a gushy too-long caption to my three thousand followers. Lots of likes and hearts.

Jack puts their arm around me. "You're living the dream."

"Just think," Anna muses, "two months ago you were a big nobody in Whatever, Pennsylvania, and now you've landed a role in a major workshop that might go to Broadway."

"I'm still wrapping my head around it," I say. "And the first show is in eight days."

"Oh my god, I'd be freaking out," Meena says, always thinking—and freaking out—like a stage manager.

"I don't have many lines."

"You read the script?" Elijah asks.

"A messenger delivered a copy to my house last night," I say.

"That's fancy," Anna says. "Is it good?"

"I honestly don't know. It's a drama about a conversion therapy camp in Florida. There's a love story between two cis gay guys, and at the end, the patients take over the facility and leave together. I'm only in a few scenes, but my monologue ends the first act."

"And then what?" Anna asks.

"My character dies by suicide."

Their faces all register shock. "That's so sad," Jack moans.

"I know," I say. "It's a dark scene."

"No, that you're only in the first act," they say.

"August," Juliet says. "You sure you want to play this part?"

"I don't want to play the part," I admit. "Where are the happy endings for trans characters? I feel like transgender characters onstage are broken, mentally ill, or suicidal. Never superheroes, love interests, or the lead. Where are those parts?"

"Wasn't your super-objective to not play transgender characters?" Anna asks.

I look at her, surprised. "How did you know?"

"Busted," Jack says.

"I kind of read everyone's paper," Anna mumbles, head down.

"Anna," Meena says, disapproving.

She waves it off. "Dad left them out. Whatever, they were all basically the same. Except for Augustus, of course."

"My super-objective is to play the great roles of Broadway like Evan Hansen, or be in *Once*, or *Be More Chill*. Basically, any role on Broadway. And those are mostly all cisgender characters."

"You'll play those roles, August," Anna assures me. "Ajax isn't the perfect role, but it will lead to more perfect roles."

"It'll be worth the pain," Jack says.

"I bet the rehearsals are going to be a bitch," Meena says, probably longing for her clipboard and headset. "When is call time?"

I check my phone and panic. "Ten minutes. I'm excused from drama classes the next two weeks to go to rehearsals."

"I'm going to miss you," Anna says.

I dig through my bag. "Shoot, I forgot a highlighter."

Meena, Jack, and Anna offer me theirs at the same time, talking over each other. They laugh and Juliet says, "Guys, he's not famous."

"Yet," Anna says.

"Better change your handle to the *Famous* August Greene," Jack suggests.

My mind swirls at the thought. Could it be happening? No way. But maybe? If I can handle the role and Joshua Downs, I could be famous.

After lunch, Juliet walks me to the basement.

"I didn't want to ask at the table—how did it go with your parents?"

I stop at the bottom of the stairs. "It was a total flop."

"Oh no," Juliet says, covering her mouth in shock.

"They found out. Then my aunt came out to them. And then they left town."

"Left town?"

"Without saying goodbye."

"Oh, August, I wish you would have called me yesterday. Are you okay?" she asks.

"Actually, I'm good. My parents did me a favor by leaving. Now

I can take roles like Ajax in *Conversion.*"

"Does this role hit too close to home? Your fairy trans-sis is worried about you."

"It's just acting," I reassure her. "I don't use my own feelings or experience. I step into the character. And how could I turn down possibly going to Broadway?"

"That director sounds like a major asshole," she says, probably sensing I'm not going to change my mind.

"I can handle assholes. I'll be the bidet of the theater world!"

She laughs, gives me a hug. "Break a leg on your first day. Just make sure the director doesn't break it first."

"Thanks, fairy trans-sis!"

"And I'm serious, August. You're dealing with a lot. Call me if you need me?"

"Of course," I say, smiling. I know she's worried about me, but I'm not worried. This was meant to be.

I get to Theater One—where *Grease* was greasing three days ago—and stop at the doors. This moment feels important. I'm about to walk into my first professional show. And if everything goes well, the Famous August Greene will go to Broadway.

I push the doors open, and organized chaos surrounds me. Way more people here than *Grease.* Actors on the stage, crew running around wearing headsets that would make Meena jealous, people making the sets, hanging the lights—it's a small army.

"August?"

"Yes," I say, spinning on my heels.

"Brady Finley," the owner of the voice says, shaking my hand. His red hair is tangled around his stage manager headset. He seems less stressed than Meena. "I'm the assistant SM."

"Nice to meet you," I say.

"Can you come with me?" he asks, then turns before I answer. I follow behind him into the audience. He points at a seat. "Sit here."

"Until when?" I ask.

"Until Joshua tells you otherwise," he says, then walks off, talking into his headset.

I set my backpack down and sit in my assigned seat, feeling like I'm in time-out.

6:35 P.M.

Things start weird and stay weird. And I have sat here, in this seat, the entire time. Before rehearsal started, Brady introduced me to the cast, and everyone politely said hello. The energy was loose and fun until Joshua Downs entered the room. Then everyone got serious and quieted down. Joshua has enough personality to fill the entire theater. Most of the time, he paces around the aisles, sometimes the stage, talking loudly and yelling notes at the two assistant directors, who scribble them down.

Honestly, I want to be onstage always, but I'm relieved to sit here and get my bearings for the rehearsals. The difference between the productions of *Grease* and *Conversion* is undeniable. There's so much talent at this school, but nothing on the level of this cast. I googled them all while sitting in my time-out chair.

These actors have been on Broadway, the West End, toured the world, and one has been in a Judd Apatow movie. Their talent is real, raw, and intense—even in rehearsal. If my life were a video game, I'd have warped to a level I'm not ready to play. Compared to these actors, I feel small and inexperienced.

I can't take my eyes off the two leads, Andy and Ben. During breaks and in between scenes, they are easygoing and funny. Always joking with the cast and crew. But once the scene begins, they turn it on like I've never seen. Another standout is Betty Lauderdale, a trans woman, whose character is trying to "do right by Jesus" by living as a man. She's in the scene with Ajax before he dies by suicide, then finds him after.

There are eight cast members onstage with two understudies in the front row writing notes in their scripts, and me on the side-lines. It's clear they've bonded from the way they talk and work together. Do they like Joshua? Are they mad about Caesar? Will they like me? Are they going to think I'm inexperienced? Instead of memorizing lines, I wrap myself in endless unanswerable questions.

Most of rehearsal is spent working second-act scenes. Joshua obsesses over every detail. He questions their choices. Pushes them emotionally. Tells them what to do. The process is slow. In five hours, they have only made it through three scenes. Joshua can be harsh and direct. It's unsettling. An actress left the stage crying.

"Let's wrap this up early tonight, gang," Joshua yells from

the back of the theater. Everyone starts clapping and circling up onstage. Even the crew joins. Joshua heads down the steps, clapping the loudest. This seems like a group activity that I should be participating in. But I don't want to make assumptions. I don't want to just insert myself into their things.

The clapping dies down. Everyone holds hands in a big circle onstage, with Joshua in the middle. He looks my way, for the first time today, and smiles. "Aren't you going to join us?"

Not wanting to make anyone wait, I take the stairs as fast as Joshua did, hopping onstage as the circle opens and lets me in. I'm holding hands with Ben and someone from backstage. I look around—there must be thirty people—as most of them look at me. "I trust you have all met August," Joshua says, "I don't know your last name."

"Greene," I say, my voice cracking a little.

"August Greene will be stepping into the role of Ajax. Chris Caesar would have been an amazing Ajax, but now we have August. Everyone welcome August."

I smile at everyone, but I don't know if they can see me, I'm so small from that introduction. "Great to be here," I say, feeling the need to say something. People say hello.

"All right," Joshua says, yanking back the attention. "Solid rehearsal today, gang. The second act is coming together, more of that tomorrow. We are eight days out. I need you all to step it up. Now, are we ready?" A few heads nod, then everyone closes their eyes. "A moment of silence for all the people who are in, have been in, or will be in conversion therapy. We do this show to bring awareness to this problem, and we're thinking of you every day as we try to honor your life and struggles."

I open my eyes and look at Joshua. That was unexpectedly touching. Maybe he's a nice guy and putting on the big bad director act?

"Have a good night," he says, then everyone falls out of the circle and heads backstage. I'm almost offstage when I hear Joshua say, "August Greene, can we talk?"

"Of course," I say, and walk toward him. The theater quickly clears out, and it's just me and him. He smiles at me, but it doesn't feel welcoming.

"August, you look scared. Are you scared?"

"No," I lie.

"I promise I won't bite," he says. "We got off to a bumpy start. I know that was partly my fault."

"I understand. You miss Chris Caesar," I say, stating the obvious.

"You're absolutely right. I miss him. I had the perfect vision of this show, and all those protesters took that away from me." He puts a toothpick in his mouth. "But here we are, and we're going to make the very best of it," he says.

"Sounds like a good plan," I say.

"You've read the script?"

"I have."

"Your monologue at the end of act one, that's the moment that drives the second act. The suicide of Ajax is what inspires the characters to fight against the therapy. I know this puts pressure on you, but the show's fate rests on your shoulders. And that means my fate rests on your shoulders. I'm going to get what I need out of you for this performance. Even if it means pushing you beyond what you are capable of. You understand?"

"Yes," I say, overwhelmed.

"Right. Glad we are on the same page," he says, chewing on his toothpick.

I should speak up. Talk back. Run away? Instead, I stand frozen with fear.

"We'll be doing a put-in rehearsal for you on Friday. Sound good?"

"I won't be onstage until Friday?"

"Correct. We will have the understudy stand in."

"But why not just have me onstage? I'm going to be here."

"'Cause we haven't put you in, son." He checks his phone, done with this conversation. "Good talk. See you tomorrow?"

"Yes, sir," I say.

"Don't call me sir. It makes me feel like your teacher."

I walk out of the theater and onto the street. I don't think anyone sees me the whole way home; I'm the smallest thing in the world.

TWENTY

Thursday, October 24

8:20 P.M.

I'm having déjà vu. For the second time in a week, I'm in the elevator traveling up forty-five floors to Justin Sudds's apartment. Well, his famous dad's apartment. Elijah texted me during *Conversion* rehearsal and invited me over. I told him I was too tired, so he demanded it. I'm worried I'll be ambushed. Maybe this is an acting intervention?

If anyone knew what the *Conversion* rehearsals were like, they truly might stage an intervention. Physically, it's been an easy week. I go to my morning classes, take a nap during lunch, then sit and watch a rehearsal for six hours. Mentally, I'm exhausted from putting up with Joshua Downs and his mind games. But tomorrow is my put-in rehearsal. For better or worse, I'll be onstage rehearsing. I don't know if I'm ready. Joshua has filled me with doubt. I don't trust myself to play the part—not completely.

Meanwhile at school, I'm playing the part of Famous August Greene. There's no denying the energy shift. Before *Grease,* I was a nobody from nowhere. After *Grease,* people were interested. And now with *Conversion,* I have their attention. Even my friends are more excited about being around me. They talk to me differently. They listen to me differently. They think I'm great, and I think I'm crap.

So, I act how they want me to act. Everyone thinks I'm the big shot, so I play the big shot. Everyone thinks I'm onstage rehearsing with Broadway actors, so I let them think that. I don't know if this is considered "making it" because I'm still completely faking it.

And tonight, they want to hang with the Famous August Greene. So, here I am. The elevator doors open, revealing the entire cast of *Grease.* They yell a loud, "Surprise!"

"What's this?" I ask, pretending to be confused. "Is this a party for me?"

Elijah hops over to me. "We wanted to congratulate you for landing the role in *Conversion,* and that amazing article!"

Playbill ran an article today about *Conversion* hiring me to replace Chris Caesar. They posted a picture of Chris, looking like a model, beside a selfie of me from Instagram. When the article went live, I ignored most of US History reading and rereading it. A small part of me wanted to send it to Mom. I wish she could be proud of me. But we haven't talked, and it would only upset her.

"Thank you, guys," I say with the biggest and most humble smile. Then I notice everyone is wearing over-the-top costumes.

Elijah has on a black corset with stockings and makeup, Tess and Kelsey are wearing nurse outfits, Justin is in a loose-fitting black suit with a back hump, Meena is a scientist (lab coat and clipboard), and Yazmin is in a leopard-print jumpsuit. But Anna takes the cake—she's wearing a glittery corset with a matching jacket, plus a red wig and top hat.

"Holy shit, Anna," I say.

She does a spin. "Don't threaten me with a costume party."

"What kind of costume party is this exactly?" I ask, feeling underdressed in my jeans.

Elijah throws his arm around me. "Only one of my most favorite movies ever, *Rocky Horror Picture Show*!"

Now the costumes make sense.

He continues, "Tonight, in your honor, we'll be doing the Time Warp in Justin's very luxurious screening room."

I know there's a cult following of devoted fans and midnight showings, but *Rocky Horror* wasn't on my radar at West Grove. Too edgy for my old school. "I can't believe I haven't seen it," I admit.

Elijah raises his arms above his head. "We have a virgin!" he announces to the crowd, which is met with cheers and whistles. "Buckle up, baby. You aren't watching it—you'll be experiencing it!"

Justin leads the way to his screening room. I walk with Elijah, who still hasn't perfected walking in heels. "Where's Jamaal?" I ask.

"Oh, he had a date," Elijah says, wobbling on a step. I'm happy that Jamaal is seeing someone—his showmance with Yaz never materialized—but I'm sad the intense cast bond is already loosening.

"Right this way," Justin says, opening huge double doors, revealing a mini movie theater with ten or so seats. There are bags of popcorn and random props spread around. "Show will begin in ten minutes," he announces.

The drink table is soda and water, no alcohol. "No drinking?" I ask Justin.

He flashes a mischievous grin. "Tonight, we're getting higher."

Kelsey passes by with a tray of brownies. "Special brownie?"

"Hell yes," I say. If my aunt Lil can eat them, I can, too.

"We should hang out soon," Justin says to me. "We could go out on my dad's yacht."

The son of 007 wants to hang out with me. On a boat. "Sure," I say, as coolly as possible. "I'd be down."

"There's the celebrity," Anna says, putting her arm around me.

I take off her top hat and put it on my head. *That's meeee,*" I sing.

"If someone told you back in Pennsylvania that you'd be at James Bond's penthouse celebrating your role in a show that might go to Broadway, would you have believed them?"

I think of who I was back there. No way in hell I could have dreamed this big. "Of course I did. I'm actually wondering why it took so long," I say.

She rolls her eyes and takes back her top hat. "I have some good news, too. I've been selected to direct a one-act play for the SPA Winter Showcase!"

"Cool," I say.

"*Cool?*" she repeats. "I know it's not *Conversion*, but this is a big deal for me."

"Yeah, it sounds great," I say. "If I don't have a show that night, I'll come see it!"

"Wow, what an honor," Anna says, and heads over to the drink table.

Elijah comes up behind me. "Let's grab a seat," he says.

I follow him while eating the brownie. I've never had edibles, but I'm guessing Justin has the good stuff. "Front row?" I ask, my mouth full.

"You'll be drier here."

"Drier?"

"Oh boy, you're in for it, my friend," he says, throwing himself into the plush recliner and popping up the footrest. "This movie was pivotal to my development as an actor and a homosexual."

"How so?" I ask, curious as to why so many theater people swear by this movie. The musical didn't last long on Broadway.

He tosses a piece of popcorn in his mouth. "Before I was out, I felt like a weirdo. I thought I was too weird even for New York."

"Not possible," I say. I've seen some very weird things.

"Don't deny me my feelings," he jokes. "I was in ninth grade, and Brad Newsome—my secret crush—invited me over to watch

Rocky Horror. I wasn't ready for this movie. It was so wrong, it was right. The actors were weird, the singing and dancing were weird, it allowed me to be weird. *Rocky Horror Picture Show* gave me permission to be me."

"Then you came out?" I asked.

He shrugs. "Not for another couple months, but I did kiss Brad Newsome that night. Right after the movie ended, I channeled Dr. Frank-N.-Furter and leaned in."

"Where's Brad now?"

"Dead to me, obviously; there's only one guy and his name is Duncan."

I check over my shoulder to see if Anna is nearby. She's at the drink table, out of earshot. "How's that going?" I ask, annoyed that it's still going.

"Well, I have a plan, and that plan involves inviting him here tonight and making him choose publicly. And I think it's a great plan."

"That's the dumbest plan ever," I say.

"Too late, he's showing up later. Let's see if he can resist all this," Elijah says, displaying his stocking-clad legs.

I laugh. "You're weird in the best way."

"Anyone sitting here?" Yazmin asks, already in the seat beside me. Eating popcorn.

I sit up a little. "Guess you are."

Elijah gets up. "I'm headed to the bathroom," he says, leaving us alone.

I smile at Yaz. "Who are you?" I ask, referring to her costume, not a deeper intellectual question.

She shrugs. "I haven't seen this movie, but I figured I couldn't go wrong with leopard-print everything. I know who you are."

"Oh, I didn't dress up."

"You're a big star."

I blush. "Hardly," I manage to say.

"Um, did you see all the coverage online about you? Broadway. com, Playbill, TheaterMania."

"I didn't read them," I lie. I read all the articles, all the comments, and watched my follower count explode. I gained four hundred followers today. Acting feels like a drug, but so does social media. And I'm getting higher every day.

"August," Yaz says, "I'm so proud of you."

"Enough about me, how are you?" I ask. We haven't talked since the cast party.

Yaz exhales loudly. "I'm *fine*. I have an audition for a short film this weekend. But I'm thinking of breaking up with my boyfriend. It's always something with him."

I nod, thinking back to the balcony where we kissed. Everything was so bright and new. Everyone was so cool and accomplished. But now I'm feeling like I've moved beyond it all.

"I'm back," Elijah announces loudly. "Got us some candy."

"Ready for the show?" Justin yells from the back of the room. The lights go down and everyone finds a recliner. There's popcorn flying around the room and lots of excitement. Red lips sing the first song as the opening credits roll. Everyone knows the words but me and Yaz. Elijah is belting every word, and when I look over, there are tears in his eyes.

The movie starts with a wedding between Janet, played by Susan Sarandon, and an actor I'm not familiar with. Confetti flies around the room, like I'm in a snow globe. "What's happening?" I ask Elijah, brushing confetti out of my hair.

"We're just getting started," he says, full of glee, as everyone sings "Dammit, Janet" along with the movie.

When Susan Sarandon puts a newspaper over her head to block the rain, everyone in the room does the same. Anna puts a newspaper over my head, then water comes from everywhere. I turn around to a full-on water-gun fight. "Don't you dare ruin my makeup," Elijah yells, covering his face. More water guns point toward him until he screams and ducks in his chair.

Things get out of control when "Time Warp" begins. Everyone's dancing and scream-singing the words. "Get on your feet, August," Anna yells. I hop on a recliner, balance myself, then go wild. The Famous August Greene knows how to shine during a group number.

I understand why Elijah loves this movie—the way Tim Curry plays Dr. Frank. No apologies. No inhibition. All sexuality. It's inspiring to see a queer character fully owning his identity. I wish I weren't playing a tragic character with the opposite of a happy ending. Ajax is the exact role I didn't want to play. I've been having trouble stepping into the character when I rehearse at home. I feel so much pressure to show up to rehearsal tomorrow and blow them away. It makes this party feel like a waste of my time.

Can you die from an edible? Maybe I'll google it.

Elijah's eyes get big. "August, Duncan is here. Come with me?"

"I don't know," I say, not wanting to involve myself.

"I threw a whole party for you—would you do this for me?"

"Fine," I say, then follow him. "Why do I need to come with you?"

Elijah stops, and I run into him. "I need you to run a distraction for me."

"A what?"

"I need you to distract Anna so I can talk to Duncan. Then I'm going to kiss him."

"In front of everyone?"

"In front of Anna. Once she sees our heat, she will stay away."

I grab his arm. "Hey, I'm serious. If Duncan isn't out about being pansexual, you shouldn't do this right now."

"This is a very accepting crowd. It's like ripping off a Band-Aid," Elijah says, and continues up the stairs to his target. I follow behind him, my heart beating fast. Anna and Duncan watch us walk toward them.

"Hello, handsome," Elijah says to Duncan, and gives him a hug.

I try to read Anna's face, but she seems unfazed. Elijah gives me the nod to run the distraction. "Hey, Anna," I say. "Look over there?"

"August, are you okay? Too many brownies?"

I don't think I like Duncan. But if Elijah goes through with this, Anna will never forgive him. I need to stop this before anything happens. "Duncan is dating both of you," I say.

All three of them look at me, shook. Then look at each other.

"August," Elijah hisses at me.

"I did you a favor," I say.

Anna gasps. "Do you think you're better than us now, Augustus?"

I shake my head. "I'm just over it," I say, then take off without saying goodbye. I am the Famous August Greene—I say what I think. When I turn the corner, I run into Tess.

"Hi, August," she says.

"Hi, Tess," I return as I walk past.

"I wanted to say congrats for getting that role."

I stop and turn around. "Do you hate me? Or all trans people?" I ask, emboldened by the endorphins and edibles.

Her jaw drops. I'm on a roll tonight. So, I continue, "I bet you're happy I'm finally staying in my lane. I bet you wish I were in conversion therapy."

"August," Tess says, but I'm already walking past her. I find my way out of the apartment, down the elevator, and call a car. Stars never stay until the end of events anyway.

TWENTY-ONE

Friday, October 25

3:30 P.M.

"This is my dressing room?" I ask.

"With all the amenities," Brady says, presenting a folding table with a desk lamp and full-length mirror. The room is basically a walk-in closet with a shelf of cleaning supplies. This is not the men's dressing room.

"Is this a joke?" I ask, hoping this is a prank.

Brady holds his hands up. "I'm just the stage manager. I don't make the calls."

There's another folding table and mirror across from mine. Same plastic chair. Tons of makeup piled up. "Who's there?"

"Betty Lauderdale."

"Oh," I say, putting the pieces together. "This is the transgender dressing room?"

"Gender-neutral dressing room," Brady says, knowing that

probably doesn't make it better. I sit down on the chair and the back nearly breaks. "I'll leave you to it," he says, checking his watch. "Onstage in ten."

"Thanks, ten," I say.

"Oh, August?" Brady says, making eye contact. "You're doing great out there."

The first half of rehearsal has been bumpy, and I can only imagine what will happen next. After this break, it's time to rehearse the scene with my monologue. "Doesn't feel like it," I say.

"Hang in there," he says, already on his way out the door. I turn toward the mirror with the horrible desk lamp lighting. Good thing I don't wear makeup for this show. This room smells like bleach. This feels wrong. I should be in the men's room and Betty should be in the women's, and that should be the end of discussion. Is this even legal?

I rub my eyes, exhausted from last night's *Rocky Horror* disaster. I avoided Elijah and Anna all morning, and skipped the cafeteria, opting for a nap in an empty classroom. I don't have the energy to deal with it. All my brainpower goes to thinking about Joshua Downs. I feel obsessed. I want to impress him. I want him to see that I can be Ajax. I can't fail at this role. This is my big chance.

Today was supposed to be my day. My big put-in rehearsal. I walked into the theater channeling the unapologetic attitude of Dr. Frank-N.-Furter. I kept my head up and pretended like I owned the room. I skipped my seat and stood onstage because it was my day. Only to be told by Brady to go sit down as they worked on the second act.

Two hours later, Joshua turned to me—sitting like a good boy in my assigned seat—and told me it was time. I was put into five scenes, the understudy showing me the blocking while Joshua gave notes. Each time we'd run the scene, I would get very specific notes like: *Your foot needs to be here. You need to look more upset. Why did you put your arm like that?* Each note whittled down my confidence. When we'd run the scene, I'd be thinking about the notes Joshua gave and anticipating what he would say next. My Ajax hasn't been great.

"Five minutes," Brady's voice sings over the speakers.

"Thanks, five," I say to an empty room. I wish I had time for a walk. I need to get out of my head. I've practiced the monologue for hours, trying different faces, pauses, and deliveries. I've put in the work, but I don't trust myself. This is my moment to prove myself. I need to show him I'm better than Chris Caesar and deserve to be here.

"Oh, looks like I have company," I hear from behind me. Betty dries her hands with a paper towel.

"They put me in here," I say, hoping she's not mad.

"I was getting used to having my own dressing room, even if it's a janitor's closet that smells like an old mop at a strip club."

"Only the best for us," I joke.

"I wouldn't have it any other way," Betty says with a wink.

"Do you want to be in the women's dressing room?" I ask.

"Those girls can get loud." She sits down at her makeshift station. "This isn't the best I've had, but it's not the worst. Like most things in life, it is what it is."

"It is what it is," I repeat, watching her powder her cheeks.

"One thing is for sure," she says. "Mr. Joshua Downs has a huge crush on you."

I laugh, not expecting that. "I think he's warming up to me," I say.

"I'm afraid he's just getting warmed up. That man can run hot, hot, hot. Oh lord, the tantrums that man-boy threw when they let go of Chris Caesar. He broke a chair that day."

"No way."

"Way."

"Was Caesar that good?" I ask, afraid to hear the answer.

Betty stops brushing her hair. "Are you kidding?" She lets out a loud laugh. "That entitled prick couldn't act his way out of a wet paper bag. Joshua wanted his social media audience to come to the show and make him relevant."

"I have three thousand followers," I brag.

"Not bad, but Chris Caesar had three million. Joshua needs a miracle to keep his career alive after the past two failures. Everyone knows that. Especially Joshua. You can feel the pressure building inside him. Bet he doesn't sleep, just paces around his apartment all night chewing on toothpicks."

It feels good to talk to Betty. Chris Caesar wasn't an amazing actor—just a big draw for tickets. I can't match him there, but I can act myself out of a paper bag.

"Honey," Betty says. I turn around and look at her. She scoots over close to me. "You have a tough scene coming up. Very emotional. And Joshua isn't going to make it easy on you. Reminds me of a show I did last year called *Tough Broads*. In the final scene, my character murders her boyfriend after years of domestic abuse. My scene partner—his name was Ronny—would hug me before and after we did the scene."

"Why?" I ask.

"He wanted to make sure I knew it was just acting, the feelings weren't real, and that I was safe. Would you like to do that with me?"

"I would," I say, feeling those tears coming.

She pats my knee. "Good. It's done, then. Keep that chin up and stay strong."

I wipe away a tear.

"And do not cry in front of that man; tears are his power pellets. Don't feed the beast."

"Places," Brady announces over the intercom.

I'm the first one onstage. Joshua is typing on his phone at the director's table in the audience with his feet up. The reading lamp lights up his face—his beard shaggy, and a messy mop of curls on his head. He's got an aura of gross around him. He looks up and sees me, smiles, and goes back to his phone. Hope he's ready. I'm going to show him that I'm a star.

After the cast is out onstage, Joshua puts his phone down, picks up the mic, and says, "August, are you ready to run your scene?"

"I'm ready."

"Fantastic," he says. "Betty and August, why don't you run the scene and we'll work out the blocking after. Other actors, find a seat in the audience."

"You got this, August," an actor yells as I head into the wings with Betty. The cast claps, and someone whistles. No matter what, actors support each other.

I stand backstage and wait for Betty. My hands shake and my eyes have trouble focusing. My mouth feels dry. I need water. There's no time.

"You ready?" Betty asks, then gives me a big hug. She smells of coconuts and vanilla. "Put your arm over my shoulder and I'll walk you to the desk. Sound good?"

"That works," I say. Ajax is coming from electroshock therapy and would be in pain. The scene is in Ajax's room. "Actually, bring me to the foot of the bed and stay close."

"I'll sit when you cry. I got you," she says. I shut my eyes. I am Ajax. The conversion therapy has worn me down and electroshock therapy has broken me. I have no hope, no fight, no future. There's only one option.

I put my arm around Betty, tighten my body, and let my head bob like it's disconnected from my spine. We walk onstage and start the scene.

"You're okay. It's all over," Betty says in a soothing voice as she walks me to the bed.

"My brain is scrambled," I mumble. I take my arm off Betty and drop down on the bed. "I'll never do that again." I curl into a ball at the foot of the bed.

"I felt that same way my first time in the shock chair, but you'll adjust. It helped me. It'll help you, too, Wendy."

"My name isn't Wendy!" I yell. "My name is Ajax."

Betty takes an audible breath. "Your name is Wendy; my name is Dennis. And you're a girl, and I'm a boy. The quicker you accept those truths, the less shocks they'll send through your body."

The script says Ajax cries. I bury my face into my jeans and make weeping sounds. Betty continues, "You need to believe that our Lord is stronger than the demons inside of you. And, Wendy, I can feel him fixing me. I'm almost there."

"Bullshit," I say.

"He does not make mistakes."

I actually hate that line because my mom used to say it. I pull myself out of the ball and sit up. "I'm not a mistake. I don't need to be fixed." I stand up and yell, "I am Ajax, and that is my truth."

"You better quiet down, or they'll take you right back to that shock chair. Is that what you want?" she asks.

I take short breaths to make my words feel winded. I know everyone is looking. I know this is my time. I stand up and begin my monologue. Once finished, I sit back down on the bed, acting dizzy and spent. Betty stands up and fluffs my pillow. "You need sleep. Lie down and I'll bring you dinner later. We can pray together."

I watch as Betty leaves, and say, "Hey, what will you do if they ever let you out of here?"

Betty smiles. "Find a wife and start a family."

After Betty exits, I pull myself up and walk over to the desk. There's a prop knife hidden under the desk table. I fish around and find it. Look at it. The lights go dark and I scream.

The actors start clapping. I can be better, but it felt good. I smile at Betty, who hugs me again. "You did good, kid," she whispers.

Joshua walks down the steps slowly, like he's thinking. The smile is gone. He jumps up onstage and walks over to me. I want to hide behind Betty.

"Was that a joke?" he says, stomping on my confidence.

I straighten myself up. "No," I say.

"What was that curl in a ball thing? Where did you learn that? Surely not this prestigious school of performing arts." Joshua swivels and faces the actors. "Did you know he goes to this very school?" He turns back to me, arms crossed.

"I was just feeling the scene out," I say. "I can do better."

"And that—what was that?—weeping? Do you think that's how a real person would ever cry?"

"No," I say, my mouth tasting sour with hate.

"And the yelling, oh my god, the yelling. Is Ajax a yeller to you?"

"He's frustrated."

"Frustrated? He's *frustrated*? You think he might be a little past frustrated?"

"What would you like?" I ask, my face red and sweat building on my forehead.

"I would like something to work with; you're giving me

NOTHING." He turns around and walks into the audience. "Do it again."

Betty and I head backstage. She gives me a hug, and we start again. I don't curl in a ball, don't weep, and act like I'm done with the world. Lights out, I scream. No claps this time. The lights come back on and Joshua says, "Run it again."

"No notes?" I ask.

"I'll give you notes when you give me something to note."

We head backstage, Betty hug, scene, lights down, scream. "Again," Joshua says.

We do it again. "And again."

We run the scene two more times before Joshua asks me to stand in the middle of the stage. I glance over at the cast, embarrassed. I shouldn't be—I wouldn't think less of an actor, watching this unfold—but I do. "Why aren't you crying?" Joshua asks from the audience.

"You want me to cry every time?" I ask.

"That's what the script says."

"I can try," I say, my throat sore from the scream.

Joshua paces the aisle of the dark theater. "What's Ajax's objective in this scene?"

I can almost hear Mr. Daniels laughing. "His objective is to end his life."

"I don't think that's what he planned at the beginning. Do you?"

"He hid a knife in his desk earlier, I think he's been planning it."

Joshua laughs. I don't know why. "And what's Ajax's super-objective?"

I think for a moment. My super-objective was to not play this kind of role. I guess if you go against yours, then bad things like Joshua Downs happen. "He wanted to be himself."

"You're transgender, like Ajax, correct?"

"I am transgender," I say, tensing up, ready for an attack—verbal or otherwise.

Joshua stops pacing. "Then why can't you connect with Ajax?"

"I don't connect with my characters, I become them."

Joshua laughs again. His laughs are menacing. "Become and connect are different?"

"To me," I say.

"How did it feel when you came out to your parents?"

If he only knew the whole story. "I was scared," I say.

"Use that."

"But Ajax isn't scared?"

Joshua throws up his hands. "Then what is Ajax?"

"He's defeated."

"Defeated," Joshua repeats. "We can make that happen."

His words send a chill down my back.

"Run the scene again," he demands. Betty and I reset and hug. This time, I deliver each word with a raw desperation, hoping that this will end soon. The lights come back up.

"Do it again."

I'm like a boxer going to the corner of the ring between rounds and coming back bruised and exhausted. This must be our tenth run. The others must be mad at me, and just want to move on. He is making them dislike me. Maybe I am worthless. Maybe I'm not an actor. "Ready?" Betty asks, and gives me another hug.

"I can't do this," I say.

"Yes, you can," she says. "Let's go."

I can't tell if Betty is annoyed by me. "You're okay. It's all over," she says, then the scene starts again. Anger comes through; every line is seething with anger for Joshua, for this scene, for myself. The lights go off. I shut my eyes and ready myself to hear "do it again."

"August," Joshua says instead. "What was your name before August?"

"Joshua," Betty says with a tone. "That's not appropriate."

"My bad," he says, holding up his hands. Betty turns and walks backstage.

"August, what's that line before the end of the monologue?"

"There's no reason to be here."

He shakes his head, frustrated. "No, the next line."

"I can't do this anymore?"

"That's the line. Take center and give me that line."

I walk into my limelight, but it doesn't feel so warm anymore, and say, "I can't do this anymore."

"Again."

"I can't do this anymore."

"Again."

After three more agains, I get desperate. "*I can't do this anymore.*"

"Three times in a row."

We continue this for a minute, but it feels like forever. He tells me to shout it. To scream it. Whisper it. My throat hoarse, my voice going, I say it over and over. And then I yell it loud enough that all of New York can hear. "I CAN'T DO THIS ANYMORE."

"I felt that one," Joshua says. "Do the scene again."

Backstage, Betty hug, arm around her, we walk out, and the scene starts again. When we get to the part in the script where I cry, I start weeping, real and painful tears. I continue with tears through the monologue. The lights go off; I scream.

"Next time, August, less crying," Joshua says. I drop into the desk chair onstage, my legs weak. I can't give anymore, can't do anymore; nothing is right. "That's enough for today, gang, we have a long day tomorrow. Let's huddle up."

The actors start clapping and get onstage. Betty puts her hand on my shoulder and gives me a squeeze. I join the hand-holding circle, standing in all my shame and all my lack of talent. Andy holds my hand and smiles at me. I try to smile back but forget how.

"Today was tough for August, but," Joshua says, looking me in my eyes from across the circle, "I'm here to make you a better actor. That's why I push you. And everyone take note, you need to connect with your character and their pain. If you don't, the audience will know. Get some sleep. Tech begins tomorrow," Joshua says.

The thought of coming back tomorrow and doing this again

is almost unimaginable. Joshua walks offstage. I think I hear him whistle on his way out.

"Hey, August." Andy grabs my shoulder. "That was really intense. Are you okay?"

"I don't know," I say honestly. "Is this normal?"

Andy laughs. "With Joshua, nothing is normal, but that was extra. You handled it well."

"I did?" I ask. Nothing feels right about what I did.

TWENTY-TWO

Saturday, October 26

9:25 A.M.

If Joshua Downs wanted to break me, I think he accomplished his mission. I woke up this morning feeling broken. No energy, no emotion, nothing. Empty. Numb. Every step I take on my way to school for hell day at *Conversion* feels forced. Even my feet know this is a bad idea.

I'm mad at Joshua. I'm mad at my parents. And I'm mad at Ajax. This isn't the character I want to play. Not over and over. I'm not connecting with him. Maybe it's Joshua Downs. Maybe it's the role. This isn't a dream come true; this is a nightmare.

And what will today be like? Twelve hours with Joshua Downs.

But I need this role to get ahead. The way people look at me at school. The news articles about me. The social media following. All that goes away if I lose the role. And I jeopardized my two best friendships here for this show. I can survive hell day. I need to be stronger than I've ever been.

Brady is waiting for me in the school's foyer. He's almost unrecognizable without his headset. "Hey, man," he says, his face serious. More serious than I have ever seen. Even his freckles look concerned.

"What's going on?" I ask, my heart in my throat.

"Joshua told me to tell you," he starts, but hesitates.

"Just say it," I say, bracing myself for impact.

"Joshua said your time would be best spent connecting with your character."

I step back. "He doesn't want me at tech rehearsal?"

Brady nods, unable to say it. I feel my knees go weak. "Look," he says, trying to level with me. "You're in, what? Six scenes. You know the blocking, you know the lines, you don't need to be here. Joshua gets extra Joshua. This is probably for the best."

Brady has a good heart. And he's right; I don't need to be here. Although feeling like I'm missing out will be unbearable. What will everyone say about me? This was my only chance to bond with the cast, and now that's gone. "So I just go home?" I ask, hoping Brady has some advice on how to spend my day.

"It's Saturday, and we have tomorrow off. I suggest you get ripped and have some fun."

"You've worked with Joshua before?"

"A couple times. The producers like me, I suppose."

"Does he always do this to actors? What he's doing to me?"

Brady raises his eyebrows. "Pushing you to be a better actor?"

he asks in Joshua's dismissive Cali accent. "He's eccentric." Brady air quotes the word *eccentric*. "He usually sets his sights on an actor and does variations of this mind game. But it's always different. Always surprising."

That brings me weird relief. I'm not alone in this torture, and others have survived. "Does it help the actors?"

Brady grins. "Have you read the reviews for his shows?"

I shake my head. My mouth tastes sour.

"One more thing," Brady says, hesitating again.

"Just say it," I say, all out of fucks to give.

"He said that if you can't deliver the monologue at Monday's rehearsal, then the understudy goes on opening night."

My mouth drops open. "Is he serious?"

"Afraid so, and I've seen him do that before."

"But the understudy is cisgender," I say. "Wasn't the point of hiring me to have a transgender person play the role?" I ask, trying to make my case.

"I don't think he cares." Brady checks his phone. "I need to get back. See you Monday?"

"Maybe," I say. Brady laughs—thinking it's a joke. He takes off toward the theater and I walk outside. This is one of those moments I'll remember forever—the bricks are red, the sky is blue, and I've never felt like such a failure in all my life. I need to clear my head. I walk in the direction of the subway, but I can't go home. If I do, Aunt Lil will know I'm a failure.

I walk past the subway, too anxious to get on, and head toward

Central Park. It's a beautiful ten-block walk, giving me plenty of time to think. I want to call someone, but don't want anyone to know. This is too embarrassing. Monday will not go well. There's zero chance that I'll perform the monologue to Joshua Downs's liking no matter what I do. Set up to fail. Doomed. I shouldn't have gone out for this part. When the understudy goes on Tuesday, everyone will find out. I'll be the joke of the school. The trans boy who couldn't even play the trans boy.

Once at the park, I walk down the cement path and hold my breath while passing the line of horse-drawn carriages. The smell of horse poop is overwhelming and reminds me of the cattle farms near West Grove. When I get to the street inside the park, I watch the joggers and bicyclists. The lawn is almost empty—too chilly for picnics in the park. I head to the duck pond, and pass by the climbing wall and chess tables.

"Well, well, if it isn't the infamous August Greene," I hear from one of the tables. Mr. Daniels is sitting on a lawn chair with a battered chessboard. There's an older Black man wearing sunglasses playing against him.

I forgot Mr. Daniels's favorite weekend activity is chess in the park. "The one and only," I say, mustering up enough energy to be human. Or act like one.

"One moment, son." He studies the board. Moves a piece. "Checkmate, Willy. I got you this time."

Willy claps twice, swears several times, then pulls out ten dollars from his pocket. Before he hands it to Mr. Daniels, he says, "I'm coming back in ten minutes to win this back."

"You can certainly try," Mr. Daniels says, slipping the bill into his coat pocket. He motions for me to sit in the lawn chair across from him. "Do you know how to play chess?"

There was a chessboard in the church's rec room, but we always went for Operation or Connect 4. "Not a clue," I admit.

"That's a shame. It's a great game to teach strategy. Teaches you to think ahead." I watch as he resets the pieces on the board. "Shouldn't you be at tech rehearsal?"

"I was told to leave," I say, with my head down.

"Oh dear," he says, looking concerned.

"You were right," I say.

"I usually am," he says, smiling.

"I skipped steps. I'm not good enough to be in this show." Tears fight their way out of my eyes and wash away the smile on Mr. Daniels's face. "I'm not a good actor. I only got the role in *Conversion* because I'm transgender. And now I'm going to get fired."

Mr. Daniels hands me a tissue from his pocket. "I've heard that Joshua Downs can be, excuse my language, an asshole."

I nod while blowing my nose.

"And his methods can be extreme."

"I have this monologue, and no matter how many times we ran it, I couldn't deliver what he wanted."

"What does he want?"

"For me to connect with the character."

"Ajax is a trans boy who gets sent to conversion therapy by his parents, correct?"

"Yes," I say, allowing him to make the next move.

"And August is also a trans boy whose parents were going to send him to conversion therapy?"

"You knew about that?"

Mr. Daniels nods, thinking. "And Ajax ends his life after the monologue?"

I nod. "I've had thoughts about that as well."

"Your aunt told me."

"Did she tell you my shoe size, too?" I ask, ashamed he knew.

"The role of Ajax is filled with trauma. Much like the life of August. Maybe you can't find Ajax's truth because you haven't faced your own?"

"I don't use my own emotions when I act."

Mr. Daniels lets out a laugh. "Ah yes, the August method."

"It's not a method," I say, disgusted at myself for naming it.

He moves a chess piece. "When you were at your old school," he says, searching for the words to not misgender me. "When you were a . . ."

"Before I transitioned," I say.

"Yes, before you transitioned, you played the role of a girl every day. I could imagine it would be easier to play that role if you disconnected from your feelings. Otherwise, it might be too much?"

"Something like that," I say, uncomfortable at how easily Mr. Daniels can read me.

"What you were doing wasn't acting—it was surviving. You had no choice but to play that character. But you don't play that role anymore. It's time to come from a place of truth."

"I don't know how to connect with Ajax," I admit.

"Mr. Greene, you can swear to me until your face is blue that you don't connect with characters or use your emotions, but you can't fool me. I saw you connect. I saw you use your emotions. And whether you knew it was happening or not, that's what made you a good actor."

"Then why can't I use my emotions for Ajax?"

"Because you haven't faced them. That's what I've been pushing you toward this whole time. You need to face your truth; then you will find Ajax."

"Checkmate," I say.

Mr. Daniels frowns. "I do regret not pushing you to get help. I suppose I thought if you kept focused on acting, you'd get better."

"I don't need help," I say, frustrated. "I've got this."

Willy starts slowly pacing around the table, wanting his chance to win back his ten dollars.

"August, do you know how the producers of *Conversion* found you? Did they tell you?" he asks.

I shake my head.

"It was me."

"You?" I ask. "But you were worried about me skipping steps."

"That was my warning to you."

"Was it only because I'm transgender?"

"That certainly helped your case. But I knew you were up for it. I still think you are."

"Did Anna convince you to let me into SPA?"

My question gets a loud laugh from him. "I love my daughter, but she doesn't have that much sway with me. Believe it or not, I think you're quite talented."

I feel more tears coming, but I push them down.

"You have to believe in yourself, son."

"I don't know how," I admit. Any confidence I had is gone.

"Face your truth. Even if it's scary. When you believe in yourself and your talent, no one can take that away from you. But no one can give it to you either. No compliment, no role, no review. That is your journey."

"My journey is into that chair to win my money back," Willy says.

I stand up to leave. I need to face my truth. And my truth is in West Grove, Pennsylvania, probably reading the Bible right now. I need to confront them about sending me to conversion therapy. I need to know if they will ever accept me as their son.

I say goodbye to Mr. Daniels and head out of the park. An hour later, I'm in Penn Station watching a bus pull up. In four hours, the bus will drop me in a nearby town, and I'll taxi to West Grove. I'll be at my parents' door by five. That's about the time Mom would start making dinner. Randy will be watching sports in his recliner.

I get on the bus and take a window seat in the front. The bus is empty, maybe ten people. I pull out my phone. I should call Aunt Lil and tell her what I'm doing. But I know she won't be happy. She thinks I'm at rehearsal until ten. If I can catch a bus back early enough, I won't be too late. I can tell her the cast went out for dinner after. I hate lying, but she wouldn't think this was a good plan.

I want to talk to someone, though. I put in my earbud and scroll through my phone, finally arriving at Juliet. There are two rings before a hesitant: "August?"

"Hi, Juliet, got any good chocolate chip cookie recipes?"

She laughs. "Of course, but I'm craving a snickerdoodle."

My stomach growls. I haven't eaten much today, only cereal this morning.

In the softest voice, to not disturb the other people on the bus, I tell her about Joshua Downs and the monologue, and how I'm going to face my truth. It feels like I'm telling her a wild dream I had, not my morning. When I get to the end, I ask, "What do you think?"

She takes a deep breath. "I don't think this is the best idea, August."

My heart sinks. Maybe I was expecting her to be proud of me for confronting my parents. For my brave journey toward the truth. "Why?" I ask.

"What if they make you stay?"

I look out at the New Jersey landscape—old factories and trees. "I'll run away again," I say. And I will.

"I would have gone with you. That's in the job description of fairy trans-sister."

"I appreciate that," I say, and I really do. "But I'll text you updates."

"Please do. And August, no matter what your parents say, remember there're a lot of people who love you for you."

"I'll keep that in mind."

I put on some music and run through all the possibilities of what will happen when I show up at my parents' doorstep. I imagine how surprised their faces will be when they open the door. They might not let me in—that's a possibility. I'll just stand outside and yell. Or they could let me in the house, and not let me back out. Randy is a big guy—he could easily overpower me. But like I told Juliet, I'll run away.

Somewhere around the border of Pennsylvania, I fall asleep.

5:06 P.M.

On the taxi ride to my parents' house, I look at the town that used to be my whole world. We pass my parents' church, my old school, and small stores and fast-food restaurants. Everything looks old, run-down, and small. New York has changed the way I look at this town. No tall buildings. No Times Square. No possibilities.

The streets of my neighborhood are lined with cookie-cutter houses, all slight variations of each other. Nothing has changed about my street—American flags and green grass and so much space. Too much space. The car drops me off in front of my parents' two-story blue-siding house. August never lived here. My dreams were so small here. But now my dreams are so big, so bright, so reachable that I will do anything for them.

I'm more nervous than I get right before a show.

I knock on the door and hear feet shuffling around the door. The light in the peephole disappears, then silence. They haven't seen me presenting as a guy. I wonder what they'll think of my jeans, hoodie, and leather jacket to go with my short hair.

"I know you're there," I say loudly.

The lock clicks and the door opens. I'm so nervous, I might faint. Mom is standing there, and Randy is behind her. They are less than welcoming.

"Come in," Mom says. Randy keeps his distance, looking at me, saying nothing.

"I'm sorry to show up without letting you know, but I have some things I need to say."

"A call would have been nice," Randy says.

"Do you need anything?" Mom asks, always a caretaker.

"Water and the bathroom? I'll meet you in the dining room?"

"Sure thing, Audrey," Mom says, making my skin crawl at my deadname.

Once in the bathroom, I catch my reflection in the mirror. This house hasn't changed one bit, and nearly every bit about me has changed. I splash water on my face and think about who I need to be for this scene. Should I be Tough Guy? Angry Guy? Any role but their daughter.

A bowl of stew and a glass of water wait for me in my usual place at the dining room table. Mom's across from me with an open Bible in front of her, bright highlighted passages and scribbles in the margins. She studies that thing like there's a quiz to get into heaven. Randy sits at the head of the table with his beer can.

I finish off the water in one long drink. When Mom goes to refill my cup, I start eating the stew. My hunger supersedes my anger or fear. Randy watches me but says nothing. The stew warms my stomach and reminds me of an average night in this house. The three of us at the table, eating, talking, and occasionally laughing. They loved to hear me talk about theater. I listened politely as they talked about church. I loved when my parents loved me. I want them to love me again.

Mom returns with my water and sits down. "Thanks," I say, then wipe my mouth with my hoodie sleeve. The bowl is nearly empty. They study me—not used to my new look. I can see the wheels spinning in their heads. I clear my throat. "Why did you leave New York without saying goodbye?"

"I was so mad at you," Mom says. "And your aunt."

"For telling you the truth?" I ask.

"What truth? You are both misguided. This is serious. We have spent hours with Pastor Tim talking about what to do."

My anger rises. I try to stay cool. "What does Pastor Tim say about me being transgender?"

Mom looks at Randy, who seems distant. "He thinks it's a lie," she says.

"A lie?" I repeat.

"Confusion," Randy corrects her.

I shake my head. "There's no confusion."

"Feelings aren't real," Mom says. "Reality is created by God. Just because you feel like a boy, the reality is that you're a girl. Biologically, you are a girl."

"So my feelings aren't real. My gender dysphoria isn't real? Every minute I hated being in dresses and skirts not real? The nights I cried myself to sleep feeling wrong aren't real?"

Randy raises his hand. "This beer can is a beer can. It can't decide it's a coffee cup. It can't make up its own reality."

"You're comparing my life to a beer can?"

He shakes his head. "I can't get the senior citizen discount because I identify as an eighty-year-old man. Your mom can't decide she's a dragon."

I sit back in my chair. Stunned.

Randy continues, "What would happen to society if we let people decide how they identify? People would be birds. They would marry animals. It would be moral chaos."

"That's dramatic," I say.

"You're sick, and you need spiritual help to get better."

Mom puts her hand on my shoulder. "Pastor Tim says a life built upon imagination is false and destructive."

"Destructive," Randy says, wagging his finger. "That's why there're so many suicides."

"That's why you think transgender people die by suicide?" I ask.

"When they go against God, yes," Randy says, pleased with himself.

Every part of me wants to scream. I think of Ajax. Being trans didn't push him, his family did. "You know what causes suicides? Parents like you. You're the reason. If you loved me, and accepted me, then maybe I wouldn't have thought about it, too," I say, shocked that I said it out loud.

"She's sicker than we thought," Randy says.

I stand up. "No, I'm fine. I'm better than I've ever been."

"Don't leave," Mom says, getting to her feet.

I put on my backpack. I almost forgot to ask the question. "Were you going to send me to Brand New Day?" I ask. They look at each other, surprised. "I saw a letter."

"What if we were?" Randy asks.

My stomach turns. "Those places are abusive and dangerous. Going there would have really hurt me."

"You need to be fixed," he says.

"You think I'm broken?" I look at Mom. "I just need to hear you say it. Were you going to send me?"

She sits back down and fold her hands, like she's about to pray. Five seconds of silence pass before she says, "Yes."

"We still can," Randy says to Mom, getting on his feet. He moves toward the door.

"You can't stop me from leaving," I say.

"Wanna bet?" he says, stepping toward me.

"Stop!" Mom screams. We freeze in place. "Let her leave," she says quietly. Randy sits back down. I look at my parents, so sad, so willing to lose me rather than question their religion.

Before I walk out, I turn around. I should say something.

There's so much I want to say, but would they hear it? Mom's not looking, but Randy has his eyes on me. I shake my head and walk out of my parents' house for the last time.

I stomp down the driveway. I'm feeling no sadness, only anger. My parents were going to send me away to be fixed. They think I need brainwashing because they are brainwashed. I disgust them, but they disgust me. I can't believe them, and they don't believe me.

I walk along the sidewalk and punch the air. Anger burns inside me, and I need to let it out. I kick the curb. The pain in my foot feels good. My parents think I'm broken. Randy and his dumb *this beer can* bullshit. I push a trash can down.

If they only knew how it felt. How much I've struggled. Why won't they try to see it from my side? Why would I put myself through all of this? I walk by a brick mailbox and punch it, the dry rock tearing the skin of my knuckle. I punch again with the other fist. Both knuckles are red, and the painful sting feels good.

My reality is that I was born in the wrong body. Their reality is an old book full of rules, and if you follow the rules then you go to heaven. How real is that? More real than me? I kick a car tire and my toe gets stuck in the hubcap, sending me to the ground. Perfect.

I pull myself up and take a deep breath. I need to calm down. I continue heading east and stop trying to fight the street. I walk my familiar route to the Wawa gas station, about a mile from my parents' house, thinking about my parents. They think I'm sick. They think I'm wrong. But when I lived in their reality, I felt wrong.

I should call my aunt, but I don't want to talk. I can't bring myself to tell her that my parents don't want me in their life. They will never be proud of me again. They will never hug me again. I turn the corner and see the gas station in the distance.

I sit at the picnic table near the dumpster. I don't know what to do next. I can't go home ever again—I'm done with my parents. And I can't go back to school because Joshua Downs will fire me, and I'll become the joke of SPA. I have nowhere to go. I have nothing left.

I pull out the soda I'd just bought from the Wawa before coming outside and sitting down. I stood in the medicine aisle for a few minutes staring at the bottles of Advil, my thoughts as dark as when I lived in West Grove. I guess they didn't go away. I didn't buy the pills, but I still could.

The sun lowers, and the streetlights come on. I don't have energy—my arms and legs are too heavy to move. My phone keeps dinging in my backpack, but I can't bring myself to look. I feel too empty. Maybe I can take a nap on this bench. I've seen others do it. I pull up my hoodie and lay my head on my backpack.

A couple of minutes later, I hear, "August?"

I look up and see my friend. Is this a dream? "Hugo?"

"Yeah, buddy, so good to see you," he says. I stand up and we hug. I can't believe my best friend from my old school is here.

"Seriously, August, you look really freaking cool."

"You do too," I say. He's wearing a Pokémon shirt and cargo pants.

"I know," he says.

"What are you doing here?"

"I knew where to find you," he says, sitting down across from me.

"You were looking for me?"

"Your friend Juliet DM'ed me. She thought you could use a friend. I was going to drive by your house, but I thought I'd check the Wawa first." He takes my soda and drinks. He always did that.

"Is it weird to see me like this?"

"Like yourself?" he asks, smiling.

"I'm sorry I didn't tell you I was transgender."

"I'm sure you had your reasons," he says.

"I didn't want to lose you as a friend. That was my reason."

"I would have never done that, man. Never."

I'm amazed at how seamlessly he's using my name and pronouns. "My parents did. I've lost my parents," I say.

"That's why you came back here?"

"I needed to confront them and find out the truth."

"And did you?" he asks.

"My truth is my parents were going to send me to conversion therapy. They think I'm sick and broken."

He shakes his head. "I disagree."

We always used to argue; it was fun. "Then what is my truth?" I ask.

"Your truth is that you have unaccepting parents. And that really sucks."

I sit back. He's right. It does suck. I thought I could be good enough and they would accept me. Succeed enough and they would love me. I played the role of their daughter; I played the role of Rizzo—I put on so many acts for them. I didn't want to play any of those roles. But I did it for them.

"Hey, August, congrats on the *Conversion* thing. I read the articles you posted. So incredible. You're famous!"

"You found me online?" I ask.

He shrugs, proud of himself. "It wasn't that tough. You liked one of my photos a while back and I did some digging."

"I did?" I don't remember that. Maybe I wanted him to find me. "But why didn't you reach out?"

He shrugs. "You looked so happy. New fancy school. All those New York parties. I figured you didn't need West Grove, and you didn't need me."

I think of my posts. So bright and cheery. Not really the most accurate representation of my life. Especially between my parents and *Conversion*. "I have been putting on acts for everyone," I admit. "It's not real."

"It isn't?" he asks, like it never occurred to him. "Well, your friends all look cool. Like, really cool."

I think about my friends. And Maggie. I never showed them my true self, always acting. They showed me their real selves, even when they were messy, and I loved them more. "I've made some good friends, but none as good as you."

"We go way back. I knew you before you were famous," he says proudly. "Tell me about some of your fancy New York friends."

"Well, my friend Meena—she reminds me of you—likes weird stuff without apology. And there's Anna—she's always got the gossip, and the biggest heart. Elijah, he's the nicest guy who was in a commercial for Gushers."

"Wait, you mean Gushers guy?"

"Yes, he's so cool," I say, feeling the darkness lifting. "And Juliet, who called you—she's my fairy trans-sister."

"That's what I love about you, August," he says. "You're so good at loving people, finding interesting things about them, and accepting them for who they are. My parents are always trying to change me. And my girlfriend, too. But you never did that. You just accepted me for me, always."

"Opposite of my parents, too," I joke. Then I think of Aunt Lil and her pineapples. Always welcoming, even when her family wouldn't welcome her truth. Sometimes the best things about us come from our broken places.

"Wait, girlfriend?" I ask.

He blushes. "Peggy Mitchell?"

"You did it! You got a girlfriend! I'm happy for you, Hugo. And I miss you."

"You too, man," he says. "Need a ride to the bus station?"

11:58 P.M.

After a long bus ride and a Lyft, I walk through my aunt's front door, exhausted and relieved to be back.

"Welcome home," Aunt Lil yells from the kitchen. "You have a guest."

Juliet and Aunt Lil are sitting at the kitchen table with empty teacups.

"Hi," I say, stunned.

"August," Juliet says. "You didn't tell me your aunt was Lillian Brooks."

"You know my aunt?"

"Of course. She's kind of famous."

"Oh, stop," Aunt Lil says, getting up and collecting the dishes. "August, you have a very sweet friend here."

I smile at Juliet. "I agree."

"Well, she's invited over anytime." Aunt Lil hugs me and it feels like home. "I'll be in my studio if you need me."

"You're my forever favorite aunt," I say. Aunt Lil heads upstairs, and I sit down with Juliet. "Thank you for calling Hugo. That saved me."

"I was worried about you. Your parents aren't the most affirming people in your life."

I nod, struggling to find the words, too upset to cry. "They will never accept me," I say. Juliet shakes her head, like she knew that already. "They think I'm broken."

"You aren't. You know that, right?"

"Things got dark before Hugo showed up. I was thinking of hurting myself."

"I've thought about it, too," she says. "In the hard times, when my life felt out of control, I thought at least I could have control over that." A tear goes down her cheek.

"That's how it felt," I say.

"I understand, August, I do. But that would leave the world

empty of your light. And you have such a bright light. You have so much ahead of you—it's so obvious. We need you here."

I bury my face in my hands. "I went looking for my truth, and my truth is so sad. Nothing like what I show online or walking down the hall."

She pets my head. "Your parents aren't going to accept you, and now you must accept that. But it doesn't define you. That's not who you are."

"I don't know who I am," I say, tired of the Infamous and the Famous August Greene.

"I can imagine," she says. "Your life has been moving so fast. No time to process anything and work through the grief of your parents."

"How do you have it figured out?" I ask.

"Oh, I don't, August. Does anyone? My story is different from yours. When I transitioned, my parents were supportive, and my friends were, too. Everyone was so happy for me. But all their support and love didn't make me feel less alone. Then I became too self-conscious to act. I retreated to quiet art rooms where I felt safe. But I was isolating, and I knew it."

"What did you do?" I ask.

"I went online. And met a guy. He said he was a freshman at NYU. He wanted to mentor me, and I believed him, which is weird because I don't believe anyone. Maybe I wanted to believe him. I went to his place one night and didn't tell anyone. He lived in a tiny apartment around Union Square. He showed me his art and poured red wine. Red wine, I thought, how adult. We sat down and looked at my portfolio and talked until the wine kicked in. Then we started kissing."

She pauses, and I take her hand. I don't know where this is going, but it doesn't sound good. "I told him I was trans, and he kind of lost it. He was mad." She squeezes my hand. "He didn't hurt me, I got out fine. But it felt like I lost a part of myself in that apartment."

"I'm glad you're okay."

"I kind of retreated more into my shell. My friends"—she pauses—"*our* friends are pretty caught up in their own stuff. They didn't notice that I was a ghost of myself. Then you came to school, and you needed help. And I wanted to help you on your journey. You gave me a reason to be less invisible."

"I did?" I ask.

"You helped me, and your aunt told me how you helped her come out to her sister. Your truth isn't your parents, or onstage, or online. Your truth is in your heart. You're a good guy, August. You care about people and dream big. You don't have to pretend to be someone else for people to accept you."

I put my head down, ashamed of all the roles I have been playing.

"August," she says, her eyes finding mine. "You have been through a lot. You need to process those feelings. You need to work through your traumas, not just stuff them away and act like everything is great. I want you to heal. Will you think about getting help?"

The way Juliet looks at me, with big eyes, wanting me to be better. "I'll think about it," I say.

"And if you ever have those dark feelings, will you promise to call me?"

I nod. "I promise."

Before Juliet leaves, I call Aunt Lil downstairs.

"What? I'm in my groove."

"Aunt Lil, I'm going to ask you a question and you have to say yes."

"I'm not doing that," she jokes.

"Juliet is a talented artist who needs a mentor. Someone she can trust. Will you be her mentor?"

"Oh, I don't know if I can mentor," she stammers.

"Can you just say yes? For me?" I beg Aunt Lil. "Juliet saved my life."

"Yes, of course. Juliet, come over next week for tea and snacks. Are you vegan?"

"Obviously," Juliet says.

"There you go," I say, smiling the biggest I have all night.

Juliet gives me a hug. "See, August, you have a big heart—lead with that. No act needed."

I nod. She's right.

TWENTY-THREE

Sunday, October 27

11:50 A.M.

Knocking wakes me. Aunt Lil opens the door and smiles. "Hey, kiddo, just wanted to check up on you."

"I don't feel great," I admit.

"I brought you a bran and quinoa muffin," she says.

"That's supposed to help?" I kid.

She sets the plate down beside me and sits down on the bed. "Want to talk?"

"I feel . . ." I pause. "I feel like I don't have a family."

"Well, now I feel like crap," she says.

"I feel lost without my parents. Maybe I was only performing for them. Maybe I should quit acting."

"Oh, August," she says. "If I painted to make other people happy, I'd be doing watercolors of ponds and ducks. We create for ourselves."

I shake my head. Rub my eyes. "I acted to *not* be myself."

"Well, it's time to flip the script." Her eyes light up. "Look at that pun."

"I don't know who I am."

"You're August Freaking Greene."

"And I don't know who that is. Not really. I've played characters for my mom, for my friends, teachers, everyone."

"Today is the first day of the rest of your life. Why don't you journal about it? That's what people suggest to me, and I never do it. But maybe you could try. Who is August?"

I nod. "Like a character study?"

"Sure, I don't know, but sounds good."

"I could try," I say. I don't have plans for today. Well, ignoring my tower of homework and running my monologue before tomorrow's make-or-break rehearsal.

Aunt Lil stands up. "I'm headed to brunch with D. We'll be back in a couple hours. Will you be all right?"

I poke at the muffin—it doesn't look good. "I'll probably starve, but I'll be fine."

"Call me if you need me, or if you think about going to Pennsylvania."

"Don't worry about me."

"That's my job," she says.

I grab my notebook from my desk—reachable from my bed, thanks to the close quarters of New York living—and open to a blank page. I've never done a character study.

I stare at the page until I hear the front door shut. The place is all mine now. I close my notebook and bring it downstairs. I can think better once I've eaten. While rummaging in the kitchen for anything edible, I open the cabinet over the refrigerator—the one with the medicine—in hopes of finding a stash of Halloween candy. But now it's empty. All the medicine removed. I shut the door like I just got caught. Panic washes over me. Did Aunt Lil hide the pills because of me? Does she not trust me now?

I pace around the apartment, feeling embarrassed. Exposed. Like some poor suicidal kid who everyone needs to be careful around. I feel sick and ashamed that my aunt thinks I'm a risk to myself. I hate that I scared her, and Juliet. Maybe I wanted my parents to realize how much their cruel words and beliefs hurt me. And just maybe, they would hurt as much as me.

But it only would have hurt the people who really care about me. Trying to end my life wouldn't teach my parents anything, only confirm their backward beliefs. I get mad at myself. Mad that I love my parents so much. Mad that I can't unlove them. I grab an apple and sit down at the kitchen table.

I start with "AUGUST GREENE: A Character Study" and go from there. I write for an hour and eat three gluten-free toaster waffles with almond butter and honey. It almost tastes like real food. Once I write the last sentence, I head upstairs and pass out.

5:35 P.M.

Another knock wakes me up. The sun is setting. I've been asleep for hours. Guess I needed it. "Come on downstairs," Aunt Lil shouts from the other side of the door. I put on some fresh clothes, grab my notebook, and head down.

Aunt Lil and Davina are seated at the dining room table.

"There's the sleepyhead," Davina says.

"Come sit," Aunt Lil says. And I do.

Davina starts fanning herself. "It's getting hot in here, being so close to this star."

"I can turn on the air conditioner," I joke.

"Can I speak forwardly?" she asks.

I look away, ashamed. "Yeah."

"I had religious and unaccepting parents, too. As soon as I had enough money, I moved from Georgia to New York. Now, you would think meeting other queer people and feeling safe to be out would make me instantly happy, healthy, and more comfortable, right?"

"Sure," I say.

"I wish it was that easy," Davina says. "I still had all these ideas in my head that being gay was wrong. And meeting people like me only made me feel worse. I couldn't get past all my old thoughts."

"What did you do?" I ask.

"Worked on it. It took having honest conversations with people who supported me, and therapy, and time. Eventually, I became who I really am." She pauses and thinks. "You, my boy, are a gift to this world, and you're experiencing a lot at once. From beginning your transition to your new school and everything else."

"That's a heck of a lot for anyone to deal with," Aunt Lil says. "I should have been more persistent about getting you help."

"Did you hide your medicine from me?" I ask them.

"Oh," Aunt Lil says. "I did, yes, when you went to bed last night. August, I love you so much. I can't think about losing you. I want to do everything to keep you here."

Davina puts her hand on Aunt Lil's. "We actually spent the afternoon looking up therapists for you. Therapy is a great way to talk to someone honestly and heal. We found a transgender man named Sam Golden; he's been working with trans and nonbinary teens for years."

"You don't have to do this alone," Aunt Lil says.

"Will you talk to him?" Davina asks.

I feel the love surrounding me, and for the first time in days, I feel safe. I dread talking to a therapist but know it will help. "Yes, I will," I say.

"That's great news," Aunt Lil says.

"Can I read you my character study?" I ask.

"Please," Aunt Lil says, sipping her tea. I can see her hand shake a bit. This must be hard for her.

I open my notebook and clear my throat. "I am August. A boy born into the wrong body and to the wrong parents, but that didn't stop him. He once believed that if he was good enough at acting, his parents would accept him for being transgender. He now knows that's not reality. He can't change their minds. So, he must change his own mind."

I look up from my notebook and see their eyes on me. I nod and continue, "Before today, August thought he was an impostor. And he was right. He was trying to put an act on, whether it be the party guy, the class clown, or some heightened version of himself. He was always trying to be someone else. August realized that if you're always acting like someone else, then you will feel like an impostor."

I flip the page. "I tried to act cool, but it's gotten in the way of being me. Of being August. And in the moments when I was genuine and real—I was August."

I close my notebook. Aunt Lil wipes a tear. "That's wonderful."

Then Davina says the four most beautiful words: "Let's go get pizza."

TWENTY-FOUR

Monday, October 28

12:45 P.M.

"Joshua Downs, please report to dressing room three," Brady announces over the speakers. I sent him a text this morning and asked him to do that. I wait for Joshua on my broken folding chair in my janitor-closet dressing room with a box of things in my lap. Betty isn't here yet—she usually makes it to rehearsal right before call time. My body is shaking and sweating, but I'm ready.

The door swings open, revealing Joshua. He's wearing one of those tattered sweaters that look like they're from the garbage but really cost a thousand dollars. "Ah, August, I was going to come check up on you," he says with a cheesy smile.

I stand up, holding my box. "My parents were going to send me to conversion therapy. That's why I left Pennsylvania."

His face registers shock. "I didn't know that," he says.

"I didn't tell you that."

Joshua enters the dressing room and leans against the sink. "Why are you telling me now?"

"Because at my audition, you asked why I was qualified to play the part. If my parents had their way, I'd be in conversion therapy right now. But I'm not, I'm here with you, and that makes me qualified to understand Ajax in a way you never will."

Joshua throws his hands in the air dismissively. "I'm so sick of this representation stuff," he says, and I nearly drop my box in horror. "An actor doesn't need to directly experience what the character is going through. I'm sorry, August, you just aren't giving me what I want."

"I'll never give you what you want," I say, keeping my voice steady and low. "You want Chris Caesar and his followers."

He crosses his arms. "Yes, I know, it's so wild for me to want an established actor to play a role. What an irrational concept! But I can't because of representation." He puts air quotes around *representation.*

"What you don't seem to understand," I say, gripping my box like a shield, "is that people want to see roles played by the people who have lived experience."

I learned the term "lived experience" last night from Davina.

Joshua rolls his eyes. "I disagree," he says flatly.

"Representation is important because these are our stories to tell, so let us tell them."

"Then why can you play Rizzo?" he asks.

Davina and I didn't prepare for that one. I shift my weight

between my feet while thinking. I want to make up a story, but I stay honest. "I played the part for my parents."

"That makes it okay?" he asks defiantly.

"Before this show, how many transgender characters have you had in your productions?"

"None."

"Exactly," I say.

"Actually, one. I did *Rent*."

"One character out of twenty shows?"

He scans his résumé in his head. "Thirty."

"And you question how a trans or nonbinary actor could make a career with that lack of representation? We need more roles, but we also need to be hired when we are the best person for the role."

"Maybe you aren't the best one for this role," he says.

"I'm not afraid of you anymore. Go ahead and fire me if that's what you want," I say, nearing the door. "But in the meantime, I'm going to the men's dressing room. That's where I belong."

I walk out of the room, expecting Joshua to say something, but he doesn't. The guys welcome me to the dressing room, and we make small talk for the few minutes before rehearsal begins. This feels like a win—possibly the only one today—but I'll take it.

An hour later, we're running the show full out—costumes, lights, mics, and nearing the end of act one. The show seems to be in a good place for the opening tomorrow. We haven't had to halt for a lighting problem, set fix, or an actor missing an entrance. And Joshua has yet to make anyone cry.

The next scene is my monologue. I wait backstage in the darkness and get focused. The crew moves quietly around me, adjusting props, helping with costumes, and moving sets. Brady cues the lights and maintains the sound levels. The actors pass by, entering and exiting the stage. I love the minutiae of theater, so many people working at once to make it happen. It's a beautiful thing. It's my favorite thing. This is what I want for the rest of my life. This is my dream. And even if Joshua fires me, it will continue to be my dream. I won't let him take it away from me.

"Hey, kid, you ready to jam this out?" Betty asks.

"Piece of cake," I say, having no idea why something being easy is a piece of cake.

Betty gives me the pre-scene hug. "You've got this—I know you do."

I put my arm around her, and we walk onstage. I am August, playing Ajax. I think of my parents wanting to send me to conversion therapy, and sadness comes over me, then anger follows. The feelings start in my chest and push on my heart. I channel them. My posture changes, and my jaw clenches. I think of how badly I wanted my parents to accept me and let the desperation boil. I don't push the pain away; instead, I use the uncomfortable feelings that I was too scared to face and become Ajax.

"You're okay. It's all over," Betty says, starting the scene.

"My brain is scrambled," I mumble, and drop to the bed, slouched. "I'll never do that again," I say.

"I felt that same way my first time in the shock chair, but you'll adjust. It helped me. It'll help you, too, Wendy."

I think about every time my parents deadnamed me. "My name isn't Wendy!" I yell. "My name is Ajax."

Betty looks shocked, calms herself. "Your name is Wendy; my name is Dennis. And you're a girl, and I'm a boy. The quicker you accept those truths, the less shocks they'll send through your body."

This is where the script says to cry. I put my head in my hands and think of my parents not accepting me. Rejecting me. Wanting to put me in one of these places. And I cry very real tears.

Betty continues, "You need to believe that our Lord is stronger than the demons inside of you. And, Wendy, I can feel him fixing me. I'm almost there."

"Bullshit," I say, wiping my eyes.

"He does not make mistakes," she says.

I let the words echo in my head. I look at Betty and pretend she's my mom. "I'm not a mistake; I don't need to be fixed." I stop and let the anger build in my body. "I'm Ajax, and that is my truth."

Betty shushes me. "You better quiet down, or they'll take you right back to that shock chair. Is that what you want?"

I stand up as Betty looks on from the bed. "Don't you see how they are brainwashing you? This isn't right. They tell us we are wrong, but they are wrong."

I walk upstage and find my limelight. Ajax's story isn't a light and happy one; it's a sad one. But it's an important one to tell. A warning. A call to change. A chance to represent the hard parts of being transgender and make things better. It's hard to use my feelings, but if it helps bring awareness to these awful conversion therapies and changes anything, it's worth it.

"Does Jesus Christ watch over when they shock us? Gaslight us? Starve us? Slap us? This isn't religion, it's torture. This isn't God, this is the Devil. Why can't you see that?"

I settle down and let defeat enter every part of my body. "They are breaking me. I can feel it. I wake up in the morning and feel nothing. I want this to end, but I don't know how to make it stop. I want to feel like my body is mine, and my life is mine. I'm sick of this place telling me I'm wrong."

I stop, shut my eyes, and think of Mom flipping through her Bible for answers. "That Bible doesn't tell you how to be a better person; it tells you how to be a follower. What's heaven? Clouds in the sky. What's hell? A fiery pit to pay for your sins. What's earth? A place to judge everyone's else life against a book. I don't know what the point is anymore." I shake my head and picture Mom and Pastor Tim talking about me. Frustration fills me up. I let it all wash over me and fall to my knees. "I will never be what they want to me to be. I'd rather die than go against who I am."

Betty stands up and fluffs my pillow. "You need sleep. Lie down and I'll bring you dinner later. We can pray together."

I let my shoulders slump. "Hey, what will you do if they ever let you out of here?"

Betty smiles. "Find a wife and start a family."

After Betty exits, I walk over to the desk. Find the knife. The lights drop. I envision those pills from the Wawa—my supposed option to escape the pain. My supposed way to have control. And I scream.

In the dark, I pull the feelings back inside. I didn't take the pills. I'm not stronger than Ajax; I just had the support I needed in that moment. Hugo was there. Juliet was there. My aunt was there. And because of them, I am here.

"And that's intermission," Brady announces. "We'll start the second act in fifteen."

"Thanks, fifteen," I hear from the actors offstage. The lights come back on and I see Joshua still in his seat. I stand there and wait to see if he will say anything. He nods slowly. "That's what I needed from you. I'm glad we got there."

I almost throw up at the thought that he had anything to do with my process. "Thanks," I say, then walk offstage.

7:45 P.M.

Once I get to Haswell Green's, I stop and catch my breath after literally running here. The open mic is almost over. I smooth out my clothes and stand up straight. Tonight, I won't be Party Guy or Flirt or anyone other than August.

I open the door to a packed bar. The place is wall-to-wall with people. Tess is onstage singing "I Hate Men" from *Kiss Me, Kate*. Makes sense; I heard that Justin broke up with her. I stop and watch her finish the song. She's actually killing it—her voice and performance are really impressive. The crowd is hooting and hollering when she finishes.

I look around for Anna and Elijah. I need them to be here. I see Jack dancing, and Meena filming them. Jamaal is at the bar with a girl, and Yaz is talking to a group of friends. I have met so many awesome and creative people at SPA. Then I spot Elijah and Anna talking by the pool table. I'm relieved they are here, and now nervous because of what I'm about to do.

On my way to the stage, I run into Tess.

"August," she says, ignoring the people trying to talk to her.

"Tess, that song was amazing," I say, being honest. "I'm sorry about the other night. I shouldn't have said those things."

She shakes her head. "No, August, I'm the one who needs to apologize. I've been beyond rude." She stops and takes a breath. "I'm sorry about how I have acted toward you. Everything you have, you deserve. I just get weird when I feel threatened. I'm working on it with my therapist."

I smile. "I have one of those, too."

"Everyone in New York has a therapist," she jokes.

"I have to go," I say. Before I leave, Tess hugs me.

I walk directly to the DJ table on the side of the stage. Mitch Oswald is the weekly host and a senior at SPA. We've never spoken, but now I need a favor.

"Hi, Mitch," I say, "I'm—"

He cuts me off. "August Greene, yes I know. Dude, how is *Conversion*?"

"Guess we'll see at opening night tomorrow."

"Any chance you can get me some tickets?"

"If you'll do me a favor?"

"Anything," he says.

After we talk for a bit, Mitch takes the stage and adjusts the mic. "We have a special guest here. A first-timer to our stage. A Haswell Green's virgin!" The crowd cheers. "Come on up, August."

I walk across the stage, owning my virgin vibes. Mitch queues up my song selection, and the music begins. I tap the mic and hear the thud echo through the bar. A couple of people scream my name, but I can't tell who. "This song is for my two best friends, Anna and Elijah."

The recorded track of piano picks up, and I sing "You've Got a Friend in Me" from *Toy Story*. The audience sings along—because every theater person knows the words—and we really lean into the chorus, practically yell-singing, *"We stick together and we see it through, 'cause you've got a friend in me."*

I try to be fully in this moment. I'm in New York singing in front of my whole school. I'm going onstage tomorrow with Broadway actors, and I've earned my spot alongside them. Maybe they call them dreams because when they happen, it doesn't feel real.

I really sing out *"But none of them will ever love you the way I do"* and hope my friends will accept my apology. The crowd is clapping and I'm dancing, letting myself get carried away in the song.

And just as the last chorus begins, Elijah and Anna jump up onstage. They circle around me and lean into the mic, and we sing together. I'm so happy to have them onstage with me and back in my life. We make eye contact on the final *"You've got a friend in me.*" We finish the last note—a nice mix of harmonies—and immediately group hug.

"I love a grand gesture!" Anna yells over the applause.

We clear the stage for the next performance, and they lead me back to their table.

"I'm sorry, guys," I say. "I was acting so full of myself at the *Rocky Horror* party to hide the fact that I was insecure about *Conversion*. And I handled the Duncan thing poorly."

"August," Elijah says, "I was out of bounds that night. You did the right thing."

"And," Anna jumps in, "we both realized Duncan is slimy. Ugh, I should have known a cello player would be no good."

"He wasn't even that good at kissing," Elijah says.

Anna rolls her eyes. "Agreed."

"So we're okay?" I ask.

"We're solid gold," he says, then puts his arm around me.

"Listen up," Mitch yells into the microphone, effectively getting our attention. "It's everyone's favorite part of the night. Our resident songstress, Maggie Ridge."

I watch Maggie take the stage. She's wearing her yellow-tinted aviator glasses, a flowy red dress, and she has her acoustic guitar. "Hello, Haswell Green's," she says. "I'll be playing a new song tonight. It's about a boy." The audience oohs and aahs as she strums her guitar and tunes a string. "It's called 'Limelight.'"

The back of my neck goes hot. I told her all about the limelight on our walk home from the *Grease* after-party. This song is about me.

You're always trying to be
What you need for the scene
But I know it's an act
Yeah I know it's an act

When the lights go down
And no one is around
Do you know who you are
'Cause I know who you are

The world is a stage
And you're just playing
But what's the truth
You aren't sayin'

Step into your limelight
There's only a few
Who can do what you do
You have what it takes
But what is at stake

Step into your limelight
Find that perfect spot
Hit your mark and stop
Tell me what you see
Do you ever see me?

The crowd claps and cheers, and goose bumps run over my body. I excuse myself and head down to the basement—the place of our meet-cute.

After a couple of minutes of awkwardly hanging out in the small space that smells like beer and pee, footsteps come down the stairs. I smile at her, and she smiles at me. "Is it vain or was that song about me?"

She laughs. "That was for you."

"I never had a girl write a song about me."

"August, you nearly begged for it."

"I'm here in this basement to tell you that—I'm here. Not some act. Just me."

"How can I be sure?" she asks.

"Can we go for coffee and I'll tell you everything?"

She smiles and nods. "I like you, but I'm scared."

"I like you," I say.

"But you're scared, too?" she asks.

I take a step closer to her. "A little. You see the real me, and I'm worried it's not enough."

"It's more than enough."

She puts her arms around me, and we kiss.

TWENTY-FIVE

Tuesday, October 29

5:45 P.M.

I exit the Starbucks with the largest coffee possible and head to SPA. A familiar walk—I could do it with my eyes shut—but tonight, I'm on my way to make history. That's dramatic, but it will be special. A warm, nervous excitement builds in my chest as I think about opening night of my first professional show. Don't know why I even got the coffee—I'm wired for all the obvious reasons.

I didn't go to school today. Aunt Lil said it was a "mental health day" and called SPA with an excuse. I wouldn't have been able to concentrate anyway and didn't want to talk to everyone about the show. I needed time to rest and get my mind right. I spent the day napping, watching TV, and trying not to freak out.

This afternoon, in between naps, I took a selfie and posted it with a lengthy caption about the truth about my parents, the conversion therapy, and how important *Conversion* will be for the LGBTQ community. I'm ready to be more honest about my life in hopes that someone else will connect with my story and feel less alone. Ajax isn't the dream role. But he's just one story—like I am one story—and I could bring awareness to trans issues. I want to make a difference, and that starts with playing Ajax the best I can. The post got a bunch of likes and new follows, but I'm going to pay less attention to that stuff.

Betty told me there will be reviewers at the show tonight. Usually there are preview performances with no press, which allows for the smoothing of small bumps of any new show, but *Conversion* is only running at SPA for two weeks and the buzz needs to build fast to make the Broadway transfer happen.

I want my parents in the audience. But they will not be there, and I need to accept that fact. Maybe even use it. I stop walking and take a deep breath. There's nothing I can do to change my parents' minds. It's out of my control. But my life, and my performance, are in my control. I start walking again and hope the empty aloneness will get better over time. I occupy my mind by running scenes in my head and saying my lines out loud. It's New York—no one looks twice if you're talking to yourself.

When I get to the school, I walk past the front entry. We've been instructed to come in through the side entrance by the dumpsters. Guess that's our stage door. I see a small group of people gathered by the doorway. Must be fans of the other actors? When I get closer, I realize I know all the people.

Aunt Lil and Davina are here with a bouquet of flowers. Mr. Daniels and Anna, too. Elijah, Meena, and Juliet wave at me and snap pictures. I walk toward the group with my mouth open, in total shock.

"What are you doing here?" I ask.

They laugh and circle around me. "August," Aunt Lil says, "we're here to support you."

"I just wanted to stand by the dumpsters," Anna jokes.

"We are so proud of you," Davina says.

"You're all coming to the show?" I ask, stunned.

"I got a great group deal," Aunt Lil says.

"Thank you, new favorite auntie," Elijah jokes.

"August," Mr. Daniels says. "Do you remember your super-objective paper?"

"Yes," I say, shooting a look to Anna, who has also read it. "I said I wanted to play male or female parts and not transgender roles. Guess I didn't achieve my super-objective. Did you come here to tell me you're lowering my grade?" I kid.

"I would disagree." He pulls a paper out of his pocket. "You did say those things, but you also said, and I quote, 'I want to move the audience, make them feel things, think about things, and leave the theater changed. I want to be a star.'" He hands me the paper. "I imagine you'll be doing those things tonight."

"Hell yes, he's a star," Anna shouts.

"But why come before the show?" I ask.

"Good question," Aunt Lil says. "We wanted you to know

something before you went onstage." Aunt Lil pulls out a note-card. She wrote a speech. "August, your parents are your parents. They are your blood and you will forever be connected to them, for better or worse. But your parents aren't your family. A family is a unit of people who believe in you, want the best for you, support and love you." She looks up from the card and finds my eyes. "They love you no matter what. They love you for you. August, we are your family. Each person here would do anything for you. Your parents may not be here, but we are. And we will always be your family."

"Your chosen family," Davina says.

I look at all of them. "I don't know what to say."

"Don't actors always know what to say?" Aunt Lil jokes.

"I guess I want to thank you. Thank you, Anna, for being my first friend. And Elijah for making life more fun. And Davina for the solid advice and loving my aunt. Thank you, Mr. Daniels, for making me a better actor, and Juliet for saving my life. And thank you, Aunt Lil, for changing my world. If you're my family, then I'm the luckiest guy in New York City."

They all hug me at once, and the warmth and love make me feel like I'll never be alone again. I am August Greene. I'm transgender. I'm an actor. I have a dream. I lost my parents but found a family.

THE END

ACKNOWLEDGMENTS

When a musical is over, the lights come up, the audience cheers, and the cast takes a bow. Being on that stage is both gratifying and humbling, and exactly what everyone who helped create this book deserves. A moment in the spotlight. Loud applause. A big bow. Thank you for helping me, you have all my gratitude. Please take a bow while I clap loudly (which makes it difficult to type.).

First bow goes to Bob McSmith. My musical cowriter. My best friend. Your heart is true. You're a pal and confidant. Life would have sucked without you. Together, we created eight parody musicals that have played around the world. And it's been an honor and a pleasure to walk side by side with you on this incredible journey. I have no doubt we created things in a past life, and I'm certain we will create things in the next. Thank you for being a friend.

Second bow is for every human who worked on our musicals over the past fifteen years. The actors, directors, choreographers, composers, musical directors, musicians, stage managers, set designers, lighting designers, costume designers, sound designers (all the designers!), the crew, marketing and press agents, anyone I forgot, and the producers. I'm proud of what we created. You are all McSmiths. We are always family. I'll never forget our time together creating something special. They were truly the best times of my life.

I was writing chapter two of this book when the world went into lockdown and theaters went dark. This book was my escape to a world where the show went on and the audience was full. The next bows go to the people who helped me survive the pandemic. Thank you to Ka-va Bar for keeping me connected (but still six feet away) to amazing people. Thanks to Rich, Michelle, Lee, Jennifer, David, Brian, Baily, Adie (my favorite!), Shane, Sam, Warren, Nazar, Taniyah, Jesse, Michael, Matt, Ming, Nikhil, Oleg, Anna, Ryan, Scott, Al, Emily, Glenn, Emma, and especially Alberto. Thanks to Vanessa and Misfits Ka-va Bar for inspiring me and raising a bunch of money for the Stay Gold Fund. I'm grateful to have a community of creative misfits and inspiring individuals.

Mom and Glenn, I love you. As you walk out on-stage, I hand you a freaking huge bouquet of flowers and give you a big hug. Thank you for all the love and support over the years. You are exceptional parents. And I will never be cooler than y'all!

Big bows for the people who helped educate and inform me about acting, directing, growing up trans, and performing arts schools. Thank you for your time, Donald Garverick and Caleb Cummings. Rachel Evans, thank you for sharing your knowledge and acting class at LaGuardia High School. Thank you to the trans community for your stories and experiences.

Two kitty bows for Bam-Bam and Bananas. You are very special cats who can't read this and will never truly know how much I love you.

To my agents at ICM Partners, I am clapping and whistling and yelling for you. Enormous thanks to the best book agent in town, Tina Dubois. Your support and encouragement and honesty has made me a better writer and person. I'm forever indebted to Nichole Borrelli Hearn, thank you for always seeing my potential. And Alicia Gordon, wow, it's been an honor to have you in my corner. You have all moved mountains so I could see my dreams come true and I am forever grateful.

The crowd goes wild for the strikingly beautiful cover designed by David DeWitt with amazing art by Little Corvus. It's been an absolute honor to have

David and Teo create all three of my covers, and they nail it every single time. Teo, you are an unbelievably talented artist. Allison Michael Orenstein, thank you for making me look so dang handsome in my author photos.

HarperCollins, take a bow! Thank you for employing me for sixteen years and publishing two of my books. You have made my life better every day. Thanks to the sales team (best in the world!), I will always be house proud. All my love and appreciation to every person and department working hard to bring beautiful and important books to the world. I always know I have the smartest and most wonderful people working on my books. I miss working beside you and have endless gratitude for what you have done for me.

I could not cheer loud enough for all the booksellers and librarians out there. I admire everything about you and what you do. You are the true heroes! Your support and friendships have been the unexpected surprise of being an author.

The crowd is on their feet for my editor, Andrew Eliopulos. Thank you for helping me navigate this story. You are a genius. I am rooting for you on your next chapter in life and am immensely lucky I got to work with you on two books. Thank you, Rosemary Brosnan, the coolest person at HarperCollins. Thank you, Bria Ragin, Laura Harshberger, and Jackie Hornberger and Jenny Moles. And to Alyssa Miele, my new editor, it's already been a joy to team up. You are thoughtful and smart and I can't wait for our time together.

Here comes the big finish. Everyone on stage locks hands and takes a bow together. The audience is on their feet and louder than ever. The stage is filled with so many people—everyone I mentioned and everyone I forgot. Thank you for making this book happen. I couldn't have done it without you. After the final bow, we hug, maybe cry, then head backstage to hug and cry some more. We are sad because it's over, but proud of what we created, and ready to do it all again tomorrow.